Hoy Polloy

David Barnard

Ebru

First published 2023 by Ebru

Cover design and map by Keith Boulton

Contents

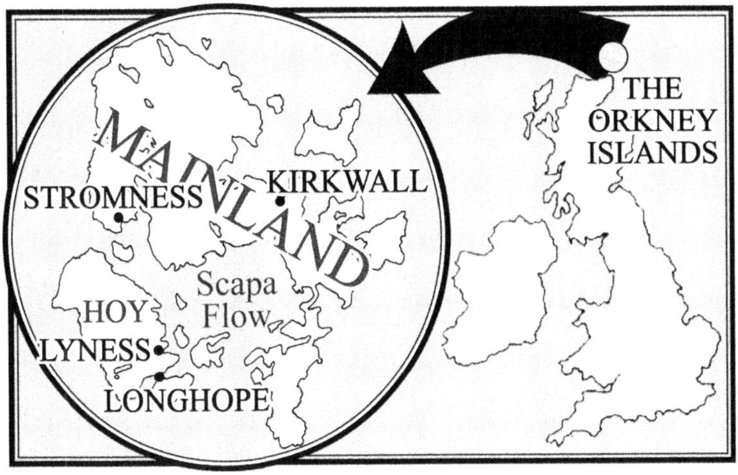
MAINLAND
STROMNESS
KIRKWALL
Scapa
Flow
HOY
LYNESS
LONGHOPE
THE
ORKNEY
ISLANDS

Introduction

Those islands to the North of Scotland, the Orkney Islands. Orkney. It's the second week of August, Agricultural Show Week. The week's gathering is rooted in the Orkney calendar and Orkney certainly knows how to put on a good gathering. *Whit like? – Noh bad. – How's yerself?* friendly is this week of coming together – come rain, come shine but mainly come rain.

The Orkney *Jahr* works its way round the calendar clock face, at its own steady pace, never to be rushed. Single-minded is the Orkney *Jahr*. Quarter past…half past…and now we've arrived at those minutes between twenty-five to and twenty to the hour.

Those days of twenty-four-hour daylight. For those who live here…a shrug of the shoulders. For those from *Doon Sooth*, a significance in search of an explanation. The

Orkney Islands? The full title? No, keep it simple and straightforward. Just Orkney, if you please. *Whit like? – Noh bad. – How's yerself?*

Twenty-five to and twenty to, the latter half of the year. Orkney has now reached autumn. Those winter winds, ring-rusty, chomping at the bit…just out of sight of the audience, side stage. Those winter winds, told to mind their manners and wait their turn. A month or two to go yet.

It's that time of year when in Orkney you receive the home call, uninvited, silent but unthreatening. Daddy longlegs arriving at dusk, drawn by the light, clamp on to the glass window-pane. They are very good at playing statues; compass-point spreadeagled.

Compass points? In Orkney, compass points are in our DNA. The North west is always the starting point with 'the North west passage' and the Hudson Bay Company and John Franklin. The Orkney *Jahr* has many a tale to tell as it works its way round the calendar clock face.

Daddy longlegs. North north west to south south east. North north east to south south west. Motionless. Lots of distancing and we're told that distancing is good, so it must be.

Top – a set of antennae sprouting out of a pinhead. Mid – east to west arms, crucifixion like, acting as stabilisers. Bottom – those spindly legs on stilts.

They never outstay their welcome, these daddy longlegs. A few still lingering, *the morn's morning*, the morning after but they are mere powder puff, spent like a

Catherine wheel after bonfire night and waiting to be wafted away by the winds. The winds here have a mind of their own.

Evening and it's time for me to light the tilley lamps, followed by the drawing of the curtains. My daily routine, from the first cuppa and gasper of the day to putting Bobby the cat out at night, is now coming ever more under the jurisdiction of the law.

Me. Inside my home. The peat fire is lit. In my comfy rocking chair, my head is rested against the brylcreem-stained antimacassar. A dram or two? Why not. I'm Orcadian, an individual. My identity is not to be defined by official blether; 'social bubbles', 'households', pamphlets on 'what to do and say without causing offence' and 'how to wear a gas mask' and 'don't go out after dusk unless you must' and the like.

Who'd have thought it? This drawing of the curtains. Mine are never fully drawn; never have done, never will be. My choice. I have the right. The bringing of light, an act punishable by law? At the start of *this* Orkney *Jahr*, who knew what those minutes between twenty-five to...and twenty to...were going to bring? And there's Johnny, Johnny Sinclair, what part does he play in this particular Orkney *Jahr* of all *Jahrs*?

Uncle Johnny, they say I look like him, that I am a chip off the old block. His moment on the Orkney *Jahr* clock face has come.

The Orkney Islands, always in the same place, set off

the North Coast of Scotland but woe betide anyone who takes Orkney for granted. It can peek a boo just when you least expect it to.

'Here's Johnny.'

1981

Summer. July. Mid-morning. Sunny day. Optimism.

I've got a brand-new Austin Metro. The open road awaits. If the road needs to go uphill, then it will be the uplands that await and the uplands are always sunny. 'A British car to beat the world.' British Leyland's ad campaign for the Metro. *The* break from the past. Trouble-free motoring guaranteed. 'British', the label that says it all. 'Send the foreigners back where they came from.' Tongue-in-cheek humour. Banter. Our speciality. North. South. East. West. Whatever part of the British Isles you're from, it doesn't matter. We are *all* special. *Banter. Billy British Banter.*

I've got my Austin Metro, Lady Di's got hers. What a lovely couple they make, her and Prince Charles. Their wedding. It's…it's…a fairy story.

GB or UK, take your pick, is in firm hands with Maggie Thatcher behind the wheel. 'The Winter of Discontent' and 'Sunny Jim' Callaghan were sent packing by 'Maggie, Maggie, Maggie'. 'Fill your boots. I know someone who knows someone who's making a pile in the London Docklands.'

Austin Metro, a British-hatchback future. In with the new, out with the old. The Falkland Islands? Where are they for god's sake and who cares? It's the summer of 1981. No clouds on the horizon, it's a sunny, summer's day. Hi-de-Hi!

I would have liked to have been a believer but, for me, summer always means itchy eyes and nose runneth over. Hay fever means my handkerchief never gets a rest. My bogie, my snot, is definitely neither eng-er-land union jack nor salty nul-points saltire blue in colour, more mucus off-white, even a bit eggy.

I'm behind the wheel, not Sophie. She has a lot on her plate. If I thought it would take her mind off things, I would have let her drive. No need to repeat myself. This sexism is a curse but I tell you again, 'I would have let her drive.'

Nothing is said between us, though there is much to be said. My Austin Metro's radio with cassette player is not functioning. There is an echo chamber of silence, both enveloping and stifling. A void that I'm not used to filling.

Trollope and *Trigonometry* and even *Latin* was on the school curriculum. Why weren't we taught useful stuff like

The Art of Conversation...and *How to Deal with Problems* and...and...and...*Life*?

We're now at the slip road for the M4, direction London. My Austin Metro is being launched down its slipway for the very first time. Foot down. Vroom, vroom. A rite of passage for a driver in their new car and it's an Austin Metro. I've just overtaken a Ford Cortina. Didn't even need to get into top gear. *Ain't No Stoppin' Us Now.* It's 1981 and I'm living the 80s' dream.

I reckon we're about halfway there. Fifty miles to go. Less than a gallon's worth of petrol needed, not bad fuel economy. Petrol's gone up to £1.44 a gallon back home. Who can afford that? 'A British car to beat the world.' I like the sound of that. You know what, I haven't done this journey before. I'm putting the car through its paces, moving through the gears. I'm in charge of it. It's not in charge of me.

But now this. On the windscreen, not one but two spindly insects, probably daddy longlegs. They have deliberately chosen my windscreen for their final hurrah. Spindly insects, side by side and splattered. Well, I feel for them but couldn't they have done their kamikaze attack elsewhere?

I press the water nozzle button but there's no jet of water on the screen. The process is repeated but no joy. The windscreen wiper blades are working but for what? All I can hear is the scrape of wiper against glass, an irritating screech. Screech and silence. Screech and silence.

The windscreen wiper lever is held tightly by the finger in the 'towards me' position to force the water jets to do what they're supposed to. Windscreen wipers are still on 'slow-active' and screeching. I am not best pleased but I can pull over at any time and with chamois leather in hand and a generous sprinkling of water from the bottle of water that I'm sure that I brought with me, problem solved.

It's all Sophie's fault. If she would only have asked for her cigarette break. That's par for the course and I'm always happy to oblige. But we're just joining the motorway and…she…hasn't…said…a…word and it's too late to stop now. I've been waiting for her to say something. It's too late to start now. Everyone knows that on motorways stopping opportunities are few and far between. Why didn't she just ask? I'm not being stubborn but I'm not going to turn the wiper blades off. Screech and scrape…a violin under the chin of a beginner.

My head is bobbing away to avoid both smears on the windscreen and the movement of the wiper blades. I can't help but voice my protest to the wiper blades' clickety-clack of a train rhythm. 'I don't want to be on this journey. I am nervous about this journey. Now she loves me. Now she does not.'

Austin Metro. Brand new. British. Hatchback. Adult.

I am the driver and instigator of this journey. She is just the passenger. The buck stops with me. I won her round. At least, I thought I had.

By not offering her support now I know I am behaving

like a spoilt child. If ever there is a time that she needs me…Adolescent, I know I am being so, though cruel is nearer to the mark.

She bursts into tears. There is a lot needing to be said. I don't know where to begin. She needs help. I need help. *A-tish-oo. A-tish-oo. We all fall down.*

I just know this is not going to end well but I don't know how 'ending well' would pan out. All my Austin Metro brio has evaporated into thin air. Mind, she's never thanked me. Not even a sniffle in that direction. I mean. I'm not looking for a round of applause. I have the best of intentions. I did this all for her. We are going *there* because I love her.

If she says 'Let's turn back', I won't be angry. I'll take the first turn-off. Should I ask her, 'Are you sure?' Maybe…no…better…not. It has to come from her. What a mess. I really feel sorry for her – though I feel even sorrier for myself.

Fresh air, I could do with some fresh air. I don't want to press the automatic window button in case it becomes another British Leyland moment. I briefly take my left hand off the steering wheel to try to open the sunroof, just a bit. The latch is jammed.

Eyes on the road. My head is still bobbing up and down and side-to-side to avoid those fucking daddy longlegs. Right hand firmly on the driving wheel. My left hand still raised, twirling anti-clockwise in search of a way in to a sunroof that stubbornly refuses to open. I must look to any car on the outside lane of the M4 as if I'm at a New Romantic disco...*Girls On Film...Girls On Film.*

'Fuck, I've never been to Stevenage before.' Ice broken?

No answer.

'Don't worry. I've looked up the...directions.' Strike two.

Silence. I try the water jets again.

'Thinking about it, I've never been to any of these post-war New Towns before.'

No answer. I'll just finish off what I was going to say. It's a case of getting it out of my system.

'Looks good on paper, the idea of these New Towns. Take your pick. Progress. Modern. Britain. That's the word, *Modern.* A real town planners and idealists love-in. A vision of the future sold to us. *New* Jerusalem. Never *Old* Jerusalem. Surprise, surprise, it always turns out differently in practice. What could go wrong? Main roads on the outside. Concrete on the inside. New housing and greenery guaranteed. *Better environment makes a better citizen.* Rest assured, money to be made and palms to be greased. Dumps. Shit-holes.'

I take a quick look at her. I think she's going to cry. I plough on.

'From drawing board to now, 1981. More than a few decades on. More than fraying at the edges.' I warm to this cold dish of a theme. 'I bet you that all these New Towns still have the original Old Town part that are still very nice but are just forgotten about in all this *New* Jerusalem *spraagle.*' Orkney-speak for *sprawl.*

Me, the *trattle-bogie*, the chatter-box. I hear myself speak but what the hell am I going on about? I glance at my watch. Whooah. Is that the time? I plough on regardless.

'I hear there's talk of a Peace Camp that's started up outside that RAF base. It's called Greenham Common. I'm not too sure what that's all about. Only be a short detour on the way back to Swindon. We can have a look on our return…if you want?'

Nothing.

'Hope I'll find a safe parking spot. Stevenage is not Orkney, after all.' Last throw of the furry dice.

So much for trying. Silence.

Finally, she speaks. 'Look at the young family in that car. That could be us.'

Me and Sophie, Sophie Fugaccia. A fine name to roll round the tongue, *Fugaccia.* We've been together for six months.

Her *faether*, she told me, had been an Italian prisoner of war in Orkney from 1942 to 1944. One minute the dusty heat of the North African desert and the next, the Nissen hut, rain noisily lashing against tin roof, on this wet and windy, inhospitable set of islands to the north of Scotland. Fate hadn't dealt a fair hand to her *faether*. Fate wasn't dealing a fair hand to me. I mean, we've only been seeing each other for six months.

I revisit her *young family* words and attach to them

something easier on the ear. She is not talking about *us.* She is just stating who was in the car. Must have been meant as a throwaway comment. First the car and now this. I'm on edge…as nervous as fuck.

Morn. Four letters. M-O-R-N. That's me. Morn. Not on my birth certificate but what I'm known as. Morn. Sorry. I'm jumping ahead of myself here. Morn.

Thinking later, much later, about her comment, maybe I had completely the wrong end of the stick. *Young family*, not words of threat but of love towards me. She is saying she wants to make her life with me.

Morn and Sophie. Sophie and Morn.

I too am Orcadian born and raised in Kirkwall, the largest and best town on the largest island in Orkney – the Mainland. Me living slap bang by the waterside, the Shore. *Stuart Sinclair*, the name on the birth certificate but known as Morn.

Why did the name Morn stick? I came kicking and screaming into this world a day late – not premature but late. Morn, the day-after baby. In Orkney, *morn* means 'the day after.' And if you think you've 'got' in all its glory Orkney speak, try working out *the morn's morning* for size.

Orcadian is a language whose prime purpose is to be unfathomable. Runes and etchings and prehistoric bric-a-brac, all wrapped up in this mysterious archipelago of islands. The largest of which is called *the Mainland.* Orkney. Norse heritage not Gaelic. Inconvenient for some.

Sophie and I live in Swindon, Wiltshire, Southern

England…South West England, to be precise. We met at Plessey – the large electronics firm and biggest employer in town.

The mysteries of mutual attraction have worked their magic art. Sophie and Morn = us. Plessey and Swindon = us. The volume control on almost everyone's tv and radio in Britain? Straight off Plessey's production lines. My current Austin Metro radio and cassette player's problem? Not Plessey's fault. I don't take kindly to snide comments about Plessey. You may think it's just banter. You may think you're being funny but…you…are…not.

Even though we've been together for just six months, there's been those moments where we've both needed to dig in. She moved in with me two months back but kept her flat and would at least once a week stay overnight at home. Space is so important, don't you think?

We share a core set of values. Orkney provides them for us. If we've had a row and are struggling to communicate, Orkney always in some shape or form opens a failsafe way back. Those sea banks rolling back to provide a path ahead to safety. Think Moses and the Red Sea. Think the Broch of Birsay and the Mainland.

We still have an hour before we reach Stevenage. Is that going to be *it* in regards to communication? An hour is far too long to put up with this suffocating silence. I'll give it another go even though I don't have great hopes. Orkney will provide the route. *In Orkney we trust.*

What now! There's a rattling sort of sound coming from

the glove compartment. Did I put something inside it or is *faulty trim* to be added to the snagging list?

This rattle for some reason triggers a memory. I'm very young, maybe five or six. I am aware of someone walking into my front room in Kirkwall. I'm playing with my model cars on the carpet with accompanying vroom-vroom noises, as if I'm revving the engines, as if I'm Stirling Moss.

This man is smiling. He's holding a tray. He puts the tray down on the carpet and ruffles my hair. Then his hand brings out from his jacket pocket a white knotted handkerchief. It's bulging but with what? This handkerchief, he unties. The contents spill out onto the tray.

The ceramic tray magnifies the sound. I can hear the sound now in my head, like dice being rolled on a metallic surface, rattling away. Four of these capsule-shaped objects, there they are in front of me, two-tone in colour and easy to swallow, if you were of a mind and I am of a mind. He playfully wags his finger at me. 'They are very, very dangerous…*lummy*.'

When you tilt the tray, these capsules seem to have a life of their own. He shows me. They fall over, they backflip, magically right themselves and yes, they are like performers at a circus, Billy Smarts. I like Billy Smarts. My uncle is smiling. He tells me they are beans. Mexican jumping beans. 'Look at those *Mexican* fellers. *Beuys o beuys. Lummy.*'

He used to say the word *lummy* a lot. *Beuys* – Orkney

speak. *Lummy* – Cockney speak. A marriage of sorts or perhaps a mish mash, a linguistic *guddle*.

These Mexican jumping beans don't stay still, never leaving the bottom of the tray. They topple over and get up again of their own free will aided by a tilt here, a tilt there. Soldiers, in my five-year-old's head, on the fields of battle. I liked playing soldiers then. It was fun. The soldiers would fall and get up ready for action, again and again…as fresh as a daisy.

Uncle Johnny watches me intently as I play with these two-tone capsules. Mexican beans rolling about on a tray. He never takes his eyes off me. 'These Mexican jumping beans are not,' he says, 'to be swallowed.'

After a few minutes, Uncle Johnny ruffles my hair and returns the Mexican beans first to his handkerchief and then once knotted back to his jacket pocket. Out comes a bar of crunchy peanut brittle from another pocket and he puts his finger to his lips. 'Hush. This is our secret.' I like secrets when there are sweets given to me. Smiling, he ruffles my hair again and leaves the room.

I like my Uncle Johnny. Some say I look just like him.

Back in the here and now, a feeling of detachment. I can hear myself speaking, fully focused on driving down the motorway miles in my Austin Metro while I tell Sophie my story about Uncle Johnny and those jumping beans that do lots of tricks but don't jump.

Take a bow, my misbehaving Austin Metro. My Orkney

route back to Sophie. Uncle Johnny and the Mexican jumping beans. All thanks to my brand-new car.

'Uncle Johnny returned to Orkney just before the outbreak of War in June 1939, long before I was born. I've still got a black and white photo of him, taken years later. Who could not be charmed by that smile and his curly hair? Popular with the ladies.

'There was something about Uncle Johnny that I hope hasn't been passed down the line to me. Did I want to be known as a ladies' man? Chewing gum on the sole of your shoe. British Empire to British Leyland. Uncle Johnny to Morn. Like a faulty gene, liable to do you no good and just waiting for the cue to cause maximum damage.

'I remember him coming to see us at home. I couldn't have been older than five or six. It was the mid 1950s. What a grey decade. No computer games like Pac-Man. No television in Orkney back then. Who could've imagined that times like those ever existed?'

'What was he like, then?'

A response at last.

'This is what I was told much later on. My Uncle Johnny returned to Orkney in June 1939…My uncle, Johnny Sinclair. He had a slight Cockney twang…and, let's not forget, a bit of an I've-seen-the-world cockiness about him. Always getting in and out of scrapes, Uncle Johnny. Falling over and getting up again, just like those Mexican jumping beans.

'Once I pretended to be asleep in the front room and I

heard Mum and Dad talk about Uncle Johnny having to leave Orkney "sharpish" and "putting you know who in the family way". You know when you're growing up and even your mum and dad's friends can be either "aunty" or "uncle"? I never knew where Uncle Johnny fitted in, inside or outside the family tree, and as you know you won't see that many trees in Orkney.'

I glanced over at Sophie. Her eyes were now closed. I couldn't tell whether she had been listening to my ruminations.

I was one of the Plessey's electronics' boffins. Sophie was Personnel, which had recently been rebranded to Human Resources. Britain was facing the future. It was at some consultants' presentation, 27th February 1981. Projector slides with graphs and buzzwords, in overdrive. 'Vision 2001 – Plesseys.' 'Plesseys must have a vision statement for 20 years' time.' 'Know where you're going.' 'Purpose.' 'Vision.' 'No organisation can survive without one.' Good Old Plesseys!

I digress. I know what my destination is at this very moment. That's why I'm in my Austin Metro and on the M4.

Sophie sat next to me at the presentation. I sneaked several looks at her. These were reciprocated. She noticed and I noticed. I was far more interested in this attractive lady than in the half-baked twaddle that was being served up. Her face was vaguely familiar but I couldn't work out from where. I took the bull by the horns.

‘I’m sure I know you from someplace. My name’s Stuart, known to friends as Morn. In Orkney, *morn* means…’

‘I know what *morn* means. Where do you think I’m from, for god’s sake?’ She points to herself. ‘Sophie, the Wynd…a *Doonie*…from Kirkwall.’ She sounded exasperated but it was jokey-exasperation and she gave me a lovely smile.

Doonie, now there’s an Orkney word. The annual Christmas and New Year ball game in Kirkwall. The *Ba*. Depending on what end of town you ‘arrived’ in Orkney, either an *Uppie* or *Doonie*. North or South of the Cross. The *Ba*, as graceful as Sumo wrestling. You’re either one or the other. Neither *Uppie* nor *Doonie* are considered to be on the wrong side of the tracks.

‘Sorry, I didn’t recognise your accent.’

‘I’ve been away too long.’

‘I’m Morn…by the way.’

‘You’ve already said.’ She points to herself again. ‘Sophie.’

We couldn’t help it. We had an attack of the giggles, attracting attention.

Different university, different degree but together at Plesseys. Always Orkney to fall back on. A pair of Orcadians in Swindon, of all places. Who’d have thought it? So much to talk about. Mutual acquaintances and the fresh air and the weather and BBC Radio Orkney. I was twenty-seven. Sophie a few years younger. She was a stunner. I was in love. We've been together six months now. You know what. She still is a stunner and I'm still in love with her but that initial excitement in our relationship has gone and it's hard work at the moment.

I knew the street well that she was brought up in. As for stuff about her folks, a mystery. Mum and Dad would always switch to a whisper when her family was mentioned. Something there that was not in front of the children, at least I supposed so. Out of love and respect, I hope I learnt to spot most of those eggshells.

She was always well brushed up, if you know what I mean, but never wore short sleeves. Was that a game changer? No but it was puzzling. Short sleeves. Long sleeves. Who cares? She was gorgeous. Really beautiful and from my hometown.

I'm sure I heard her crying at night, though nothing was ever said about it. I didn't know whether this was something to challenge or tiptoe round.

Still, the frequency of these dark moments increased to such a point that Sophie couldn't brush aside her inner despair. 'It's nothing, just stomach cramps.' I wanted to show her that I was there for her. I pursued the matter, gently but persistently. Visits to the doctor followed. I did offer to accompany her. I did.

Helplessness. It wore me down as well.

Traffic was heavy on the M4 that sunny morning. Three lanes filtering into two didn't help. I hoped we weren't going to be late. This was the West Country. 'Picturesque', so *Visit England* said. There was nothing in the scenery for me to be captivated by; no lush verges.

Roadworks. Hard Shoulder. The Open Road. Austin Metro. Britain. Next stop, Reading. On our way to Stevenage. The first of the New Towns. Stevenage, the exciting future…once.

Morn and Sophie. My turn to be silent. So much for the failsafe, recuperative powers of our shared Orkney Islands heritage.

I'll just carry on with my story about Uncle Johnny's exploits but keep it to myself. Not being wilful but realistic.

Someone had once said to me, "You know what Morn. You and your Uncle Johnny. You're a chip off the old block." So, in more ways than one, this'll be *my* story. *Me* time. I don't see why I should always be indulging her moods. If she doesn't want to listen…that's up to her. We're not talking right now but I do love her and I do understand. I am on her side. I can't imagine being without her.

I'd been aware of those marks on her arm from the start. Not eye catching but there to see. Not for the many, only for the few…probably just for the intimate. Long sleeves, the veil in other cultures. Some deep unhappiness in the past, certainly before we'd met. My goodness, I pray that's the case.

If Sophie wanted to protectively wrap her past around her, who was I to tell her she couldn't? Has to be her time and place. I didn't want to stumble in and make matters worse. 'Tell you a secret, then tell me one of yours.' Didn't want to trick her by playing *that* game.

Those marks; no longer fresh pickings, well past the blood red and raw stage. The stains faded now, part of the furniture. Long sleeves, the cover up keeping her despair away from prying eyes, that's her right and so it should be. Not Morn and Sophie. Not Sophie and Morn. Sophie. In no way does she answer to me.

A month ago. Cinema night but a tearful last-minute cancellation over the phone. That for me was *the* moment. I needed to see her and put my hands round her and hold her tight to me and tell her that everything would be alright. Orcadian holding Orcadian in Swindon. She lived only a short drive away. I turned up at her flat unannounced. She was pleased to see me.

She talked. I listened. Proper listening. Not going through the motions. It all spilled out. Her dad, a merchant seaman, had come back for shore leave before going away…never to be seen again.

Uncommunicative, that would be the only way of describing Sophie's mum's relationship with Sophie. She was cruel to be leaving so many things unanswered. Sophie was fourteen then. A succession of dads would follow. Some nicer than others. Some friendlier than others. Some too friendly. A blind eye turned by those who should have known better.

Sophie's happiness is my number one priority but this Stevenage journey was my suggestion and I have made all the arrangements. I do have a nagging doubt. Is all this purely with Sophie in mind or is it more about me and my needs?

Anxiety like any contagion spreads too easily. I need to look confident and reassuring. '*May the day turn out well.*' The Open Road. Austin Metro. New Town. Britain. Jerusalem, Old or new, within touching distance. Well, we've passed Reading anyway.

Who was I to put in train such a powerful sequence of events? Why hadn't I shared my misgivings out loud to Sophie before making *that* phone call?

This thread of thought welling up inside me becomes overpowering. There is no room now to continue Uncle Johnny's story. Uncle Johnny's story will have to wait. Maybe Uncle Johnny's story was ready for a break anyway, for an intermission. Like at the cinema with the plush curtains drawn and the lights on and the usherette walking down the aisle with her ice cream tray…I worry that I have been thinking out aloud. I worry that Sophie has heard every word of mine. Sophie's eyes are shut. She's asleep. I'm sure she is. I hope she is.

Her dad came across as being extremely friendly. He was neither abrupt nor suspicious in tone. I did my best over the course of a few phone calls to reassure her actual father that it wasn't money she was after but self-worth. It was easy for me to do so because I was not spinning a line, I was telling the truth.

I hope my honesty shone through. I had tried to put

myself in *her* position. I now was trying to put myself in *his* shoes. Me, a wet-behind-the-ears, 27-year-old now turning this stranger's world upside down…

M4 to M25 to M1. M4-M25-M1. Reads like spy craft. Morse Code. Enigma machine. My foot down. My car. Motorways. Modern. Movement. Despite my best wishes, Uncle Johnny pops up again uninvited. Demanding to be the centre of attention.

'You listen to me, Stuart. I'm your uncle.' I hear his voice. 'Aldwych-The Strand-Adelphi Hotel, heart of London. 1939. On the cusp of War, the cusp of…'

I see him before me, arms akimbo. 'That trumps your hand,' he says. My Uncle Johnny, he's a bit of a bluffer and not one who wants to lose even to his young nephew at cards.

This is 1981, though. A strong feeling that 'M4-M25-M1' is somehow predestined. A longstanding family wrong to be righted. The treating of someone with respect. Different people involved from different generations but the principle everlasting.

So, there's not far to go now. Reading and the M4, long past. We've turned onto the orbital M25, which is like the outer ring of the London dart board. Twenty miles left. Roughly, twenty minutes' drive. This *New Town* of Stevenage with its road network and landscaping will be a box of tricks. I have to find Sophie's father's house within this town planner's Rubik's Cube.

But enough is enough. My patience, fully tried and

tested. That moment has arrived. The squashed daddy longlegs on the windscreen have to go. At the first service station on the M1, I pull in. I forgot to bring a bottle of water with me. One duly purchased and chamois leather in hand, I get to work, clearing the debris. It doesn't take long.

For Sophie, this is an opportunity for fresh air and a ciggie break. Why hadn't she asked earlier? Back in my brand-new Austin Metro I have a clear view of her now. She's totally wired. I pick up my Filofax. Do you know that I was one of the first people in Orkney to own one? Gives me a cutting edge, don't you think? Ciggie finished. She gets back in the car. Ten minutes out of our future and then off we go.

Underpasses and flyovers. Not much point looking for a guiding green light. Green and glass. The outskirts of Stevenage. Roundabout after roundabout but no traffic lights. New Town. A consultant's vision statement.

My Austin Metro draws to a halt. I don't need to gently nudge Sophie. Her eyes are open. She knows that before the hour is out, she will be seeing her actual father and not the ever changing one presented to her by her mother.

'Are you OK?'

'Fine.'

'Please, I won't be angry. If you don't want to go ahead with this.'

'No. I'm fine.'

More by luck, I found his house. Stevenage once must have had a lustre about it, long faded. New Town?

‘Right, we’re here.’

I park outside and make doubly sure my Austin Metro is locked. I wouldn’t be without my krooklok – steering-wheel lock. Hand in hand and we are walking up the driveway to this semi-detached bungalow. I give her a quick good luck kiss on the lips. There is a tremor in the response, and not from passion. I hold her tighter. I hope this reassurance of mine isn’t being misconstrued.

The next two hours flowed like a benign river. No blockages. No waterfall. Many tears and hugs and laughter and introductions aplenty. ‘…And my name is…I’m the son of him.’

Sophie’s father, wife and family there were so welcoming and friendly. Gathered as we were in the large walkthrough front rooms, it was a joyously warm, intimate experience. A fine buffet provided. She certainly did not need me to act as a chaperone. The occasional glances between us were of affirmation, Dutch courage not needed. We left at about 3pm. Time does fly.

If there’s nothing else that I had done in my life, I had done this.

‘What do you think? That went well.’

‘Yes.’

I didn’t get that much more out of her. In fact, not a peep.

It was a long drive home.

From time to time, I glanced at my rear-view mirror and then at her, to be met with a blankness, a void.

Sophie didn't stay the night.

1981. Thatcher's Britain. Out with the Old. In with the New. Austin Metro. Motorways. Stevenage. A New Town. Aspirational.

It was asking too much to expect our shared Orkney upbringing to be able to ride to the rescue this time.

Those fucking daddy longlegs didn't bring me any luck.

Morn and Sophie. 1981. The start of the decade. Facing the future. Separately.

I just had Uncle Johnny's story for company on our return drive back to Swindon.

Uncle Johnny…inside…my…head.

Uncle Johnny…the only company I've got.

Uncle Johnny's story helping to deaden the pain.

Uncle Johnny's story and what a story it is.

'You listen to me, *beuy.* I'm your uncle.' I hear his voice.

'Aldwych-The Strand-Adelphi, heart of London.'

'Aldwych-The Strand-Adelphi.' No mumbo jumbo, more of a swirly incantation like an Orkney piper at the gates of midsummer dawn.

SPRING 1939

Paper. Paper. Read all abou' i'.

As many double decker buses as cars and vans, the honking of horns and aroma of exhaust fumes, you're left in no doubt that you're in the heart of a city. Hurrying and scurrying of folk on to and off of the pavements. Eyes down and not for a full house. Mind the gap. Hit-or-miss. Stay alert. People spilling in and out of shops. Time, a precious commodity. Excitement. Hubbub. It's no ordinary city. It's capital. It's the Capital of the Empire. It's London. 1939.

Eyes up. The sky peek-a-booing through those tall buildings. There are British-Pathé-News sandbags placed round them. Some of the special buildings even have a barrage balloon flying above. Let those enemy bombers just try. An inflatable fish in the sky with strings, that's what they look like. London is full of surprises. You wouldn't be able to hear a birdie above the cacophony. As for actually seeing our feathered friends – fat chance.

Johnny takes a deep breath in. It's worth the cough and splutter and is far more exciting to this 19-year-old than Orkney with its clean but boring fresh air. London. Try and top that. Johnny is not going to disparage where he has come from. Orkney has its fresh air and farming and fishing, but London. *Beuys o beuys*, full-on London. Early afternoon London. Heaving London. Capital London. A different world. A different class to this 19-year-old.

'Paper. Paper. Read all abou' i'. 'Grea' Bri'ain guaran'ees Poland's fu'ure. Ge' your paper.' *Ts* are cockney optional from this newspaper seller. A newspaper to be read and then discarded. A double-page spread lies on the pavement. Uncle Johnny bends down. Curiosity behind this bending down, not picking up litter – couldn't give a fig about keeping the streets of London free from *bruck*. Centre pages displayed and it's that large advert for Anchor Butter gawpin' at him that gets Johnny *finkin'*.

Not the Anchor-butter-support-New-Zealand-part-of-the-Empire bit, nor the wholesome image of milk spurting from the udders into the steel pail ready for the churning bit. It's the picture of the spreading of the butter on to the piece of toast that gets Johnny smacking his lips. It's the means of delivery for this gastronomic delight. The knife but a non-serrated, rounded edge, useless sort of knife. An imposter of a knife. A knife in name only.

'A butter knife is only good for spreading butter. Only the best butt-er knife will do for spreading butter. The best butter needs the best knife and so on and so on.' Catchphrases jumping about in Johnny's head. No, Johnny wants to be taken for a Cockney. *Bu..ah. Bu..ah. I really fancy a nice bit of toast and bu..ah,* cor *blimey, luv-a-ducks.* All good-natured Cockney nonsense filling his Kirkwall head.

You see he's got a butter knife in his back pocket anyway. It's from work. They use it to slit open envelopes, to have a poke around if you get my meaning. Not every letter, 'cause management wouldn't be able to turn a blind eye if it was so much in their face but maybe a few letters a day, the ones from abroad. You'd have your excuse ready then. *Just checkin' from the le..er inside that the address on the envelope is okey-dokey. Foreign, innit.*

Johnny, a messenger boy from the post room walking the mean streets, knife in back pocket bringing an edge to it all now, causing no harm with his adolescent nonsense. Here comes menace. Here's Johnny.

If you are after my girl, I'll get my knife out and you'll regret it. Tough guy. Accompanied by a hard, you'll-be-sorry-if-you-mess-with-me smirk. He is *Rocky Sullivan.* All in his head. Played by James Cagney. His hero. *Angels with Dirty Faces.* His film. As he walks towards the Adelphi. To no one in particular he delivers a James Cagney warning, *Someday, you're gonna stick your nose in and get something you didn't expect in it.*

Films, not just entertainment for Johnny. Films. How else in Orkney was he going to see with his own two eyes what goes on off the island. *Doon Sooth* – those words encapsulate anything and everything that goes on in the outside world. Albert Kinema in Kirkwall, the *Toon's* cinema brings the School of Life early to Johnny. 'Cause he'd be under age, he'd have to sneak in, fire exit, side lane entrance and hope he wasn't caught.

The result? Here, now, before you. It wasn't *Mither* or *Faether* talking about uncle-this-or-uncle-that that took him to sea. It wasn't *Mither* or *Faether* talking about London that brought him to the Strand, heart of London. He'd seen what it was like on the Big Screen. The films offered Johnny the only image of his future that he could trust… one of success and well within grasp because he'd seen it with his very own *mince pies* on the Big Screen.

What You See, You Can Be.

This one, he saw just a few months back. It was right good. *Angels with Dirty Faces.* Johnny is practising staring guys out and *tellin em* straight, *You do know what guys get who talk.* Johnny from Kirkwall, from the *Toon*, from Orkney is a natural. Johnny (James Cagney) Sinclair personified on the mean streets of London. Pats his backside trouser pocket to make sure he is not without a weapon. No shooter for him. A knife, just as effective. Even a butter knife. He knows how to use one. Let someone just dare try it on.

Always with his left hand he'd pat his back trouser

pocket. Yes, the knife is there. Yes, the butter knife. Left pocket. Had to be the left hand. Even if Johnny wanted to use his right hand, it's out of action, rendered inactive. Left hand, good. Right hand, out of action.

All things Cagney, is how Johnny likes to fill the silence in his head as he walks from Bush House, Aldwych to the Adelphi. The heart of London. A short walk, certainly less than half an hour. Half ten in the morning. Same time, every day. The Embankment and River Thames, nearby. Trafalgar Square with Lord Nelson and them pigeons (coo coo), Big Ben and the Houses of…, nearby. Same route. Aldwych to the Adelphi. A to A.

'Jock, do not deviate.' He has been told. 'Out of Bush House, left. Then right at the Strand. Straight ahead. Past access to Waterloo Bridge. Past the Savoy Hotel. Third left. Adam Street. First right. John Adam Street. Bob's…your… uncle, the Adelphi. Should take fifteen minutes tops. *Got it, Jock*?'

All is said friendly like, not sneery. No point in pointing out to Mister Rennison sir that Johnny's name is Johnny not Jock. No point in pointing out to Mister Rennison sir that Scots aren't all called Jock. Mister Rennison sir is not a bad egg. He is in charge. 'I will not tolerate any use by my staff of in-fucking-temperate language in my presence, an offence I consider worse than in-fucking-subordination. Have I made myself clear, Jock?

'The fucking Adelphi. Art Deco. Brand New. Marble foyer. Spotless. You'd be honoured to eat your dinner off the…Take the lift. Second Floor. Next to the lift, the offices of Walter Gibbons. They have the key to the attaché case. They will take out the papers and replace with new ones. Speak to no one, no one. *Have you fucking got that, Jock?* Speak to no one.' He holds one finger up to his lips.

Mister Rennison sir, staring hard at Johnny. 'Do…not… examine…contents of. Do…not…talk…to…anyone…on… the street. Straight back. Got it. If your nose itches, use your left hand to have a fucking scratch. Got it, Jock? So, fuck off and start doing what we're paying you to do.' All said with just the right balance between friendliness and menace. Iron fist in a velvet glove. Cagney to a T.

Walter Gibbons. They're partners of Stanley Gibbons (just around the corner) them postage stamp people. Stanley Gibbons, they're world renowned. This lot, different line of business. He knows that Bush House, where he works, is the home of the BBC. Walter Gibbons, never heard of them. *Shipping Agent.* That's what the nameplate on their door says.

A few months in. Sunny Spring day. 1939. Johnny's done his drop off and is just about to retrace his steps. The returning attaché case is unusually empty. He's so close to the water and being a good-Orkney-Islands-boy he does miss the water, he thinks wouldn't it just be grand, just dandy, to see Old Father Thames? Just a few minutes' walk away. What's the harm?

He is temporarily distracted by a fine-looking lady who other things being equal he would like to get to know better. But Johnny isn't tempted. He wraps himself up in his Cagney persona like a safety blanket. Cagney doesn't do loose talk. Johnny doesn't do loose talk. He'll keep schtum about this little diversion. My goodness, the River Thames certainly does not disappoint.

The following day, Mister Rennison sir hauls him over the coals. Mister Rennison sir's applecart well and truly overturned. No attempt at friendliness now. Rollocking delivered for transgression and a first and final warning, all rolled into one.

How did Mister Rennison sir find out? Some bastard ratted on him, but who? Doesn't matter. Johnny never did it again. Johnny had learnt his lesson. If you transgress, you get found out. Isn't that the sort of twaddle they teach you at Sunday School? Father Thames will have to wait for out-of-work hours. He makes an effort to put all daydreams and distractions to a lock-up garage in his head and Johnny becomes more observant at street level throughout his short, daily delivery-and-collection walk. He pays more attention to the here and now.

But the silver screen fantasy won't go away. It won't be constrained. *They* are so scared of what he, Johnny (James Cagney) Sinclair can do. Johnny Sinclair is a man to be reckoned with. Just giving them a peep at this blunt, round edged knife and they know what's coming. A curl of the upper lip and a patting of the back left trouser pocket…with his left hand. People on the street must understand. *No one messes with Johnny.*

Hang on. Hang on. That same man, every day. He's following me. I see him now. I bend down to tie my shoelaces. Quick glance and peek behind. This side of the Strand. No traffic obstructing my view. He's looking in the shop window. Light coloured mackintosh and wearing a 'titfor'-tit-for-tat = hat, that's Cockney talk. That same man. Always there. Too much of a coincidence. The bugger's following me.

Just happens to emerge from a doorway next to the Savoy in the Strand as Johnny walks by and barges into him. 'Guv, can you tell me the time?' A *Paddy* from the Emerald Isle, on hard times. A man on his uppers but he does not whiff of piss and pints. A man of the street but pong free. A king of the road but pong free. There's the thing. We help people in Orkney. Automatic. But Johnny's promised to talk to no-one, *no-one.* Johnny knows he'll be well and truly in the proverbial with Mister Rennison sir if he doesn't keep to his word.

Johnny lifts his hand, the active one, the left one, 180-degree flip so that the tramp can see the time for himself, from his watch. The tramp tugs his forelock. Johnny's *north and south = mouth* keeps schtum. No breaking of his word…

Johnny's done his bit. Doesn't want to have to listen to any begging bollocks. Walks right through the down-and-out feller as if he's not there, shouldering the *Paddy* out of the way.

All the way from Orkney, 1939, in the centre of a

London putting on an air of normality as the skies get ever darker. That was Johnny. Happy. Happy as a pig in shit. Who'd have thought it? At the top of his game, our Johnny. The dog's bollocks. Him, the lad from Kirkwall. Him, the lad from the *Toon*.

All so different from the horse-and-cart-and-bicycle-and-no-pavement world of Kirkwall's Bridge Street and Broad Street. Here in the midst of this thrilling city. London and it's going to be his future. Not paved with gold but all these possibilities. As malleable as putty, our Johnny. Only one thing on this 19-year-old's mind.

A handcuff placed round Johnny's right hand. Johnny, not under arrest. The handcuff supposed to be under the sleeve but visible if you look closely enough. The attaché case tight to the wrist, not dangling. Him. A lad from Orkney. A messenger boy cum courier, that's Uncle Johnny. Entrusted with promise-not-to-tell secrets. No, not James Cagney fantasy. Reality. He is paid to do this. A work duty. Legal. Above board. Must be important.

They get to know Johnny there at the Adelphi. The concierge at the door. Formally dressed. Posh. Authority. Doesn't matter where he fits in the hierarchy, the doorman is authority and therefore to be kowtowed to. Never says a word to Johnny but always winks at him as Johnny is let through, not even now needing to sign in. Johnny finds this winking right-confusing.

Johnny then takes the lift. Second floor. Offices immediately to the left. There is a brass nameplate on the door. He rings the bell. The same person always lets him in.

This first and only contact point at Walter Gibbons, always very stand offish, unforgiving, almost barking at him, though nothing censorious – 'fine day', 'you're right on time', 'see you tomorrow morning'…nothing chatty-like.

Johnny is never told this man's name. Johnny doesn't know the bloke's name. Johnny does not want to know the fucker's name.

Yes, you fucker, see you the morn's morning. My black shoes are better polished than yours, you Berkshire Hunt.

But over the course of a few months this stern feller's manner towards Johnny softens, becomes friendlier, draws him out into conversation, shows interest in him. Johnny's confused…doesn't know where he stands with him. Then… one day…in a I'm-not-talking-down-to-you sort of way, after the documents are exchanged and Johnny's heading for the door, he calls him back and says, 'How are you getting on, Jock?'

'Fine, thanks.'

'You're doing very well. *We're* pleased with you. There's something I have to tell you…When you walk down each day from *the Bush,* do you ever notice a man?'

Johnny feels like playing such a ridiculous comment for laughs. Of course, he is aware of loads of passers-by, men and women in the hustle and bustle of the big city. Holds his breath.

Mister Walter Gibbons man repeats, 'Do you ever notice a man?'

'I do…sir…the one with the light fawn mackintosh and hat…other side of the road…always ten yards behind me… never in front…walking slowly…always the same coat… never looks at me. I never let on that I know he's there. He never lets on that he's seen me. What a palaver!'

Mackintosh man and me. Lay it on thick with a trowel that the penny had dropped long ago.

'Sir. He's armed. Isn't he?'

'Johnny, don't take any notice of him. Yes, he is armed. Revolver. He's guarding you…' he laughs, 'but more importantly, he's looking after those papers in that attaché case, making sure they reach the right destination. When did you first notice him?'

'Over a month ago, now.'

'Very good and neither he nor I ever had an inkling that you knew.' The Walter Gibbons man paused. 'See you tomorrow, Jock. Oh, by the way, what's the time?' He puts on a stage Oirish-begorrah accent and then holds his nose. He's smiling.

Johnny's smiling. The sun's out and the sun is joining in the smiling. Bright light splashing through the window. Attaché case papers replaced. Locked. Handcuff clicked. Under sleeve. Johnny senses that he's passed some sort of test.

'Jock? Just a minute. We've got it right about you. You're a smart lad. Here at Walter Gibbons – Shipping

Agent – we're good at reading people, sizing up their character. Strike me as being perfectly capable of looking after yourself.

'Confidential papers. Strict security arrangements. Walter Gibbons is always on the look-out for new staff who can be trusted.

'You're too bright just to be working as a messenger boy. You've got it in you to be doing more in our line of work. Helping King and Country in our moment of… Rest assured more and more barrage balloons are going up, the sirens will be sounding, sandbags everywhere – not of the bucket and spade variety. We'll all be masked up. Not going to one of these posh balls.

'You, Jock. There's an exciting opportunity for you. Something a bit dangerous but you'll be back on home turf. We've already squared it with Bush House. Let you know a bit more tomorrow morning. Remember. Never let the left hand know what the right hand's doing. Won't let us down, will you?' A challenge, perhaps an order.

Johnny's right excited. Sold on it even before he knows what *it* actually entails. Has to be undercover work. Top secret. Johnny's lip curls up – Chicago style. Rocky Sullivan, eat your heart out. Johnny (James Cagney) Sinclair.

I will need an alibi…no…alias, that's the word. Those men on the street corners. I will be like them, smartly dressed in black. I will be known as 'The Spy in Black'.

Johnny believes he is one of a kind. Orkney is great.

London is great but as sure as eggs are eggs, you can never top the Land of Make Believe in your head. Johnny is playing out his remarkable life on the big screen. 'If you see it, you can be it'…and this is the holy wonder…*it is coming to pass*…a leading role certainly and not a walk-on part in a 'B' movie.

Opening scene. Bush House – BBC. Him, just sorting out the mail, pigeon hole compartments, basement post room and no natural light, caged. He is allowed to spread his wings, a messenger boy, daylight – fourth floor, fifth floor and typist pool. Then outdoors, Aldwych-The Strand-Adelphi, blue skies and Johnny (James Cagney) Sinclair sometimes likes to make room for Johnny Sinclair (soon-to-be RAF pilot, the Distinguished Flying Cross (DFC) medal comes his way after his first skirmish with the *Luftwaffe*) in his head. And now he doesn't even need to pass Go, to become a spy.

All the details to be fleshed out the *morn*.

There is a cloud on the horizon, though.

She had come back into his life. Found each other working on the same floor at Bush House, the Aldwych, London. An Orkney lass. Kirstin. Kirstin Rendall.

Whit like? – Noh bad. – How's yerself?

One of the Rendalls. Kirstin was at Papdale Junior in Kirkwall with Johnny. She's a great looker and they fall once again for each other.

She thought he was quite a catch. One thing leads to another and within the month, May 1939, he's got engaged.

Whit like? – Noh bad. – How's yerself?

Kirstin's working as a typist, also at Bush House, London. Left home because she wanted to travel. Why should travel and fortune just be the preserve of men?

Whit like? – Noh bad. – How's yerself?

Eighteen years old and Kirstin is well and truly smitten with Johnny.

'Johnny, I've got a pen friend in Ostend, Belgium. Her parents run a guest house on the sea front. Johnny, we could go there for our honeymoon. "The season tails off by mid-September," that's what my friend says and throws in, "we can get a special end-of-season rate." Just think of it, my love. Ostend in early October and Xmas not far off. Belgium, in October. What could be better? It'll be so peaceful. Those sandy 1939 beaches all to ourselves. Romantic.'

Johnny is strong on 'romantic', providing he can get his leg over.

'Perfect.'

An October wedding in London is planned. It's mid-summer now, end of June. Plenty of time to make arrangements.

'London…here in London…that's where we'll put down roots…away from all of this everyone knowing everyone else's business…London for us. Wouldn't it be nice to receive a canteen of cutlery for a wedding present?' Kirstin whispers and then nibbles Johnny's ear. She's a wee slip of a girl, but with a determination to make something of herself.

'*Whit like? – Noh bad. – How's yerself?*'

'I've never been so happy.' That's what Johnny tells Kirstin that evening. He's not being straight with her. Kirstin had been moving far too quickly in this wedlock malarkey for Johnny's liking. He doesn't tell Kirstin what's making him so happy.

It's that clock, it's that Orkney Jahr clock. The Orkney Jahr clock is holding me back.

Johnny wants to put a bonfire-night banger of a rocket under the arse of the Orkney *Jahr* clock so that he can find out what Walter Gibbons has in store for him. For a 19-year-old, patience is no virtue.

Come *the morn's morning*, Johnny more puzzled than disappointed. The detail is sketchy to say the least.

'Jock, you have been chosen because you're a local lad and can fit in easily back home in Orkney. Alumni of Kirkwall Grammar School, weren't you?' Diddly squat as to what he was to be chosen for. No option to think about it.

'Yes, sir. Anything to serve King and Country.' Johnny didn't believe this King and Country guff but thought it sounded good.

'You'll be starting immediately.'

'Yes, sir.'

'Here's your ticket for this afternoon's 1.30 Thurso-bound train for Orkney.'

'Thank you, sir.'

My goodness, that's cutting it fine. Only a few hours to pack my bags. Must be very important and dangerous this job that I'm having to start immediately.

Johnny leaves the attaché case at Walter Gibbons, handcuff and all, looks at his indented right wrist ruefully and gives it a comforting rub. He is never to return to Bush House, goes directly home to his lodgings, packs his bags and heads for Euston Station.

'By the way, Jock, you'll be met at Inverness Station, *the morn's morning.* Did I get that Orkney expression right? Tomorrow morning. This contact lady will dot the i's and cross the t's for you.'

I'm going to be a spy. Undercover. I might even get to wear a mac.

Johnny's going to be going home, Orkney bound. Home. Having made it. Not as a piece of flotsam and jetsam. Not someone carrying their tail between their legs. Important. Secret mission for His Majesty. At Inverness he looks forward to being provided with his cover story.

Only an hour in Inverness before catching the Thurso train but if this contact lady turns out to be a smasher, I can always delay the second leg of my journey home. I didn't say anything to the Walter Gibbons man about Kirstin. This job offer has saved my proverbial bacon. I'm just not the commitment type. She'll be snapped up straight away. Kirstin's a smasher. Why do girls always want more than a bit of slap and tickle?

From Hudson's Bay Company times, Orkney folk have

always valued adventure and travel over the humdrum. Is Johnny excited? Like fuck he is.

They'll be making a film of my life. I'll be on the screen at the Albert Kinema in Kirkwall and not just as a B-Movie bit part player...a star in the Main Attraction, no less...and I'm not even 20 years old.

Paper. Paper. Read all abou' it. Johnny Sinclair.

TUESDAY 27TH JUNE 1939

Still Tuesday. 13.30pm. It's half past one. The London Euston to Thurso train is packed full. The time it takes to change trains at Inverness Station in the Scottish Highlands, his only break in the journey. Johnny finds his seat. Twenty-four hours travel to come, to all Orcadians over in a click of the fingers.

06.00am, the *morn*, the Wednesday, that's when his contact will be meeting him. Such an ungodly hour. Chuff-a-chuff-chuff, up to Thurso on the northernmost tip of Scotland. A bit of rocking and rolling on the Pentland Firth ferry. Early afternoon, arrival time, in Orkney. That fresh air, take a lungful.

Johnny is Orcadian and is used to the feel of long-distance travel. He will be engaging in shut-eye for most of the journey, but will always remain alert as befits a special agent. He is in moggy-mode but knows with what had happened in t*he Malacca Straits* he had already used up one of his nine lives, eight left. Johnny is an Orkney Tom – an Orkney Octopuss.

This time tomorrow, I'll be seeing the Old Man of Hoy. This time tomorrow, give or take an hour, I'll be seeing my old man in Orkney.

Johnny's rail ticket includes a seat reservation but here's the thing, the ticket issued just takes him as far as Inverness. If his contact doesn't turn up during the hour changing trains at Inverness Station, Johnny's well and truly buggered. Not impressed, my Uncle Johnny. Not impressed.

Passing the time will be a challenge. Johnny can look out the windows 'til his heart's content but they haven't been cleaned and he'll see nothing. Smokers fug fills his compartment, a real pea-souper. Panoramic view? Puffer steam billowing from the front engine? Come on, we're in the here and now and not the make-believe world of tourism and films.

Johnny needs to distract himself. He gets into the part of being secret agent. Wants to learn the knack of observing without being observed. After all, how does he know that one of his fellow compartment passengers isn't a German spy? On the other hand, how does he know that there isn't a guardian angel from Walter Gibbons just checking he's safe and secure? Only one way for Johnny to master this. Give it a bash. It'll be easy-peasy.

The toot of the whistle. We're off. The seat next to me

empty. Who's going to fill it? Restaurant car's in third class. I'll check it out. Restaurant car normally means tea and a bun but you never know.

Johnny doesn't feel remorse but it's nagging away. He knows he's treated Kirstin very badly. He feels guilty and so he should. Not even telling her to her face. A letter or note would have been a poor substitute but at least she would have known he wasn't a missing person.

I'm only 19. Conscription kicks in for me on my next birthday when I'm 20 but who knows what's around the corner? Kirstin...I couldn't have found a sweeter girl. Well it's too late now...spilt milk and all that. I'll make a new start, I promise. Thank goodness we were always careful but I left those matters to her. I must steer clear of Kirstin's mither and in fact of all them Rendalls when I'm back home. I'll make it up to Kirstin, promise.

Newcastle Station. 18.35pm. Still daylight, still Tuesday – early evening. The seat next to him still empty.

A young lady, very attractive, enters the compartment and sits next to Johnny. She has a bit of a problem putting her bags in the overhead rack but gets there. Johnny takes in this wonderful, unexpected view. Her dress clings closely to her backside. He would normally be in there like a shot.

Good pair of 'hams' (ham and eggs = legs). What a glorious 'bottle' (bottle and glass = arse). This is a test, though. Temptation.

She crosses them; those legs. Mid-length skirt. She's wearing the latest fashion, elegant, certainly not tarty.

Pretty face. Demure. Johnny suspicious. He has to get in there but decides on waiting and seeing how it goes. He'll button his lip and wait. Johnny crosses his legs, mirroring her action.

Very shapely legs.

'Monsieur, I'm sorry to bother you. Have you possibly got a light?' Such a sweet voice. Soft accent, foreign though. Be careful.

'Of course, ma'am.' She is looking intently at Johnny. He looks away. This isn't at all easy. It's against all of his natural, male predatory instincts.

'Excuse me, sir. Could you ever so kindly bring down my carrier bag from the overhead rack?' She points to a spot above Johnny. What a delicate wrist she has. 'It's got some food and a thermos flask. Such a long journey.'

'Pleased to oblige, ma'am.' The carrier bag is full. Nestling on top of it is a large white envelope, quite bulky, possibly sealed.

Johnny carefully takes down her bag without saying a word. Next to the large white envelope, is something submarine shaped, wrapped in white paper. He has never seen a sandwich that big.

'In France, monsieur, we call this a *baguette*.'

'Bag…Ate', ma'am?'

'No. It's said all in one word, *baguette*.' She is chuckling but not laughing at him.

'Please, I have a knife to cut the *baguette* into portions.'

Did she say a knife?

Johnny is truly on guard now.

'It is too much for one. I had a late lunch but how do you say in your country, I am *pecker...ish*. Will you please join me?' She chuckles. 'You English always "Please", "Thank you", "Sorry", "Excuse Me". You, English...So polite but never straight to the point.'

Johnny, having been called *Jock* for almost all of 1939 in London, does not react kindly to being called *English*. Johnny's *Orcadian*. He is right proud of the fact but doesn't feel the need to spell out that he is Orkney born and bred every time he opens his *mooth*.

'It is a cheese and ham *baguette*...with some mustard from Dijon.'

Johnny nods as if he has a clue where this Dijon is... foreign, definitely foreign. *Foreign* means to be treated with suspicion. That mustard could contain poison.

'No thank you, ma'am. I've already eaten.'

'I am visiting *maman* in Pitlochry on Thursday. But I thought I would like to spend a day on my own in Inverness and travel down the day after. I have heard that Inverness is such a beautiful town. I have come to collect *maman* for a stay with me. She has an appointment with a specialist in Glasgow. *Maman* is unwell...her chest...with the cough. Glasgow. I have heard it is such a cultured city. It is well known for Charles Rennie Mackintosh.' Emphasis placed on the *Mack in Mackintosh*. 'Am I not right?' A pause, then: 'You are very quiet, *monsieur*.'

Maybe she is a recruiting sergeant for the French

Foreign Legion? A bloody attractive one, though. No. I am serving King and Country. I will not be tempted.

Johnny nods and then closes his eyes.

I should have told Kirstin but what would I have said? More importantly, what happens if I don't get my onward ticket from Inverness? The jingle jangle of small change in my pocket? Not enough for a rail ticket. Inverness? Don't want to be stuck there.

The train pulls into Inverness Station. 6 o'clock, Wednesday morning. Sun already up, a true Highlands welcome. The seat next to Johnny is empty.

I thought she said she was stopping over in Inverness. What happened to her? Fishy. Very fishy. The contact and drop will be made here. Just a handful of platforms at Inverness Station but a lot of passengers will be spilling out of the train. Not going to miss the reception committee of one. Less than an hour between trains.

The man at Walter Gibbons saw something in me. I will not let him down. Invisible. That's what I'll be. I will watch, listen and note down while not being seen...

'Walter Gibbons.' More of a bark than an entreaty. Johnny falls into step with a stoutish, matronly lady who seems to know him – an old bat of a lady.

She locks arms with Johnny and he is frogmarched across the station concourse in the direction of the station cafe. It is open even at this ungodly hour. He is firmly deposited like an errant nephew at the first free table, still to be cleared.

Johnny is told in no uncertain terms to sit and wait. She returns carrying a ceramic tray, on top a plate with a pair of well-handled rock buns and a couple of cups of *rosie lee = tea*, filled to the brim and splashing over the sides into the saucers, a brown splish-splashy waterfall. Johnny doesn't want to spend longer with this old bat than he needs to.

The old bat's loud voice cuts right through. She could give a foghorn a run for its money. It's as if she wants all of the Scottish Highlands to know that she's there. A rum do.

Johnny has of now no rail ticket for the final six-hour leg of the journey. He is becoming more and more anxious. Fuck the instilled patience of the Orkney *Jahr* clock, time isn't just ticking away, it's wooshing out like one of those angry Orkney winds.

'Here's your ticket. Sign for it.' The old bat finally produces the goods, comes up trumps.

At last and thank you. No small talk. No pleasantries. No, 'Hello, Mister Sinclair. Did you have a good trip?' A cat with a mouse on the end of the paw. Sign for it? What does she think I'm going to do with the ticket, flog it?

'We'll be making sure you get on that train.' She does not engage in eye contact.

Probably pissed off at having to be up so early in the day.

'Shouldn't you be at Army camp?'

Old bat thinks I'm dodging the national call-up. So that's it. Oh no. Not going to justify myself. No spilling of the beans. Careless talk...I've met her type before.

'Are you sure you don't want this? "Waste not, want not. Sixpence is as sixpence does." That's what they say.' She paused, waiting for Johnny to say or do something, then made a grab for the bun.

I wouldn't even pay a tanner in toto for that piss water and unclean gobstopper. To hell with it. I'm going to tell her that. I've got the rail ticket now in my hand to get me home to Orkney. Old bat.

Johnny lets her know that he is dissatisfied with the standard of catering at this establishment. He fears the worst but here's a surprise. She nods in agreement.

I am being listened to.

She returns to the counter having barged in at the front of the queue and demands to see the manageress. What a foghorn of a voice. Everyone in the Caff is staring at her. Everyone bar Johnny.

This could be another test, after all. Must look disinterested.

Johnny pretend whistles away the time with that current snappy favourite of his, a Joe Loss tune. *Hands, Knees and Boomps-A-Daisy.* He looks at his watch. Just twenty minutes to go before the train to Thurso pulls out. No seat reservations for this leg but at least he has his rail ticket.

Get on with it. She does. No magic envelope. Instructions communicated by human voice, by foghorn.

'Thursday morning. Tomorrow morning. *The morn's morning,* as you Orcadians say, the 29th. Half past nine sharp you'll be expected at Kirkwall Hotel. Ask at the desk for Commander Winifred – SNO and King's Harbour Master, Scapa. Scapa Flow. The Flow. Lots of work there for the Navy to do. Getting defences shipshape. Make sure you're wearing Number Ones.'

Christ. Louder still. I'll call her Foghorn Fanny. Why not make the announcement over a megaphone outside Carlton House Terrace No 9, the German Embassy in London? In fact, with a boom-boom voice like that, why bother with a megaphone?

Johnny's out of his chair as if a wasp had stung his arse. Bun and tea replacements left untouched. Rushes to catch the train. Ticket is for third class. Standing room only. Not surprised but feels he deserves better.

Finds a space at the top of the corridor. Shoulder drops his kit bag and makes do. Happy? If Johnny had played his cards right, he could have been snug in the arms of the lady from Dijon.

This much smaller train from Inverness to Thurso puff puffs its way through the Scottish Highlands, one of the most glorious landscapes in the western world.

The train snakes its way from the capital of the Highlands to the northernmost tip of the Scottish Mainland. The promise of wooded glens and moorlands; lochs and waterfalls; stone cottages dotted here and there, deer emerging from the heather is there for all, to be enjoyed through the much cleaner carriage windows.

Johnny though seems more interested in admiring his face in the tiny mirror that he is holding. He'd *half-inched*

= *pinched*, her powder compact case for the sheer hell of it. Powder compact case. That'll teach her. *The old bat.*

Practising my tradecraft. I'm not going to be just good at this game, I'm going to be the best. I'll set my sights high. That watcher in the Strand, he was good, but I've got my sights on being better than the man at the top of the organisation himself...Watch out Walter, this oik will be wearing your crown...in its entirety...not just 'alf a crown.

WEDNESDAY 28TH JUNE 1939

There he is. The prodigal son and he's back outside his home. *Toon* centre, more or less. Clay Loan. Just beyond Victoria Street which leads off Saint Magnus Cathedral. Front doors are always open in Orkney, so he could just walk straight in. No fuss, no pack drill. But Johnny wants, no he demands an entrance. Him, kit bag slung over his shoulder and all. Johnny, returning from the World, from *Doon Sooth* as they say here, peeks through the bay window…and there's that familiarity but that unfamiliarity like putting on your slippers for the first time in ages.

Johnny decides to spread out arms and legs, as if about to be frisked. His nose is squashed against the bay window. He rat-a-tat-tats with the index finger knuckle against the glass. Johnny is playing the fool, playing the daddy longlegs. Five minutes, he'll give this being-noticed lark, about five minutes.

He would have been back on leave anyway at the end of August. His first furlough as merchant seaman, his first job. August 1939, as good a month and year as any. Not the first one to look older than his years. Not the first one who goes to sea and no questions asked. As far as he was concerned, it's better that he keeps to the merchant seaman story. It's only the last week in June and far too early to catch the real daddy longlegs spreadeagling themselves, playing motionless. Johnny has to prepare the ground.

His folk are expecting him. He rang ahead from the telephone box at the Pier head, Stromness. Just didn't know what to say. Saved by the pips. Couldn't let on the real reason for his return. Back in Orkney but even more important he is back in the land of hush-hush. Orkney's a haven but from what?

Of course, *they*'ll be listening in. Our lot? No. The Germans? No. Those nosey parkers in the Kirkwall Telephone Exchange at the Big Tree, down the Close. Yes. Them. You can count on it. You know what they say in Orkney. You can fart at one end of the street and by the time you've reached the other all Orkney will find out from a reliable source that you've just had a shit. The telephone operators, inside track.

Mind Johnny doesn't know himself what the story is to be. Whatever lies in store, he will give his best. Now that'll surprise folk. He has had time to work out the *dutiful son* version on the bus taking him from Stromness to Kirkwall.

He plumps for keeping it vague, keeping it familiar. *Merchant seaman. Off the Dunster Grange. Shore leave. In between consignments.* Will throw in *Malacca and the Straits of.* Enough of a grain of truth, somewhere in all of this babble to still their curiosity. Johnny was brought up proper. He will not fall foul of any of the Ten Commandments, in particular the one that says, *Thou Shall Not Lie To One's Parents.*

'How long you staying for, *buddo*?'

'I'll be hearing something, the *morn*, *Faether*.'

He's landed the big one – 24 points, 1st Dividend, jackpot on the football pools – but it's all top secret.

Shh...mustn't tell.

THURSDAY 29TH JUNE 1939

Commander Winifred – Senior Naval Officer (SNO) Scapa Flow and King's Harbour Master, Scapa – keeps Johnny waiting in the outer office at the Kirkwall Hotel, on the Shore.

The Commander has already served his country once in Flanders. He is getting on but could still walk into any rugger team, well built, stocky not overweight, still to reach the jowly stage of three score years. An upright, firm handshake sort of feller is our Commander. A hail-fellow-well-met is our Commander. Some though say of him, 'that Commander, he can lose his rag easily.'

Bet he's got more than one room here at his disposal.

The Navy base, his patch, is at Lyness, over the water on the Orkney island of Hoy, not a hop-skip-and-jump away. It mightn't make sense but of course in Royal Navy order of priority it does.

Yes, accommodation is available at Lyness but here's the catch. The accommodation-is not-in-keeping-with-that-which-his-position-warrants. The HQ of the Senior Naval Officer is to be found in the Kirkwall Hotel, the most palatial hotel in the *Toon* and his HQ since April, just the few months.

Royal Navy *modus operandi.* One. Two. Three. Task number one. Find the most comfortable quarters. Number two…requisition. Number three…comfortably furnish.

Let's not pull our punches here. Navy HQ is nowhere near the workplace.

Born the previous century is our Commander. Full name Oswald Geoffrey Winifred. What sort of name is that? Oswald. No Mosley lover, he. No Blackshirt he. No fascist he.

The Commander is related to Winston Churchill. The first cousin of…happy to let people know this fact.

If I had a penny for every old feller rabbiting on about what they did in the trenches and I bet I'm going to be getting an earful from him of 'It's A Long Way To Fucking Tipperary'.

The door slightly ajar, a raised voice. You can hear the Commander, crystal clear, on the blower, on the *dog and bone. Cockney speak = dog and bone = phone.* You'd expect though the Armed Forces up here would have their own secure line.

He speaks frightfully la-di-dah. The Commander's secretary, not much to write home about. Desk name plate –

Miss Val Garson. She's from Stromness. You know what they say about lasses from Stromness. Like their town, Alice-In-Wonderland. All over the place. Don't take pride in their looks. No Saint Magnus Cathedral there. No central point for the eyes to focus on in Stromness. Just a higgledy-piggledy warren of lanes. Always takes too much time to get where you want with them. After a while you say to yourself, 'Can I really be bothered?'

'Look here…I am Commander in Charge of Scapa Flow Naval Defences…Put me straight through to Admiral Sir Charles Forbes…Yes…the Admiral…I'll hold on…Right…You're telling me, he's busy…This is a matter of extreme urgency…Get him to ring me back when he's free…A launch…My own boat…Commander Winifred…Based in Scapa…S-C-A-P…Winifred…W-I-N-I…

Have to beg, steal and borrow from the Brylcreem Boys…Fucking RAF…

'What for?... What for?... The French Navy here…Two battleships…Three cruisers…Yes, the *Dunkerque* was here…Lyness Base…earlier this week…Not a good look… your SNCO in a loaned bath tub…Hello…hello...'

He's about to say, 'Courtesy visits…don't happen every day.' But if he does, he's snookered. It'll weaken his case for his own boat. *Courtesy visits*, sounds more like a Sunday afternoon church fete.

'Damn, the line's gone dead. Damn.' Ear piece slammed down on receiver. Silence.

Johnny told that he can go through now. Secretary doesn't deign to look up.

She's from Stromness. Why would anyone want to live there, when you can live in Kirkwall?

Johnny knocks on the door.

'Enter.'

The man to be in charge of Johnny's first mission is in full regalia, seated behind a large desk. Three rings of gold braid – the final one *with* a loop – on each jacket sleeve. Look at those brightly polished brass buttons – six each side, perfectly spaced, symmetrical. There's a bit of a Spencer Tracey's older brother look about the Commander. Avuncular.

He's well ancient. Must be over 50.

Johnny knows he must play the game. Keep his thoughts to himself. Be respectful. Yes sir, no, sir, three bags full sir. Take it all in but be very observant.

On the desk – a desktop bell, the Commander's naval cap, an ashtray with stubbed out cigarette, a mug of tea and newspaper, *The Chronicle* (needed contacts to get his own copy, that early in the day).

No need for a desk name plate. The Commander is the Commander and this is *His Office.*

Johnny can make out markings on the opened pages of the aforesaid daily newspaper. Certain words are circled and underlined.

Next to the newspaper, a large jotter. A few words are scribbled down. Months in the mailroom at Bush House have honed Johnny's technique of deciphering things upside down.

Sees a time: '3.20' ringed. Sees a name: 'E. Hide' underlined. Sees another name: 'Pickles' encircled. A line having been put through the words 'Syrup of Figs'. Farther down the page the letters 'E' 'P' 'S' 'O' 'M', and numbers '5/2'.

We're not talking five shillings and twopence here. What's that word he sees repeated on the page, upside down? 'FAV'.

Bottom of the page, outline of words 'FRENCH' and 'RAF' in large block capitals, not just scrawled. The shading-in spills over, more bludgeoned than precise.

Take it all in, Johnny. Take it all in. On the wall behind, a framed picture of His Majesty. Weak light coming through from the side lane window. One vase, slightly chipped, with red and black flowers on the 'sill in front of.

The Commander is the person to provide the answers for why Johnny has been handpicked and brought all the way back from London town. He stands to welcome the prodigal son.

Johnny stands to attention. Johnny. Suit, tie, and boots so well buffed up that he can see his reflection in them. Johnny's 'Number Ones'. Johnny's dad is a farm-labourer-come-odd-job-man. Him this man who he now 'yes sirs and no sirs', from monied family. Different worlds. The Commander, aristocracy. Johnny, *hoy polloy.*

'At ease.' Commander Winifred's anger has evaporated

into thin air. He meets this young recruit in the centre of the room. Informal-chat, neutral territory. Ushers him towards one of the three comfy armchairs in a circle. Pastel pink. Military issue? Doubtful. There is no reason why Johnny should take an instant liking to this man…but he does.

Smiles. Soft manner. 'Good to see you, young man.' The Commander with chummy voice does not need to shout as he issues the instruction in a seductive, playful tone, 'Miss Garson, a pot of tea please for my coffee table and there's one more visitor to come, so there'll be one more for the pot.'

Coffee table in the middle. Yesterday's *Daily Express*, pride of place. Johnny can't help but take in the front-page headlines. *Britain must stay clear of European war*.

'You come recommended, Johnny. William Gibbons from London. Bill Craigie, your chief engineer on the *Dunster Grange*. Craigies, well respected family in *Toon*.

'They say you're a sharp lad. You've got a head on your…Loyal and…ah…not too full of himself. We need a *weel kent face* here. Someone well known. Someone who will not attract attention in Kirkwall and here you are. Welcome, young man. Welcome.'

Johnny has to pinch himself. The Commander flattering him, putting him at ease.

'You're spoken of highly…Just between you and me… young man, why did you swap the *Dunster* for the bright lights of London?'

Johnny is working out what to say. He is watching the

Commander's right hand closely. The hand extends forward, picks up the slim folder from the coffee table, rests it on his lap and opens the folder. All this takes place in one graceful, one handed movement. Automata? No. More like a conductor introducing an adagio – slow, stately and composed.

Slim pickings inside. A copy of the *Orcadian* prominent, not the current week's issue. Surprised the old edition hasn't gone the well-worn route of ending up either as a fish supper wrapping or portioned out for the lavvy. *The Orcadian.* The weekly local newspaper, the bible.

Commander looks Johnny straight in the eye. 'This causes me great concern…'

Someone else walks in. The Commander looks up. The newcomer could be a twin. 'Dressed in civvies' doesn't do justice to this prosperous looking feller from a prosperous solicitor's practice.

He is wearing a homburg hat like our dashing foreign secretary, Anthony Eden, lounge suit, white linen waistcoat with fob watch chain visible and a precisely cut almost pencil-line moustache aka movie star Ronald Colman.

'Ah Colonel Victor, so pleased you could make the time in your appointment-filled day to join us.'

Us. He is treating me as an equal. Different class. What manners.

'Johnny, this is Lieutenant Colonel Dundas. He is Officer Commanding Heavy Regiment, Royal Artillery. As you're aware I'm sure, one of the town's top legal beagles.

And, if he hasn't got enough on his plate, Colonel Victor is the Orkney Honorary Vice-consul for Germany.'

Johnny once again stands and salutes. Plays it safe.

This feller's ancient and justified as well but he's built like an ox.

Miss Garson brings in the tea. Her smiles are for the Commander and Colonel only.

'Thank you, Val. No lapsang souchong?'

'I'll put it on the shopping list, Commander.'

'Miss Garson, those red and black flowers in the windowsill vase…such a lovely touch. Displaying flowers is an art and you have this skill in spades, in spades.' The Colonel knows how to speak and say nothing. The art of small talk.

'The flowers are a belated thank you to Kirkwall for the hospitality extended to Captain Jung and his crew. Delivered first thing this morning by Muir's. The flowers came with a card from the German Embassy.'

'Red and black flowers, I should know their name Val, shouldn't I?'

'Black dahlias and red roses, Commander. Dahlias and roses.'

'Oh, of course. Black dahlias and red roses it would be. Cheerful. Gives one a lift.'

Johnny nods in agreement.

'That'll be all, Miss Garson. Now gentlemen. Down to business.'

Both of these men. Jowelly. Fleshed out faces. Wonder

whether they still get their leg over or even want to. Used to be a nice bit of stuff working in the barbers in Tankerness House. She could put it about. Concentrate, Johnny. Concentrate. This is your first day.

'You don't find me in good humour, Victor. I've been holed below the Plimsoll line…blue on blue…the RAF providing the friendly fire. Having to grovel to them for the right to have first say over usage of one of their launches. Me in charge of Scapa Flow and…all this is undignified.

'Don't care that the Fleet Air Arm has returned to where it belongs, back to the Admiralty. I am Senior Naval Officer here and no fucking boat is available for me to do my job. The RAF, just Johnny-come-latelies.' He jabs his index finger like that Lord Kitchener did in his Great War recruitment poster.

The Commander's got a temper.

'Anyway, old chap. Thank you for finding the time to be here. I know you're busy. What I'm going to be reading out, you and I are well aware of but it gives our new eyes and ears an insight into the enormity of the security problem that we face in Orkney.'

He takes out the *Orcadian* from his folder. Thursday the 15th June's edition. Definitely,1939 but a fortnight old. He selects the passage of interest. No easy come, easy go jollity. Deadly serious now. No runners and riders for the 3.20 at Epsom. No more tea-break joshing. Business. Security business.

GERMAN NAVYMEN IN KIRKWALL. HAPPY SOCIAL MEETING WITH ARTILLERY MEN.

"Last week Kirkwall received the German Navy fishery protection vessel *Weser*, of Wilhelmshaven, commanded by Captain Karl Jung.

The crew played out a 2-2 draw in a football match with Kirkwall Rovers at Bignold Park, and then attended a dance with members of the Orkney Territorial Army (Royal Artillery) at the Junction Road Drill Hall.

British khaki and German navy blue mingled in the best of spirits, and the men of both countries – and the girls of Kirkwall – made up a very jolly assembly. When the Germans returned to their ship at midnight, 30 Kirkwall Grammar School students sang the German national anthem at the Pierhead. The *Weser* left at 6.30 the next morning to the salute of ships in the harbour."

'Oh. I missed a sentence from the article. My apologies, Johnny. My apologies, Colonel. You need to get the full picture.'

"Captain Jung paid a courtesy call at the Kirkwall office of the King's Harbourmaster, Commander O. Winifred R.N."

Commander speaking of himself in the 3rd person. He is saying something about himself that could be incriminatory. As a top wallah, bet Colonel Victor was also involved in the arrangements. Why a football match and not rugger? More their game. Grim faces all round but all this happened a fortnight ago. Could be serious egg on face.

The Commander slides the two-week-old copy back inside the manilla folder.

Johnny, don't say a word. You'll find out where you fit in. There has to be more to come here...

'Johnny, I'm so sorry. This must appear to be terribly impolite. Can you please give us a minute or two? Something that I need to discuss with the Colonel. Of a private nature. You understand. Please wait in the outer office.'

Miss Val Garson and myself are going to get further acquainted. A mutual pleasure? I don't think so. No raised voices are heard. Nothing for my ears as I wait for the recall. Not long to wait.

'Johnny. Please do come back in. We're finished.'

He doesn't wait for Miss Garson's say-so. Johnny reoccupies the same comfy armchair. No turning the clock back though, there's a different atmosphere. Strained.

Accept it as it is. Say nothing. I look at the Commander.

It is Colonel Victor, though, now who leads. 'Welcome on board, Johnny. Welcome to the team. I'm sure you've got a story or two to tell.' Colonel Victor smiles. 'All that travelling you've done…'

He's appraising me. Don't want to slip up here. Don't want to be seen to favour one over the other. Certainly, don't want to appear loose tongued, nor one of those thickos who's got nothing to say for themselves.

The Malacca Straits. I'll tell him about the Malacca Straits. Yes! The Colonel's hanging on my every word. I'm just getting to the really interesting bit about...

Colonel Victor stands up. Shakes Johnny's hand. Moves towards the door. 'Next Tuesday, 2 o'clock at the Kinema. Upstairs. Punctual. You'll have your weekly report ready to hand to me.'

Albert Kinema. Why there? Weekly report on what or whom? How many words?

'Two copies. Typed. Welcome to the team. It's been so nice to have met you.' Colonel Victor departs.

I have no typewriter, have never learnt to type and have had no need whatsoever in my life for carbon paper. It just makes your hands dirty, all this interleaving of blank paper with these flimsy, black inky sheets. If a girl was to walk out on me, the way he just did to me...curtains...no second chance for her. Now there's just me and the Commander.

Who the hell is senior to whom? Army to Navy? Navy to Army?

'Don't worry, I'll get Val to see to the typing up. The Colonel is a bit of a stickler for correct indentation of paragraphs. I'm more relaxed in that area. It's intelligence we're after, not a diploma in English Grammar. Your intelligence findings. Make sure Val has the report first thing every Tuesday.

'Now. Here's the good news, Johnny. I've opened a bank account in your name. £3.10s.0d a week will be paid in plus expenses. This money is not to be used as your slush fund. Any indication of misuse…they say about me… “the person who crosses the Commander will live to regret it”…we’ll leave it at that, shall we?’ A broad smile on his face.

‘Ah yes, there’s accommodation thrown in - it’s grace and favour. Here’s the keys for you.’ The Commander winks.

Johnny smiles back.

‘I’m giving you the keys now but you’re to wait until tomorrow before you move in. Friday…not a peek before… Friday is your *flittin’* day.

‘Job in Lyness, Golden Wharf – that’s your cover story. It’ll stop people scratching their heads trying to second guess what you’re up to. It must all be quite unfathomable. That German Navy visit. I’ll fill you in.

‘That jolly social and football match. Us and the Germans. When was it now? A fortnight ago. This fishery cruiser of the German Navy visited us just for the day.

Roll forward a week, on the 22nd. Yes. Last Thursday. A German navy chappie was arrested in the streets of Kirkwall. All hush-hush. His name was Herr Hermann Schneider. Picked up by the police in Bridge Street, much the worse for wear. Would hardly merit anyone’s attention but documentation on him showed that he was from the *SS Weser* of Wilhelmshaven. Yes. *That* German Fisheries Protection boat that left the week before.

‘The visit may have looked like a good old Fisheries Knees-Up, washed down with more than a dram or two of our *Highland Park*, talking shop and drinking and playing football and dancing and canoodling, if you get my drift.

'Hans Across the Water stuff…sorry, that's a terrible joke. That's what they'd like you to believe but these Germans are guilty of 2+2 = 5. Offering friendship and hospitality does not make us Orcadians simple and gullible.

'We showed the Hun before on the fields of Flanders what we're made of and we're ready to do it again.

'I have it on good authority that the German Admiralty send young navy men to a different type of ship each year to 'gain experience'. You can bet your bottom dollar that the *SS Weser* was not 100% crewed by fishing wallahs. Anyone could be on board, even Gestapo…though more likely to be a few U-Boat wizards. A large number of new faces this year, certainly not *weel kent* ones.

'The police counted them in and counted them out. Even checked their passports. Same number. Twenty-five. Names matched. Something's afoot here. A substitute used, maybe. Convenient way to take an agent off Orkney Mainland. Presumably the person left behind has a support mechanism to fall back on here. I don't like it. I don't like it.

'So, what would our Herr Schneider have been up to during the last week? Sightseeing? I don't think so. Lyness is being readied for the Royal Navy fleet to be moved up to Orkney from the South Coast, Portsmouth. More to the point, where's Herr Schneider been staying? Is there a Nazi safe house here in Orkney?

'Would have been nice if Colonel Victor had kept me in the loop on this. Disappointed. Very disappointed. Intelligence. From a reliable source. This is where you fit in, Johnny. Eyes and ears.'

He adds a bit more. All concisely presented. Ten minutes later, like a clockwork toy, Johnny has been fully wound up and is now raring to go.

'Oh, and by the way, you may report on a day-to-day basis to Colonel Victor but *you are answerable to me.*

'Don't let me down. You must finish off telling us about your travels some time. Most interesting…Where was the place again?'

'*The Malacca Straits.* We had just…'

The Commander looks at his watch. 'What a pity. Is that the time? *Tempus fugit*. Those Straits will have to wait for another time. Important phone call expected… Admiralty.' The Commander gets up. Johnny follows. Johnny is being shown to the door.

'Johnny. We need spies because there are people out there who mean us harm. Never forget that.'

On his way to the door, the Commander has picked up the newspaper, that very newspaper with the ringed and encircled names and numbers. The *Chronicle*. The *Racing Chronicle,* not the other one – the *News Chronicle*.

There's important business outstanding for the Commander, more important than affairs of state. He picks up the phone.

'Five guineas each way…'

FRIDAY 30TH JUNE 1939: 1

It's Friday morning and Johnny has only been back a day and a bit. He would've preferred to be left in peace. I mean it's not asking much, is it? No one does a better breakfast fry up than *Mither*. *Faether* though is giving him the third degree. Johnny's having to duck and dive as greasy, runny egg is dribbling down his chin.

Johnny, in between mouthfuls, tells *Faether* that the *Dunster* is going to take longer than expected in dry dock and he's managed to get fixed up with some temporary work over in Hoy, in Lyness. All this is said casual like and he throws in for good measure that there's still the last bit of salvaging of the German Fleet to be carried out in the Flow.

Faether rises to one of his favourite themes.

'What's the point, *buddo?* All this bringing them sunk

German boats up to the surface when the *Luftwaffe* tomorrow will be sending our Royal Navy battleships down to fill the hole that's been left? Davy Jones' Locker? Ha bloody ha. Ha bloody ha. *Them Huns* always have the last laugh.'

Mither, a pushover…her *buddo*...truth shines out of his…*Faether* not convinced. Keeps on prodding him, force feeding him, down his gullet until like a goose he's gagging. *Faether* wheedles away. 'Why not consider this?' 'Why not consider that?' 'A to-ing and fro-ing delivery job of stone from the quarry outside Kirkwall to Hatston just inside the *Toon* boundaries?' 'It'll be more than a temporary job' 'You'll earn good money.' 'You're only really going to be working flat out for half a shift but getting full pay.' 'Put in a word for you, *buddo*. Laying a runway there. I'll find out for you, shall I?' 'The runway…just give me the word, *buddo*.'

'Runway', it sounded like. 'Run-a-way.'

War stuff, Johnny's being offered. Little does Johnny's *faether* know what Johnny's really up to. Just one day back and Johnny's already picked up on some such aerodrome, or whatever it's called, being built on the outskirts of Kirkwall.

Easy to say nothing when your mouth's full of rashers, sausage, beans and eggs. Mither's a star.

'More fried bread, Johnny?'

'Yes please, *Mither*.'

'Hope it's Orkney stone that's being delivered for the *run-a-way.* You never know with the Council where it gets its stone from. Council always a bit hush hush about this, a bit protective. Well, Orkney does good business with tourists seeing its Stones. Ring of Brodgar and them Standing Stones of Stenness.' *Faether* is opinionated.

Johnny knows he can get away with 'everything will be clearer job-wise for me next week' and sticks to this line.

What's worse? Telling 'em a downright lie or the gospel truth? They're doing my head in already and I've barely been back a day. I heard 'em say, 'What are we going to do with the lad?' Why don't they just stop naggin' and just leave me be?

'Got to be going *Faether*, I'm running late.'

'*Buddo,* with *Mither's Full Orkney* inside you, any running and you'll be just like Metal Industries…heavy lifting them Scapa blockships…bringing back up what's just gone down.' *Faether* feels because he's *Faether* he has the right to the final word.

Johnny is in a mad rush to inspect his hidey-hole, grace and favour room – top floor of the Albert Kinema, Kirkwall's cinema. Him, actually being allowed to live in the Albert Kinema. Hollywood comes to Kirkwall. Johnny is not just going to be one step from Hollywood, it will embrace him and not let him go, like many a conquest who's found Johnny's charms irresistible.

Albert Kinema. Kinema with a block capital 'K'.

Orkney's got a 'k' in it as well. That's not Orkney. Ordinary letter 'k' will do, thank you very much. Understated. Orkney just gets on with it…always has done…always will.

If you pay heed to the Orkney *Jahr,* you would have got that by now. And if you don't pay heed, more fool you.

FRIDAY 30TH JUNE 1939: 2

8.30am. Dead excited. Pure dead brilliant. First visit to my hidey-hole. The Kinema is only a short walk away. The *Toon* is waking up. I better think about what route I'll take. This isn't Aldwych-The Strand-Adelphi, predetermined and not to be deviated from. I have options. No messin'. I'll take the direct route to Albert Kinema until I'm within spitting distance. Clay Loan-Victoria Street-Broad Street-Saint Magnus Cathedral.

Hello, who do we have here? By the bus stop…a good looker…a face you're not likely to forget. She must be waiting for the Scapa Pier bus, for the Hoy boat to take her over to Lyness. That's a large holdall she's carrying. Pity… I'm in work mode…other priorities…an intelligence agent…my destiny… I've already earned my boy scout badges.

I'll be too conspicuous if I use the main Albert Street

entrance. There's the side door down the alleyway. This is the clever bit. I'll walk down the main drag, Albert Street, go past the Kinema, bold as brass, whistlin' my favourite tune, *Hands Knees and Boomps A Daisy,* and then take a left here at Mounthoolie and left again…and left again.

Kids like to get up to a bit of mischief down this *peedie Kinema* lane but as it's before nine in the morning it'll be as dead as a dodo. I'll enter the lane by the drill hall, Junction Road end. I'm bloody excited.

8.45am. Arrived. I'm in full Aldwych-to-Adelphi mode and look round a final time. The coast is clear. The key is in the lock but the door won't open. Blast. I'm using the wrong key. Got the right one. I'm in. I've as much time as I need to explore my new surroundings.

What's that noise? The almighty clatter of things being knocked over. Where has that come from? Upstairs. Phew. Only the Kinema cat – Katy Kustard, she was there before I went to sea. Meeting me on the first landing, me-going-up-she-on her-way-down fleeing. Besides her, there's no one about. Friday is no Kinema matinée day, after all. I tiptoe up to the top landing like a prowler, and take a click-click photo in my head of what I see.

Some doors are shut. Where will my grace and favour room be?

The large room. My goodness this can't be the one, can it? Door wide open. Quick peek in. A few boxes and cups and saucers strewn over the carpet. Big enough for a tennis court, this room. The room's not going anywhere, let's just park it.

Three other doors.

One leads to the lavvy. That's class. *An indoor lavvy.* The two remaining doors are shut. Neither key fits the first of the doors. Must be the projectionist's room. Forbidden to enter. As top security goes in the magical world of cinema, the projectionist's room, always strictly *verboden.*

Let's just have a look at that room opposite. Keys in hand. Is that the one? The door opens. The room's a bit on the small side, disappointing. Dingy. There's the light switch. That's more encouraging. A box room containing a bed with desk and chair. A small mirror and an empty waste bin. A sink with a clean towel and a new bar of Pears soap…that clean smell!

A window, so we have some natural light. It looks out over the fire escape. Curtains, so complete privacy when drawn. A radiator under the window, so heating provided. Storage space; just under the bed. The bed, made up, clean sheets.

You know what? *It'll do. No. More than that. Credit where credit's due. It's perfect.* Spotless. I wonder whether the cleaning lady's been vetted. *I wonder what she looks like.*

I've nothing to drop off yet. Early days. Now it's back to that first room, the large room, the one that's big enough for Centre Court, Wimbledon, the one with the door open. Let's just first put the boxes back in place.

We've got the shrine to Hollywood. I am immediately transported to Cal-i-for-ni-a. I am on the studio lot. No looking back now. I hear the sound of clapper boards and directors yelling, 'Lights, Camera, Action'. I shut my eyes. I have entered this magical land where all my dreams can be fulfilled.

Let's see. My boxes of intelligence-stuff will fit nicely in here amongst the magical, Hollywood tinsel. *Tinsel and Gretel.* Posters and photos of Hollywood's greatest. Yes, James Cagney is there. Bette Davis as well. There's one even of Errol Flynn. I wouldn't be seen dead in a swashbuckling outfit. Not even for a dare. Give me Cagney any day. As for the Snow White and the Seven Dwarfs poster, *heigh-ho.*

Magical. Reminds me of London's West End, stardom in the core of this Capital city. You can see them for real on stage. You can actually do the latest dance to these twelve-piece bands on the dancefloor, not on the floor of your front room. They're in front of you, on stage – in the flesh, no longer hidden inside your Bakelite radio. I'm not bragging but I took Kirstin once to see Joe Loss. Yes, I did. *Joe Loss* in London Town. She was very grateful. *Beuys o beuys…*

London…there's more than one cinema there.

Kirstin. I can't stop thinking about her. We're in the back row, the posh seats at the Leicester Square Empire. What a first date. I remember she wasn't backward in coming forward. I didn't see much of the film.

She let me rest my hand on that soft part of her upper

leg just above the stocking-top and at the end of the evening a long goodnight snog. Over the months…well, we'd done more, much more.

I'd gladly spend 1/9d just to be sitting next to her now. Can it have only been a week ago that I last saw her? Neither of us knew it was going to be for the last time.

Maybe war would be like that. Tearful farewells, up and down the land. She would have found someone else by now, no problem but I'll never forget Cristina, I mean Kirstin. Slip of the tongue, sorry.

'Monday night at 8 o'clock at the Albert Kinema. They hold classes upstairs in the large room. Eyes and ears, that's why we brought you back home. Your first assignment.' That's all the Commander had said.

There must be a list of what local groups use this room. Maybe there's something pinned up on the wall. While I'm at it, what films are showing over the next few months? Success. On the top of that box there. Some flyers.

I like the look of that one. I 'alf fancy Greta Garbo. I never got to see the whole film. Thrown out before I got to see *the dance.* So were my mates. I was only 15 at the time. She ends up starkers. *Matty Hair* we called it at school. *Mata Hari*. Greta was an enemy spy. I knew what she was up to straight away. Would I be tempted? No. I'll get my leg over but I'm not going to be giving away top secrets to any good looker. If I time it right, I can take my seat as soon as lights out. I'll already be in the building. Diddly squat, it'll cost.

Large room. A large oblong table hogging the middle, could seat twenty. Stacked chairs against the far wall. Natural light in short supply. The street window hadn't been cleaned for some time. The other window boarded up. Up there on the far wall, a framed photo of Edward VIII. No other royalty.

All good stuff for my first report.

Beuys o beuys. They should have changed that framed picture by now. Nearly three years back. That's when Edward VIII was kicked out. That woman, an American Jezebel…At least Bette Davis is a looker. That American floosie. Not Bette Davis, *her*. What's her name? Wallis Simpson. The Royal Family will never make the same mistake again.

Walls freshly painted in lavvy brown. Must have been a job lot offer. Dingy. Uninviting. A high ceiling. A cobweb or two. Worn carpet.

What a strong, musty smell here. *Gas*. Won't mention this as well. The Commander would not thank me for this reminder of the Great War. Don't want him to think that he's got a right namby-pamby working for him.

I've seen loads of people wearing masks on the streets of London, gas masks. Didn't see the need for them then. Don't see the need for them now. Wouldn't 'alf look stupid wearing one.

Time for a fag. Where's my Craven 'A' s? It's not my first of the day.

Tomorrow night. Saturday night. Could get *blootered.*

No, let's *just* see whether *she* still works there at Tankerness House. I'm in need of a trim anyway. I'll ask that one out. 'You've ended up as a snappy looking dish,' I'll say. She'll be eating out of the palm of my hand. After the film…no messing…straight upstairs…to my Room at the Top. You can guess the rest.

Just the weekend to come. Monday 3rd July 1939. I'll be starting for real…for King and Country. Isn't life exciting? I'll show them on Monday that *I ain't no cream puff.* That's Cagney for you. *Heigh-ho.*

MONDAY 3RD JULY 1939

8.05pm. Just a tiptoe across the corridor. I'm a few minutes late. The class has already started. I've done this deliberately, being a few minutes late. This late thing. Any pre-class chit chat and I might give the game away. With my guard down I might say something that I shouldn't. No knocking on the door. Take a deep breath and in I go. I feel as conspicuous as a camel in Kirbister. Mind. There are many Kirbisters in Orkney. That's Orkney for you. Just the six sitting round the table. One of 'em must be the teacher. Six minus one, that makes five students. That must be her over there. Loads of clutter in front. The seat next to the teacher, empty.

Apologies all round from me. I briefly introduce myself to the teacher and class. No *weel kent* faces here but I've been *Doon Sooth* for three years. First impressions, none. This won't do. In this dangerous world of espionage, first impressions count. First impressions, the difference between life and death.

A quick scan round the table. Well, two lookers. *Beuys o beuys*.

Another quick 'taking it all in'. No one else to write home about. Down to security business.

Why didn't the Commander give me a stronger steer? Maybe this is always the way in matters of national security. I did ask around over the weekend.

'That upstairs room in the Kinema? Always in great demand, *beuy*. The room can be hired out for free to any local group and is slap bang in the centre of *Toon.*'

I found out that Tuesday nights, it's hired out to the Woman's Institute; Wednesday, the Episcopalians; Thursday, Life Form Drawing – a very popular class with a waiting list a mile long. As for tonight's class...well…no one could keep a straight face.

The teacher is speaking.

'Ben Nevis estas alta monto...alta monto

sed Everest estas multe pli alta

Repeat after me please.

Ben…Nevis…es…

And again, class.'

These are s*lim pickings* to go on…

'La rivero Forth estas mall rapidflua.'

A foreign language class but I'll be buggered if I know what one.

'*La rivero…*

'Now divide into two groups and translate what's on page five of your textbook, then we'll go through last week's homework.'

Blink. Blink. Blink. Click. Click. Click. Snap. Snap. Snap. The flashbulbs have gone off. I'll be like one of those hardboiled-Noo-Yawk-photographers. I've seen them on the Big Screen. The deceased…down an alleyway or laid out on the back seat of a mobster's car.

First, I'll get the pictures in my head. Then, their pen portraits to match but I mustn't give the game away, mustn't.

One. Elderly man. Thick glasses. Looks foreign. Is foreign. Speaks with accent. Suspicious. Can't follow what he's on about. I'll bet the farm on him being a Nazi.

Two. Matron looking lady. I saw her Saturday through the shop window. Local hairdresser. Not, I say *not* the one in Tankerness House.

You know what. She's worth a second look. Blonde curly hair. Tight fitting dress, large buttons all the way down the front. Large…Needs them done up right to the top to keep *them* in. That dress. Figure hugging. Stripes, blue and red like you get outside the barber shops. Candy stick. Bet she knits socks for the Nazis in her spare time. Bet you she's a seamstress as well. A real *Mrs Sew and Sew.* I'll call her that. She keeps on interrupting the teacher.

Whoops. She's staring back at me. That's two out of two… Nazi candidates. I must quickly move on. Now who do we have sitting the far side of her?

Three. A man of the cloth. Dog collar. Grey haired. Quietly spoken. Always clearing his throat before saying something. Straight and upright.

He is irritating though. Continuous loud contact with table using his middle three fingers as he speaks. Doesn't stop. Will…no…*has*...got on my nerves with this drumming or is it thrumming of his fingers.

Now who's this feller?

Four. Dressed in bohemian fashion. Artist type. No jacket and tie. Beard. Nondescript. A bit of a Micky Angelo in our midst. Their type, never happier with an easel and a bowl of fruit. A bit of a banana.

Micky is now talking to Mrs Sew and Sew. She's giving him a spare pen and some paper.

'Don't worry, Mister Halbert. It happens all the time.'

Mister Halbert…and here?

Five. *Lady, in her late twenties. Extremely polite. Bland. Unlikely to be of any interest to the authorities.* That's how I'll describe her in my report.

Beuys o beuys. It's her. The one I saw at the bus stop last Thursday morning. Red lipstick. She's made an effort, without any doubt whatsoever. Maybe I'm going to enjoy this language class after all. Wedding ring on her finger, pity…but… no…obstacle.

One to go. The teacher. A bit of a plain Jane. Schoolmarmish.

So, I've memorised their faces and have their descriptions in my head. Just their names remaining. The teacher's bound to have a list of the runners and riders. Then even if nothing else materialises, I'll have more than enough for tomorrow's report.

The teacher's folder is on the table, immediately in front of her. It is open.

Now's my moment. She's distracted. I'll just lean over to take a peek. Yes. There must be a list of names nestling inside on a bit of paper. I'll either commit them to memory or *half inch* the list.

Mind, I need the teacher's name as well. That's easy enough. *MISS JANET SHEARER* written on the cover of her folder in block capitals. Then there's a dash and then what must be the name of this class.

'Class, repeat after me, once more.

Ben Nevis estas alta monto, sed Everest estas multe pli alta.

Now class. What is so interesting about that sentence? *Ben Nevis estas alta monto.* Who can help? Think grammar – *alta monto...alta monto.'*

The elderly man with those thick glasses and a thick foreign accent. Maybe he's the person the Commander has in mind for me to run the rule over. The man raises his hand to attract the teacher's attention.

He looks a bit like that Hollywood Claude Rains feller. A very precise, stiff-arm action. I almost expect him to do a Heil Hitler salute. Come on. Someone, please engage in conversation with ... Give me a name.

'Yes, Mister Oertel.'

'Madame. *Estas* is the verb. *Alta* is the adjective. *Monto* is the noun.'

'Well done, Albert.'

Albert, first name. Sounds like Urtle, the surname. Albert Urtle – Number one.

'In the language we're here to learn, nouns always end in *o*. Adjectives always end in *a*. Does anyone want to give me another example of how simple the language is? A noun with an adjective.'

'*Bona lallies.*' It's the man of the cloth's turn to speak.

'Thank you, Mister Firth. I'm afraid, though, only half correct.'

Mister Firth.

'You were right with *bona* as an adjective but are you sure about the noun? This so-called noun of yours, *lallies.* Rules are rules. We must always follow the rules. The grammar is straightforward. Nothing complicated.'

The teacher suddenly raises her voice. Her voice is trembling with emotion.

'With this easy-to-learn language all nationalities will be able to communicate with each other. All the barriers in our troubled world will be broken down. By understanding each other better, there will be no need for war.

'I have seen the new Germany at first hand. The trip was organised by the National Union of Students…to promote peace and understanding…as does Esperanto…we all must work unceasingly for the cause of international fellowship.'

Janet Shearer. The teacher.

I've already got *Mister Halbert.* That's the three men sorted, A strong poker hand. Now that just leaves the identity of the pair of ladies in the class. If one name comes, the other is bound to follow straight away - like the London trolley buses.

Mrs Sew and Sew is well stacked. The other one with the red lips. I 'alf fancy her. That list in the teacher's folder. My moment can't come fast enough.

Patience, Johnny. Patience. The Commander wanted me to be here for a reason. This class must either be a recruitment centre or it's been infiltrated or it's another test or it's a complete and utter waste of everyone's time. Patience.

The folder on the table.

Block capitals. Black ink.

MISS JANET SHEARER – ESPERANTO EVENING CLASS.

So, we are learning *Espe...Esperanto*. Never heard of it. Where do they speak it? Somewhere in Europe? Or maybe it's got something to do with what they speak on the Western Isles. These Western Isles, off the coast of Scotland but in the Nordic Sea. Esperanto…but…but… why would anyone want to learn this Esperanto here? *Es-per-an-to*.

'Class. We'll break for ten minutes. When we resume, everyone will have their chance to say a sentence or two about themselves in Esperanto. Don't worry. You're not being marked on this exercise and I'm sure I will see or rather *hear* progress from you all.'

Miss Janet Shearer's buff folder is precariously balanced on the edge of the large oblong table. Now's my chance. I accidentally-on-purpose tip the folder onto the floor. Papers scatter. Just a few in there.

On all fours now. Under the table. Gathering. Found what I was looking for. A sheet of paper with names of the attendees. As fast as a sleight of hand in the find the lady card trick, I fold the list up and squirrel it away in my jacket pocket.

Mission accomplished. While I'm on all fours let's have one final look before I come up for air.

That one with the red lipstick and smile. What a pair of lallies!

I apologise for my clumsiness to one and all and then move away from the table.

Time to give the time-honoured signal to the ladies. A pack of ten is opened. I ever-so-casually take one out. Tap it on the box. Craven 'A'. *So easy on the throat.* Filter-tip. It was Kirstin's favourite.

She is walking over to me. I return her smile. Squared and tripled. Promising. Lighter at the ready. More than promising.

Blast. The man with the dog collar is buttonholing me. It's the dog-collar man, the Minister. I'm trapped.

'I'm Mister S.M.D Firth of Stenness. Pleased to make your acquaintance. Sorry and you are…'

Fate. You win some. You lose some. *Mister S.M.D Firth of Stenness.*

'The League of Nations was deliberately rendered ineffective by Great Britain and France. What we need is a *People's Peace Pact.* War will be swept from the earth forever. People must get together and tell their rulers and leaders that they will not fight each other. Esperanto, a common language, will…'

'Suppose we two were fond of a dog-fight and each of us are dog-owners. We train our dogs to fight each other and arrange for the fight to take place next Saturday. They snarl and snap at each other and then fight like mad. General excitement all round.

'We then arrange for a return fight to take place, a week Sunday. We might even put a five-pound bet on the outcome. But on the day before the contest something strange happens…unknown to their owners, the two dogs have got together. They give each other a good sniff all over. Presently their tails begin to wag and they start talking to each other in a doggy fashion and by-and-by each discovers that the other isn't such a bad sort after all. Quite a nice fellow, in fact.

'The upshot is that they decide fighting is a mug's game altogether and they agree they'll have no more of it. Their owners can thrash them all they like.'

The lady with the red lipstick is walking over to me. Not before time. I point to my pack of Craven 'A' cigarettes.

'And that's what happens on the day of the fight or non-fight. Common sense. A common language. A common understanding. If the armies of the world refuse to fight each other, there will be no war.'

He hands over a pamphlet. It'd be rude for me to refuse. It'll pad out my report.

'...do you know Zanres Cafe? It's just over the road from here. 16 Albert Street.'

I nod and of course smile.

'Our Peace Group meets there. Like-minded people, in friendship. Every Wednesday morning at 10 o'clock. Zanres. Please join us.'

'I'd be delighted. It'd mean so much to me to be with like-minded people.'

'Class, tea break is over.' Miss Janet Shearer ended this announcement with a couple of claps of the hand.

I catch *her* attention. We both shrug...

'Now Mrs Tulloch, Isobel. Tell me in a few sentences in Esperanto something that you have done since last week's class?' The teacher has found her first victim.

Isobel Tulloch. Isobel Tulloch. Mrs.

Everyone bar Johnny takes their turn. The after-break session of the class has run its course. 9.30pm.

'*Bonan Nokton.* See you all next week.'

'*Bonan Nokton,*' is the refrain.

Isobel is first out the door. Quickly followed by Mister Halbert, the artist.

Mister Oertel and the hairdresser, Mrs Sew and Sew, are deep in conversation.

'Mrs Craigie…'

Claire Craigie. Mrs. Number two on my list. Could be the most important of the lot. Claire Craigie. Craigie, not an Orkney name. Hang on. Isn't there a Craigie family from Aberdeen living in Clay Loan, just a few doors down from home?

'…In London there are gun emplacements in the parks and open spaces. The authorities say that we need guns to meet the possibility of air attack but you and I know that this is more likely to attract than ward off an enemy attack.

'It's a hostile gesture. A hostile gesture. Where do our children play? What about the geese and birds? The guns if fired will shatter all the windows nearby. Where is the sense in all of this?

'Mark my words, they'll do the same here. Yes, it'll happen even in Kirkwall. How can anyone justify putting a gun emplacement next to Saint Magnus Cathedral? Provocation. Mark my words, there'll be broken glass all round and not a paper airplane in sight. Absolute folly.'

'Sometimes it's good to break windows. Kristallnacht showed *them.* Hitler wouldn't pick on *them* for no reason,' Mrs Sew and Sew replies. This is accompanied by a glance over each shoulder.

What does that mean? This 'Kristallnacht'? Must be another of them Esperanto words. Maybe it's code but it'll go in the report. Help pad it out. 'Kris...' Not sure of the spelling so I'll make sure it's got a '?' next to it.

Johnny quickly slips out. He doesn't want anyone to see that he'll be going straight to his room across the corridor. Doesn't want his cover well and truly blown before he'd even got started. He rubs his hands together in self-congratulation. The report will be in that Val Garson's hands first thing the *morn* for her to type up.

The Commander and the Colonel will be impressed. *Heigh-ho.*

TUESDAY 4TH JULY 1939

'Report to be presented for typing by 10'o clock Tuesday morning *at the latest.*' I was banging on the Commander's door in the Kirkwall Hotel at nine.

'Do you know what time it is?' Miss Val Garson, not in the slightest pleased to see me.

'Here's the report. I'll be returning at noon.' *That told her*. I was not going to argue the toss. She's from Stromness.

Midday on the dot I collected the two typed copies from her.

'I can't thank you enough Miss Garson for such a fine piece of typing.'

Bu…ah spread thick with my bu…ah knife.

'The Commander wants to see you back here, 5 o'clock sharp.'

2pm. I am ready to hand over the typed report, as instructed, to Lieutenant Colonel Victor Dundas in my grace and favour flat, top floor, the Albert Kinema.

I wasn't sure whether I was a *postie* on a merry-go-round astride the same gee-gee, or a clothes whirligig being blown this way and that by the strong Orkney winds.

'Johnny, *saluton.*' I look round and salute the Colonel.

How did he get in? I didn't hear him. I never leave my door ajar. The old boy must have his own set of keys.

The Colonel chuckles. 'No Johnny, please at ease. *Saluton* is Esperanto for *Hello*.'

I grin.

'Let's see what you've got for me.'

'Typed…double spaced…good…full marks.'

'Johnny, in future there's no need to put yourself to such effort. A bit too gold plate all this, isn't it? We're not presenting a warrant for court, are we? I'm sure your handwriting is perfectly legible. A handwritten report will do fine. Just print everything in block capitals to make doubly sure. Important though, it has to be delivered straight to me. For my eyes only. Message understood?'

'Now let's have a read.' I can hear his breath. The Colonel is not to be rushed. He is taking his time. Legal beagles love nothing more than *minutiae*, getting lost in the weeds. He finishes poring over my report.

'That's exceedingly fine work.'

'If I was you, I'd accept our Mister Firth of Stenness' kind invitation. Join him and his friends at Zanres tomorrow morning for their weekly Peace Group blether. You're not expected in Lyness at the Golden Wharf until first thing Thursday.'

The Colonel looks slowly round the room as if he's seeing it for the first time. He then locks eyes with mine.

'Oh, by the way…a word of advice. Ensure you're punctual. No cutting corners, please. No good going AWOL when something meaty crops up. Be the first to arrive and the last to leave.

What time did you say… at Zanres tomorrow? 10am? Aim for a quarter of an hour earlier, no later. 9.45am. Esperanto class timekeeping won't wash…'

How did he…?

'I know what these Peace Groups are like…can talk the hind leg off a donkey. Most of them are as inoffensive as a budgie in a bird bath, bit of trilling, some water gets splashed, nothing more. However, the gullible can easily be influenced by the wrong sort of birdie. Could be a Nazi cocksure *bonxie* in their midst. Make sure you're there for the whole shooting match, the full shebang. I'll be in touch.'

Johnny is left with plenty to ponder.

5pm. On the dot. Back at the Kirkwall Hotel. Appointment to see the Commander.

I flash my best smile at the *wifey* in the outer office.

Miss Garson points to the Commander's office door. Her and Foghorn Fanny at Inverness Station must be related.

The Commander with pen in hand is poring over the newspaper. I'm greeted like a long-lost friend.

'4th July. It's a special day for me, Johnny. The Memsahib…fine woman. Today's our 35th wedding anniversary. It's also American Independence Day. I hope that if the balloon goes up, the Yanks don't faff about and join us on Day One. It took them all of three years in the Great War. That's Yanks for you. Rest assured, My Memsahib didn't need any time to make up her mind...35 years.'

'Down to business. That report, excellent. Yes, Val managed to work out that word *Kristallnacht*. A giveaway, that's one Nazi sympathiser flushed out. Suffice to say that the Nazis treated Jewish people as being no better than animals on that particular night. November 9th. Just eight months ago, one month before Christmas 1938. An absolute disgrace. We're on to something here. Rest assured – the Esperanto group will attract Nazis like moths to light.

'Yes. This schedule works well. You attend the Esperanto class on a Monday night. Hand your report in first thing the *morn*, the Tuesday, for typing. And we round things off at this time with a confab every Tuesday afternoon at around 5 o'clock.'

The Commander is up and running. Just like his gee-gees.

'By the way Johnny, *the Colonel may be your*

pointsman but I'm in charge of the whole fucking railway network. Never forget that.'

'Bit of background for you. Orkney is going to be receiving a very important guest here soon. This guest is *the top of the tree.* It's just at planning stage so must remain the *toppest* of top secrets.'

He takes a slow deep draw on his pipe after *top* and then after *secrets*. As sure as eggs are eggs, the Commander exhales and out pop those wisps of insider knowledge smoke.

'The visit will take place after County Show Week and well after those daddy longlegs carry out their last August hurrah but it'll be before Santa even thinks about trimming the reindeers' antlers in Lapland. Let's leave it at that.

'Identity of our guest only known to a handful. If any news gets out, the plug will be right *royally* pulled. Let's hope that our Winston can continue to shake things up.

'It gives us a bit of breathing space to weed out enemies of the state. You're not the only one helping us on the inside but you've been brought in to strengthen the team. Can I say, Johnny, you've proved a fine addition to our ranks. Having travelled the world, gives you that international perspective on things…'

'What happened in *the Malacca Straits*…was remarkable. Only an Orcadian...'

The Commander raises his index finger from his right hand to his pursed lips.

'Indiscrete talk will assist the enemy. Hundreds of

people are working over in Hoy at the Lyness Base in close contact with the general public and our Naval personnel. Lyness, that's our Achilles heel.'

I nod.

'Lyness is full of malcontents, shit-stirrers; rates of pay, working conditions that sort of thing. 1/3d an hour makes, with overtime and bonus, £3.10s a week. That sort of money is not to be sniffed at. Johnny, your brother worked there, didn't he?' The Commander's tone is no longer affable, no longer avuncular.

Both the Commander and the Colonel can change horses, just like that.

'One of the ringleaders was your brother, wasn't he? Stevie isn't it? Stevie Sinclair. You're bound to get a few accidents on any construction site, aren't you? Of course, I'm sorry for him but putting my sympathies to one side it's easy for any troublemaker when you're on the inside to be able to fuck things up from the outside. Your brother. Doesn't work anywhere near Lyness now, does he? *Doon Sooth.* Malcontent to collaborator, easy step for some to take…isn't it? When was Stephen last at home? Now that's the question for you to answer, isn't it?'

I'm being stared at now. Hard eyes of suspicion and interrogation. Made to feel downright uncomfortable. The sins of my brother placed squarely on my shoulders.

'Johnny, I know you've only been away a few years but you wouldn't recognise Lyness now. We're not talking the Wild West and Dodge City but it's grown like topsy.'

The Commander switches back to playing the uncle. He's spoon-feeding me loads of information. Am I listening? Am I fuck.

'Lyness, a naval fuel oil depot and shore base in the Great War. A place of remembrance for all those Germans laid to rest in the Cemetery nearby. HQ for the post Great War salvage of the German scuttled fleet. Continually reinventing itself is our Lyness. Change after change in little more than a couple of decades.

'Now the Admiralty are going helter-skelter, reinforcing our defences for what will be the home of the Royal Navy. Tunnelling and road making, that's the name of the game.'

I nod.

The Commander stops speaking, hands me a folder. Stamped on the front are the words *Top Secret*. I pore over the contents. I'm fully engaged now. Photograph after photograph of those currently under surveillance. Suspects, one and all.

My brother Stevie is in the pack, hardly surprising. I feel the piercing eyes of the Commander boring down on me as I pick up Stevie's photo. I spend a lot of time considering it even though I want to move on quickly to the next *weel kent* face.

'Take your time, Johnny. Take a good look. You have an excellent memory for faces. Some may be new to you. Some…more familiar.'

And that's what I do. I take my time. Picking up, putting down, memorising click-click and then on to the next photo. Well. Who do we have here? Jim Rendall. Jim Rendall's Kirstin's older brother. He's as hard as nails. The Rendalls. You don't want to get on the wrong side of that family. His photo in the gallery of shit-stirrers? No surprise.

The Commander drones on.

'Scapa Flow? What marvellous anchorage. Fifteen miles long from north to south and eight miles wide. There's about 100 square miles of deep water there. Never mind just the Royal Navy, Scapa is large enough to accommodate all the navies of the world if it wanted to and this Commander here before you Johnny is honoured to be appointed the OIC – Officer In Charge.

No, it can't be. As *one of those under suspicion?*

She is looking at me now, captured by camera. From the Esperanto class, it's Isobel Tulloch, with her ruby red lips. To stop my hands from shaking I pat down my pockets, as if looking for my pack of Craven 'A' cigarettes. Breathing space in short supply. It's like fortune hiding, never there this breathing space when you need it.

Isobel Tulloch.

'The German Navy must know every nook and cranny of Scapa Flow by now. You tell me how many Nazi spies in the guise of holidaymakers have been on fact-finding pilgrimages to Orkney. Camera and notebooks at the ready. All for the Fatherland! Sieg…fucking…Heil.'

The Commander pauses, just a hiccough of a breather and then the words quickly resume pouring out of his mouth.

'There are rumours of mystery lights last week being seen in the Flow. Some folk, those who you would expect to have more sense, are convinced that the German submarines are already at it. I've never heard of submarines with full beam headlights before. Folk once scared will believe any *cobblers*. They'll be telling us next that Nazi submarines are bringing a virus to infect one and all.

'We've laid enough nets and sunk enough blockships to stop U-Boats from getting in. Nothing more corrosive for civilian morale than nonsensical rumours doing the rounds. They'll even be mistaking the cries of seal pups on the Hoy sandbanks for subs surfacing.

'Johnny. See you next Tuesday at 5 o'clock. You've enough to be getting on with now.'

My goodness he doesn't 'arf go on and on. What do we have here? Hardly a surprise. That 'foreigner' at the Esperanto Class. Albert Oertel with the pebble glasses. He looks as creepy in the photo as he does in real life.

The Commander puts on a from-the-pulpit voice to recount what some fellar or other has said.

'Why does all this foreboding and unpleasantness have to wash ashore on our islands of Orkney? Why can't these German spies and the British military leave us to our ways? We don't need our population here to be doubled, trebled or even more…interrupting our peace and quiet?

'We don't need our lush landscape concreted over. Just leave Orkney to our ploughing competitions and Women's Institute meetings and church services and County Week agricultural shows and our bringing in the peat and our corncrakes and our daddy longlegs and our cold winds but above all leave us to the sea and the land and above all to ourselves and our own ways.'

'What do you make of that, Johnny?'

Damned if I agree, damned if I disagree. Play for time.

'Sir, with all due respect, it's tricky to...'

'Well said, Johnny. Well said. We have many of our feathered friends here but some folk who should know better are *living in cloud cuckoo land.* I kid you not, those exact words came straight from the mouth of the Minister at last Sunday's service.'

It's silly really...I know I've been Sooth for a few years but I'm back now and I wish in a funny sort of way that Orkney could have stayed exactly the same as when I left.

'We're part of something bigger and we must take the lead. We are a seafaring island. We'd be letting down the great Saint Magnus himself if we just shut our eyes to the outside world. The darkness that's enveloping us won't leave us be.'

That photo can't have been of my Isobel.

'The sooner Winston Churchill comes to power the better.'

The Commander has finished. He has had the final say.

He has every right to have the final say. He *is* the Commander, after all.

He is not the pointsman he runs the whole fucking Orkney rail network.

WEDNESDAY 5TH JULY 1939

Zanre is not an Orkney name, it's Italian. *Zanres*. The coffee shop and tearoom and ice cream parlour, all rolled into one. We are lucky to have it here in the *Toon*. Zanres is the best.

It opened just a few years back, in 1934. I was a patron even before I received the call to go to sea. Ice creams to die for. Just ice creams, me in my short *troos*. Too young to appreciate the delights of their frothy, steamy coffee.

Always on the go, these De'Longhi coffee machines. Pump and hiss, their getting-down-to-business sound. No different in their way from the Flying Scotsman's steam engine. Hiss, hiss; toot, toot.

Zanres, Number 16, Albert Street. Less than a hundred steps down the road from Number 49 the Albert Kinema, a couple of minutes on foot at the most.

Zanres, the Central Café. Zanres, Central Station. Hiss, hiss; toot, toot.

Livio, honestly. Just look at him. Those Italians, always with a smile on their face and never short of an arm gesture or two. A song at the ready, even a bit of the old Verdi. What singers. Uninhibited in their happy ways, could teach some of our sourpusses a thing or two about how to enjoy life.

Livio, it's his premises and he will not give the time of day to queue jumpers in his cafe nor to *fascisti* Mussolini salutes, *Il Duce*.

'Only banter, Livio.' 'No offence meant,' as he's kneed in the crown jewels with this long running Mussolini non-joke that brings tears of the wrong sort to Livio's eyes but it's a larf because *it's banter*, isn't it?

Zanres biscuits, especially those crunchy almond ones – Cantucci, sugary, almondy heaven. A chat with Livio would brighten up anyone's day but it's Zanres' pistachio ice cream, as exotic as a gondola plying its trade to and from the island of Shapinsay, that makes the place special.

Like the room upstairs at the Kinema, Zanres is open to local groups. He is generous minded, open to one and all. No block bookings, there's more of a tacit understanding. Not during peak times, of course, Livio's got a business to run after all. A few tables at the back are reserved during the off-peak times for bletherers, those of like mind, free thinkers, arty types. Signore Livio Zanre is making his contribution to the community and it keeps the cash register purring away.

9.45am. I'm there well early for the 10 o'clock start. Don't want my knuckles wrapped twice.

'Hello Livio, I'm with Mister Firth's group.' I announce my arrival. He points to the tables at the back of the establishment. His finger wafty; not pointy, not Kitchener-Your-Country-Needs-You mode. His arm limp, not fascisti erect. The Mussolini joke has well and truly worn thin by now but it won't stop. He's *foreign* after all so considered fair game.

I have a quick look round the back. The tables are empty. I order a coffee.

Tables at the front start to fill up. I stand at the counter waiting for the first attendee to arrive. I make the crema last and enjoy my blether with Livio who remembers me from before I went away to sea, or says that he does. I am just getting to the most exciting bit. *Beuys o beuys and then there was the Malacca Straits…'*

The first attendee of the day has arrived and sits down at one of the tables at the back.

I join her, cup in hand.

Saluton.

Lovely smile I get in return and the here and now is all I want to think about.

'Mister Firth invited me. He was very keen to introduce me to…'

'A pity that on Monday night you preferred to talk shop

with Mister Firth than say *saluton* to me.' Flirtatious. Those lovely eyes. Her photo in the Commander's rogues' gallery must have been a mistake.

'I…I…' Tongue-tied.

'You mean you couldn't escape?'

We both laugh.

'Johnny. Johnny Sinclair.'

'A pleasure, I'm sure. So very pleased to make your acquaintance, kind sir. I'm Isobel, Isobel…'

'Tulloch.' Johnny provides the surname.

Cups are raised from their respective saucers and chinked. Mock formality. I know I'm supposed to be unobtrusive at all times when intelligence gathering but what the hell.

'You have to be so careful nowadays. If you were to express any slight doubt over the path we're taking, you run the risk…'

I had rehearsed this tempter of an opener to the first person I was to speak to. As good a way as any in getting a member of the Wednesday morning coffee club to be indiscreet. But before I could throw it into the ring…

'Zanres is my favourite coffee shop in town. Mind you, my Saturday morning treat is to go first-thing to the Ballantyne Tearoom.' Isobel is staring at me. It is a world apart from being stared at by the Commander.

I nod. *Ballantynes* is a right smartish sort of tearoom, at the start of Bridge Street, no distance from here. Message passed and gratefully received. My eyes move away from her face and settle on the hand holding the coffee cup. Settle on the fourth finger, left hand – the one next to the tiddler. No wedding ring there today.

She has seen me look.

The tables quickly fill up. No opportunity to talk further but I make sure that whenever our eyes meet Isobel's smiles are reciprocated.

Now down to work. The seat next to me is now filled. A brute of a feller by the name of Robert Eunson introduces himself. Not a *weel kent face.* He was not at Monday night's Esperanto class. No shilly-shallying, no opening pleasantries, Robert's not straight out of the blocks. He bulldozes the blocks out of his way.

'Even the British Legion here in Kirkwall had to put an end to the annual Armistice Day parade due to the poorer and poorer turnout. I admit they did bring it back last year but who in their right mind would willingly want to celebrate the horrors of the Great War? The past is there for one purpose and one purpose only, to be forgotten.

'As for this Hitler. He has his detractors but is very popular with his people and who can deny that the Germans don't enjoy as much personal liberty as us British. Germany is a country back on its uppers. Look at the tremendous pride shown on their faces during the '36 Berlin Olympics. A bit of flag waving does no harm to anyone. What's wrong with showing a bit of pride in one's country?'

'Mister Eunson. I go along with you totally on this. People tend to make a mountain out of a few scuffles and the occasional disappearance of…I tell you I get sick and tired of listening to some of our lot. Especially Winston and his like. I was born in 1920, too young to remember the horrors and futility of the Great War. What can we do in Orkney to get those-who-should-know-better to see reason?'

Robert Eunson lowers his voice. 'We need to put a brake on all this rearmament work taking place at Lyness, at Scapa Flow. At this speed we're *clewing* top speed towards another war.'

In there like a whippet.

'Look, I'm completely with you. A breathing space. That football match in the Great War. A 365 days of the year truce is needed, not just for Christmas Day. Otherwise, it'll be tit for tat. Every aggressive move from us will be more than matched by Germany. We should be friends.'

The line has been cast. The bait too tempting. The fish has nibbled. Time to reel in…

'Sh…not so loud please. You don't know who's listening. Careless talk…'

I raise two hands in apology.

Robert Eunson continues, his voice growing ever louder.

'Our countries share such a glorious rich culture. Both have a common problem, a bacillus within. There's a lot of anti-Jewism in Germany, as there is here. You get my drift. I mean Hitler wouldn't just be picking on them for no reason. There's a trait in their character…'

That's word for word what Mrs Sew and Sew said at Monday's Esperanto class.

'If only we could turn the clock back a year or so. That service in Saint Magnus Cathedral when the two German liners, *the General von Steuben* and *the Milwaukee* came to town. One thousand Germans. The Cathedral was packed. I was there. The sermon was even delivered in German. There was a Lutheran choir singing. Heavenly. Uplifting. Our nations, united as one. Northern European, Nordic, Anglo Saxon…as one.'

Mister Eunson has closed his eyes, no doubt remembering the wondrous occasion. I lean over to him, making sure my voice is as close to a whisper, as can be.

'If I can be of any help, please get in touch. I'm starting at the Golden Wharf in Lyness, Hoy tomorrow. Sorry I haven't introduced myself. Apologies. My name's Johnny Sinclair.'

Robert Eunson. Double chin, over forty years old. Flabby face with rubber lips. Bushy eyebrows. Wide neck. Gigantic hands. Wrestler build. Never mind a Half Nelson, he could easily deliver a Full Nelson. This Robert Eunson. One to be closely watched but kept at a distance. Hand round the windpipe. Knee in the back. Quick snap of the vertebrae. All in a day's work for Robert Eunson.

I look over towards Isobel, missing her smile. Her seat's empty. I for the first time feel a shiver of self-doubt. This is not a game. It's as if time stands still. A Zanres' tableau. All tables occupied. Silence; no conversation. Cups being held up. No crema froth signature line yet above the patrons' upper lips.

A new table and new companions. There's a lot of musical chairs going on here. Mister Firth who gave me the invite is now on my right, with the artist-looking type from the Esperanto class facing. Who to talk to? I've had quite enough of Mister Firth from Monday night, thank you. Him and his sniffing-up-the-dog's-backside allegory for peace. So that leaves…without any expectations here…the artist-looking feller from Monday's class…Mister Irvine Halbert.

'*Saluton.*' I get in there first with my Esperanto, like those freemason fellers, quick to give their recognition handshake. You have so many new friends with Esperanto, perfect for the world of spies.

'*Saluton.* Esperanto not only provides a common language to bring nations together but it helps activate our spiritual liver bile to cleanse our souls.' A superior air about him. His liver bile has gone straight to his head.

He is looking me up and down. Mister Halbert is keen to talk.

'Moral standards slacken when excess uric acid and other harmful impurities remain in the blood. Orkney is a cesspit, a veritable Sodom and Gomorrah. It rains a lot here, maybe I should be saying *Sodden* and Gomorrah. Most people in Orkney are morally inept. Esperanto can lead the charge towards moral rearmament and away from the path of sin. Esperanto cleanses.'

I try to keep a straight face. Isobel gets up from her

table and leaves. Damn but at least I have her calling card. Ballantynes.

The Colonel's words of advice or admonishment come to mind. *Stay the course and remember you're our eyes and ears, everything else is my responsibility.* I try to nudge the conversation with Mister Halbert into safer waters.

'Isn't that upstairs room in the Kinema perfect for the Esperanto class? Shame the class isn't held on a Saturday then we could fit in a film as well. The Kinema is one of the world's greatest…'

'…The Kinema's an abomination. Hollywood is synonymous with Hell.' Johnny had unintentionally lit the blue touch paper. 'The Kinema deserves to be burnt to the ground. Lightning looking for Beelzebub will do the Lord's bidding. Temptation will be removed once the Kinema is burnt to cinders. It's all in the scriptures.'

I'm not having that. Too far. He has gone too far. I'm not having the Kinema disappear up in smoke. Fire? No. Over my dead body. This tripe is coming from an artist for god's sake. You'd have every right to expect better.

'Doesn't matter whether it's arson or a random act of nature or a spark from the nearby timber yards. Only a sick mind like yours could think like that. You might as well wish ill on our Saint Magnus Cathedral.' I'm shouting, can't help myself.

All at Zanres can hear me now.

'No. The Kinema will never end up as ashes. *Never.*

Never.' I pound the table like an auctioneer at the Farmers Mart using his gavel.

The Luftwaffe *would never dare bomb the Albert Kinema*, on the tip of my tongue. Needed to be said but… but…my cover would have been well and truly blown. If I think about it, it's a silly thing to say anyway. German planes could *never* reach Orkney…though London's well within range.

The Kinema is off-limits.

I count to ten, taking deep breaths. This dimwit is told in almost a whisper but in no uncertain terms that the Kinema is fireproof, that it is far too solidly built to ever end up as dust and ashes, that it is built to the highest standards, that it even has the latest asbestos lining for the roof to keep the heat in. *Game Set and Match*. Or to borrow the title from Joe Loss's Big Band hit, *Hands, Knees and fucking Boomps A' Daisy (*with or without the profanity). I do not care. My dander is well and truly up.

The Kinema is strictly off-limits to this Halbert feller, this Orkney trow.

I say no more. Keep my true feelings hidden below the surface like an iceberg. This Mister Halbert is right *doolally* but is he harmless? He could be that away-with-the-faeries type. Like that *The End Is Nigh* feller. I'd seen him on my Aldwych-to-Adelphi run in London, that one wearing the signboard. *Less Lust by Eating Less Protein*. What's wrong with lust anyway? This Mister Halbert is a disgrace. He doesn't even smoke. What sort of man is he?

Mister Halbert leaves Zanres briskish. Flea in the ear.

Nearly 11 o'clock, an hour and a quarter has flown by. Nature calls. I then return to my table and join the hairdresser, Mrs Craigie, Mrs Sew and Sew and Mister Firth. They are the last ones there. I haven't yet spoken to Mrs Sew and Sew. I must make sure that my gaze doesn't wander below the Plimsoll line, that revealing dress and all.

Mrs Sew and Sew has taken over the seat vacated by Mister Halbert. Difficult to catch what she's saying. The odd word, that's all. Mind, don't all Aberdonians speak in an odd way? Lovely coiffured hair. You'd expect that, wouldn't you, from a hairdresser. Did I just hear her say, 'my salon in Lyness is more of a barber's than a hairdresser?' Bet she gets to hear a lot of stuff from her male clients as they get a short back and sides.

'Will see you Monday night, Claire.'

Claire, that's right. That's Mrs Sew and Sew's name. Mrs Claire Craigie.

Claire, no I prefer to call her Mrs Sew and Sew, gets up to leave. Shapely legs. Puts her napkin on the table, neatly folded. Fumbles with the cup and saucer. What's this? With a now-you-see-it-now-you-don't movement of the hand, she slides something under the napkin. Mister Firth readies to leave.

Johnny's and Mister Firth's napkins still in their holders. The waitress comes over to clear the table. Slides her hand under Mrs Sew and Sew's folded napkin and pockets something…probably just retrieving a tip but very secretive in doing so.

Mrs Sew and Sew goes to the counter and talks to Livio.

'I'll be round this Friday evening, Livio.' she says in a loud voice, 'to cut your hair. Straight after you get the deliveries. About 9pm.'

'Yes *Signora*. I will have something for you then.'

I hear people saying that Livio has decided not to apply for British citizenship. Why would anyone not want to apply for British citizenship? 'This Friday evening…'

That's it. Enough is enough. Half past eleven, on the dot. An hour and three quarters. Time to leave Zanres.

It's bright and sunny with a westerly wind. Not too blustery, that's typical for Orkney. Rain is always just an aitchoo away. I'm in no rush…will take in the fresh summer air. There's always going to be someone to have a blether with. I've been half way round the world over the last few years as a merchant seaman…visited many places…a lot of yarns to tell…*the Malacca Straits*…that's the best one.

Turn left to Saint Magnus Cathedral? No. I turn right towards the harbour. There's just the filter tip left of Albert Street and then I yank left into Bridge Street. Fast approaching lunchtime and the streets are getting shopping-busy with folk and carts.

The waterfront, the West Pier and there it is…high tide with the sea washing to shore. The familiarity of the swell of the Bay of Kirkwall. Time has stood still. It's like I've never been away. This is what I've come back for. This is part of my being. This is where I truly belong. It's Orkney. It's home.

My musings are interrupted by a crescendo of sound from the direction of Shore Road. Orkney reservists are being drilled. Marching. Good for morale. A parade but somewhat raggle-taggle.

'Eyes front. Left-right. Left-right.' 226 Anti-Aircraft Battery are soon to be going *Doon Sooth.* Hobnail boots on the tarmac road, a metallic, clacking sequence of sound filling the air not yet drilled into precise, rhythmic step. 'Left-right. Left-right.' Arm firmly gripping whatever's available. A rifle if you're one of the lucky ones, a stathe will do, even a mop handle gripped tight to the shoulder. All are in uniform. There's none of this goose-stepping nonsense. Them Germans take themselves far too seriously.

I just know what *Faether* would be saying about all of this. 'This marching and playing around is all very fine but who's going to be feeding the *kye* = cattle, and who's going to be cutting the peat and bringing in the hay?'

I recognise many of my old classmates from Kirkwall Grammar School.

If they are sent to war, how many of them will return? If

they're shot, how many of them will be able to get up, brush themselves down and start all over again?

I fumble about in my pocket and bring out trinkets that I'd picked up on shore leave in Tijuana. Tijuana, *Doon Sooth*, the Pacific. They are no bigger than capsules and topple over of their own free will but always get up again. Them Mexican jumping beans. More lives than a litter of cats.

All this thinking of war, it puts a spring to my step. I'm 19 and only another year before I sign up. Too young to worry about whether today will be the day that a bullet has my name on it.

I'm starting to feel peckish.

Great fun, this spying lark.

But even more important. Ballantynes on Saturday morning. She'll be there. I know she will.

Beuys o beuys.

THURSDAY 6TH JULY 1939

'You can let folk know that you're back but do not draw attention to yourself,' the Commander had said. 'You're just plain Johnny Sinclair, one of the *hoy polloy*. We don't want your cover well and truly blown. Word quickly gets around in Orkney, even quicker around Hoy. Thursday's going to be your first day. Good luck and remember eyes and ears…report to the Golden Wharf at 9.00am. There's a spare place on my launch if you want it.'

Ridiculous. *Hoy polloy* don't travel on private launches. Thank-you-but-no-thank-you. It'll be the public timetabled motor boat run for me. The Marne II leaves from Scapa just outside the *Toon* for Lyness Pier, the Naval Base over on Hoy. Marne II, that's my boat.

The bus to Scapa leaves in forty-five minutes time from outside Saint Magnus Cathedral, the heart and let's not forget, the soul of the *Toon*. Up early, I want to give myself enough time to wolf down the full Orkney before heading out. *Mither's* a star.

On today of all days I want to avoid *Faether* bending my ear. Anyway, out of luck, I've company at the breakfast table. *Faetherly* advice, as welcome as a slice of bread, Anchor-buttered on both sides. *Faetherly* advice laid on thick.

'*Buddo*, you never said how the job in Lyness came your way?'

I take my time removing that bit of bacon rind trapped in between my molars.

'Got talking to someone in the Bothie Bar who said he was on the lookout for someone who can do a bit of heavy lifting in a warehouse but most important of all can use a clipboard and ask awkward questions. "Has to be an immediate start." That's what he said.

'As soon as I gave him my name, he recognised me. "You're one of the Sinclair boys from the Clay Loan." Gave me a quick look up and down and we shook hands there and then. I was to report to the Golden Wharf in Lyness – first thing, *the morn's morning*. The Golden Wharf.'

'*Buddo what's golden about it?* I'll tell you. The Golden Wharf? The colour of the piss being taken. That's what's golden. Orkney, the first place in the world to have a circular pier, 360 degrees in the round. Saw a hospital once like that. A merry-go-round money pit. Complete and utter waste of money.'

Faether's off on one.

'Well at least all this getting-things-up-to-speed-in-case-of-war is putting more than a few bob in folk's pockets. About time, too. You, you're now going to be working over in Lyness. Me, I'm delivering stone from Cursiter's Quarry – to lay down a run-a-way (*the old man and his 'run-a-way'*) for Hatston aerodrome. Good Orkney stone. Can't beat it.

'There's a real buzz about Orkney. East Mainland. West Mainland. The Isles. Not just the shopkeepers but the farmers are raking it in. More workers here, more mouths to feed. Money goes round and round in local folks' pockets. Different place, *buddo*, from when you left. Different place…

'Exciting times for a young feller like you. If only I was your age, *buddo*. Nothing weighs heavily on yer shoulders. Too young to have been through the mirk of The War *yerself*. The knock on the door. The regret-to-inform-you telegram.

'But *buddo*, we have to do our duty. We can't turn our back on the world. Hitler means us no good. When our country comes callin', *we have to do our bit.*

'That sermon last Sunday at St Nicholas' was a thundering disgrace. That silly old bugger. Him wanting us to look the other way. "Weak nations must take their chance and we should mind our own business." Absolute twaddle. Makes as much sense as a *coo* wanting to pluck its own eyebrows. You have to stand up to a bully. If we look the other way, it'll be our turn next.'

All this goes in one *lug* and out the other. When Faether holds court in the Bothie Bar, they say that he can clear it in one-minute-flat. The management always tries to wind him up near closing time, saves them the bother.

The Old Man has said his piece…

'My goodness, is that the time? Don't want to be late on my first day, *Faether*. Want to make a good impression. Lyness work.' Off out the door I go, still munching my piece of toast.

I don't really know what I'll be expected to be doing in my Lyness-job-that-isn't-a-real-job. Storeroom assistant stuff, I imagine. Rack upon rack of supply materials, all with serial numbers. Issuing out, receiving in. Army would call the whole caboodle, Quartermaster Stores.

My Lyness-job-that-isn't-a real-job is a skive. I mean you have to laugh. Generous tea breaks. In need of a light up – authorised fag break. Working out who's going to win the 3-o-clock at Uttoxeter. I'm a bit tired, so let's sit down on the lavvy, A card school continually on the go. We stop if it's raining…union rules…and it never rains in Orkney. And the double and treble lashings of jam in the donut…the clocking-in machine always needs fixing – strange that! Getting paid and not having to clock in and clock out. Getting paid and not even having to be there. I can feel the jam just oozing out all over my chin.

The Golden Wharf. Named by someone taking the piss.

Hive of activity? Ought to be. Work in progress? Ought to be. Up-to-date record keeping for issues in and issues out. Ought to be. Card index filing system. All over the place.

I look out to the Flow. Warship after warship after warship. Each one needs supplies. I know that it's just supposed to be an alibi sort of job, but skiving is not right, not right at all. I agree with *Faether* on that one and there aren't many things that I agree with *Faether* on.

A lot to look into here. Never mind the enemy within, Nazi sympathisers and the like. Not just cardboard boxes put in the right order on shelves. Pilfering, the number one enemy. Never mind the nuts and bolts, it's the desirable items that *have walked*, are *walking* and always *will walk.* Power drills, that's what I'll focus on today, my first day.

Security, a joke…an absolute fucking joke. I don't want to be like a puppy throwing myself into anything and everything 100%. Remember this is only a *nom de plume* sort of a job, a cover, a costume, a pretence. That's all. A pantomime sort of a job, like putting on makeup and stuffing something up your jumper to make you Widow Twankey at Xmas time. *Oompah, oompah, stick it up yer jumper.*

My hours aren't going to be regular. I don't want word to get around that I'm a gumshoe = private dick. I'll be down on them heavy from the start, then the men will not see farther than me being *the Man with the Clipboard.* No messing…authority…I'll act the bastard. It might run counter to eyes and ears but…

It's Day One. A lot to take in. Is that the time? Better late than never, time to stretch my legs - lunch time. Who knows? Is the rest of Lyness Base as slack happy as the Golden Wharf? Look at those hangars, workshops and those big fuel storage tanks. The size of the place, I cannot take it all in. *Beuys o beuys.* Lyness is getting to be as big as Kirkwall.

Accommodation blocks, bungalows, dormitories, standalone houses for those at the top. Men. Women. Sailors in uniform on dry land. Royal Navy or Merchant Navy? You can tell by the cut of their *troos*. I might even recognise some chums from my *Dunster Head* days.

Lunchtime. First Day. Just away from the main road, I'm walking past a derelict bit of ground, a wasteland – a place where kids meet up at night time for a bit of canoodling and drinking – but this is in broad daylight and all. It's just half past twelve.

Two vans; one with army insignia, the other a right jalopy…and hello what's going on here? There's a lot of taking goods out of one and putting in the back of the other and you can guess in what direction the tide is flowing. They see me and drive off sharpish in their respective vehicles. Van number plate. Click. Click. Click.

The parade of buildings down this street looks interesting. There's a Social Club. Some shops. Look, there's the Chippy. Look, there's the Hairdressers. The Salon. It's open. Too good an opportunity to turn up. I'll just take a peek-a-boo through the window.

There she is. Our Mrs Sew and Sew, the Craigie woman, from the Esperanto class. She does work here after all. The blowsy one. All the clientele is male. Salon, no. Barbers, more like. Let's do a quick walk in and walk out. The doorbell ting-a-lings.

Both chairs occupied. Men with a blue cloth tucked in to the back of their necks. Snip. Snip. Staring at themselves in the mirror. Wanting to pull a gurney face to look as grotesque as possible. If they get Mrs. Sew and Sew to laugh, their reward will be the reflection of her heaving bosom.

What, Johnny wonders, are they telling her? If ever there's a place for a spy to operate from unnoticed, this is it. Spilling the beans as readily as their discarded hair dropping on to the floor. Men, not yet in the barber's seat, waiting their turn. Talking shop to pass the time. Loud voices. Johnny doesn't join them, quick about turn before being noticed.

Mrs Sew and Sew, Mrs Claire Craigie. More than sympathiser. A Nazi suspect, out and out. Bulls eye. *I'll be round this Friday evening Livio to cut your hair. Straight after you get the deliveries. About 9pm.*

This can't wait until my next weekly report.

Only a day and a bit to go and then the weekend. Saturday morning. It'll be tea for two, Isobel and me, at Ballantynes. A pot of tea and then those ruby red lips…all for me.

3pm. Where did the time go? I've already read out the

riot act to a few of the thieves. That's it. I'm back at the Golden Wharf. Have put my shift in. Better clock out. Oh yes, I forgot. I collect coat and duffel bag from the stores room. It's time for the boat home.

'Hey Johnny, there's a man wanting to see you about something.'

I don't recognise the man who's keen to see me. Hardly surprising, it's my first day. Nothing *Whit like?* Nothing *Noh bad.* Nothing *How's yerself?* friendly about this feller. He's looking at me as if I'm as welcome here as a plate of cold sick.

I'm not backing down. We're like two bulls locking horns, a stand-off of a staring match. Mexican stand-off probably. Like those jumping beans. He'll be the first to topple over. Easy-peasy.

'You're new here, aren't you?'

'And…?' Could be talking to the union man, the shop steward. Could be talking to the butcher, the baker, the candlestick maker. I'm being given the once over.

'*Adiaū.*'

Ady what?

'*Adiaū.*' He gives me a hard man look.

This Esperanto lingo can be spoken at the most unexpected of moments.

But I do now remember him.

My new Esperanto friend is the driver of that jalopy, helping himself to stuff he shouldn't be. Esperanto man walks off without uttering another word.

FRIDAY 7TH JULY 1939

Early evening – 7.30pm. Saint Magnus Cathedral, always there – any time of the day, any day of the year. Inspirational, our Saint Magnus Cathedral. Buildings are permanent fixtures. No one's going to knock down Orkney's spiritual pride and joy. Dominates the *Toon* does Saint Magnus. Its spire-praiseworthy and spire-prayerworthy.

'Johnny. Number Four, that's where we'll meet up… just a vespers away from the Cathedral…up the Watergate. You can't miss it. Big tree. Front door has a bronze name plate.' The Commander finishes with a laconic, 'casual dress of course, not number ones.'

The rendezvous, easy-peasy to find. No friendly chit-chat. No *Whit like? – Noh bad. – How's yerself?* Straight in to the operational briefing.

'We're being joined by that right pair of C's',

Constables Craigie and Cormack. Let's hope that Constable Craigie is not related to your Esperanto friend, Mrs. Claire Craigie.

'I had all sorts of difficulty getting the support of their chief wallah, another 'C' – Chief Constable Campbell. His manner was a bit too high and mighty for my liking. Smacked of *Auld Reekie.*

'The Chief Constable was not slow in telling me that Friday night is one of his busiest nights of the week. "Drunk and Incapable…far easier to deal with than…Drunk and Disorderly…last weekend a few Lyness louts even decided to commandeer one of our buses." He told me that he needed all his men for action at chucking out time and there'd be merry hell to pay if Craigie and Cormack weren't returned by then.'

'Commander you're a good mimic, got him down to a T, that faint hint of a lisp. Chief Constable Campbell? I would blackball him from the Masons, if ever he had the audacity to try and join. Hoy polloy. Hoy polloy.' The Colonel was chuckling, a rare occurrence.

'Chief Constable, he just turned his back on me, yes… me…the Commander…and walked away just as I was telling him that I had requested a back-up vehicle should things not go to plan. Not impressed. Manners no better than a…

'So, let's get this right, Johnny. Say once again what you heard at Zanres.'

My moment.

'Livio, I'll be round Friday evening, to cut your hair. Straight after you get the deliveries. About 9pm.

'*Yes, Claire. I'll have something for you then.*

'It's some sort of code for an illegal delivery, I'm sure it was…

'I'd heard from a reliable source that Livio has decided not to apply for British citizenship. Why would anyone not want to apply for British citizenship? There's something very suspicious going on here…at times like this you have to publicly declare who's side you are on…especially if you are a foreigner.'

'That last bit about "Livio not applying for British citizenship." Who told you that?' The Colonel not prepared to accept hearsay, wanting chapter and verse.

'…One of the Wednesday group…I heard it from the adjoining table…I think it was from the…Minister…Mister Firth from Stenness.'

The Colonel still staring at me…expecting more from me?

'I'll give the signal when it's time to move in.'

The last word, it had come from the Commander. There's a surprise.

———

8.15pm. We walk down to 16 Albert Street. Zanres. Zanres, also known as *the Central.*

Albert Street is already busy. It's Friday night after all,

come rain come shine. Zanres is just on the abstemious, the dry side of the *Toon*, the Saint Magnus Cathedral side and not…

…on the other side. The other side that's where you'll find the Bothie and the Albert and all the other waterfront hotel bars and drinking establishments. The Shore and Harbour Street. The other side is where fine Orkney men having toiled all week will be looking for a bit of the action.

New life had been breathed into this getting-oh-so-predictable, weekly argy bargy with the arrival of them upstarts from Lyness, Hoy. Them East Mainland lads now unite in Orkney brotherhood with them West Mainland rickets-ridden-roughies.

Those West Mainlanders, no less Orkney than the East Mainlanders, come to Kirkwall in search of a drink. The capital of the West Mainland is Stromness but it's dry…

Orkney lads now as one…united…against the Lyness *ferry-loopers* = Orkney speak for incomers.

This weekly argy bargy is all good training for the *Ba*. The *Ba,* an Orkney tradition, is the contest that takes place every Xmas and New Year's Day in the centre of the *Toon*. Bridge Street- Albert Street- Victoria Street but the *Ba* can spill every which way.

The *Ba,* it's nothing like *Baa Baa Blacksheep Have You Any Wool?* The *Ba* is as predictable in its direction of travel as a flock of sheep in a hurry without the farmer and sheep dog. Baa. Baa.

The *Ba,* it's as easy to follow as listening to someone using-plain-speak-and-education-and-letters-before-and-after-their-name instructing you on how to tie your shoelaces.

So, it's Friday and not at all rowdy in the centre of the *Toon* but there's still a few hours to go before chucking out time and that's what's making Chief Constable Campbell twitchy.

The two constables had already taken up their position. Both in plain-clothes. PC Cormack, ciggie in hand, in the doorway of the ironmongers directly opposite Zanres casually passing the time of day. The other constable, PC Craigie, looking to any passer-by as if he's giving his reflection an admiring once over in the Pomona Café window.

A White Austin Seven van parks outside Zanres. The engine is left running. The back doors of the van ajar and Livio, with another man helping, is loading up the wheelbarrow with the first of the boxes taken from the back of the van. Zanres is still open for business and doing a roaring trade.

The start of the weekend. Summer months. Not quite up to chippie closing time hours but those ice creams and coffees and cantucci biscuits…what a grand way for *Toon* folk of all age groups to enjoy the long summer daylight. There's just a few outside on the street, them scamps trying to make that difficult choice of whether to slurp, lick or bite the head off their flakey 99s.

'Odd that they're doing this unloading in full view.' The words came out louder than I had intended. We're just a few doorways away from where the raid is due to take place.

'Shh, lad, shh.'

Zanres. The two Cs – Craigie and Cormack. Two more Cs – The Commander and the Colonel – That's four Cs and then Me. All of us in position, primed for action. In our sights, Livio and the Austin Seven driver. Five of us against two of them.

Me and the Colonel and Constables Craigie and Cormack move in, pincer like. The kids hanging outside scatter. So much for their let's-be-adult bravado at the first sign of menace. A few of them drop their precious 99s. What was chocolatey heaven is now just a mish mash of chocolatey shards in a white vanilla puddle on the pavement with a few kids' tears.

The Commander holds back, in watching position…just far away from the action to be able to direct it.

Livio instinctively shouts. 'Help. Police. Get the Police.'

'We are the Police you, stupid fucker.'

Constable Cormack grapples with Livio and pushes him face down on the pavement. Blood pouring from his nose mingling with the vanilla puddle – a right raspberry ripple.

'Robbery, Robbery. Help. Help. Get the Police.' *Aiuto! Vi prego aiutatemi! Prego. Prego.*

Folk inside Zanres are gawking. Some seeking safety

have moved to the back of the cafe. A member of staff rushes from behind the counter to shut Zanres front door and locks-and-bolts it from the inside, to protect one and all. This is unheard of. This isn't Chicago or even Aberdeen. This is the *Toon*. This is Orkney.

Things like this just do not happen here.

A passer-by answers Livio's cry for help. Three now against the five of us. The passer-by is holding an electric flash lamp, a sturdy object useful at moments like these, and strikes the Colonel's head with it. The odds are in our favour but I know from my education at the Albert Kinema that the baddies are more likely than not to be in possession of a shooter.

The driver of the Austin Seven is quickly handcuffed. The member of the public coming to the rescue is handcuffed. Finally, it's Livio's turn. The Colonel and myself get right stuck in. We ignore Livio's – *Prego, Prego*. Quite right to. He does not even want to take up British citizenship. A semblance of order is arrived at. Job done.

The Commander steps forward. Now is the time to make his presence felt. Bowie knife in hand. Today's Friday. Tomorrow this kerfuffle will be forgotten, it'll be a 'Drive In Saturday'. The Commander means business.

I watch as the Commander gets to work. He strides towards the wheelbarrow and picks up the top box from the stack. The Commander may be ancient and justified but he can look after himself. I've no feel at this stage as to the heaviness of this top box. There's a bit of rattling around inside. Could be weapons with Nazi propaganda literature acting as the packing material. Maybe a bomb or two, fuses – ready to be primed.

I see powder spilling out from the underside of the box. Contents intended for the disruption and destruction of the Lyness Royal Navy Base. The sharp blade of his Bowie knife is put to work, as he slashes open this first of the delivery consignment.

Packets with foreign labels. Stacked up neatly in bundles of six. Perhaps drug smuggling as well as... That's what foreigners do. Foreigners take every opportunity to undermine British and in particular Scottish morale.

The sharp blade is used to initially stab the top of the packets and then go every which way around the compass – NSEW. Out spills this powder. I see the Commander bringing the tip of the index finger to his lips. It's the colour of granulated coffee. It is granulated coffee.

Livio, handcuffed and therefore firmly in the grip of the law, can see every moment of this debacle unfold. The Kinema just one hundred steps away. It is the worst of all Hollywood movies for him.

The Commander was trained for the Great War, with its Trenches and the Bayonetting of… The Commander doesn't want to believe his own eyes. Box after box gets the same treatment. Each plunge of the Bowie knife, another step away from sanity. The Commander becomes unrecognisable, a contorted face capturing his louder and louder grunts as he's succumbing to an inner demon.

My fists are still primed but it's not that sort of self-defence I'm readying for. I had to say something. I needed to justify. Justify, that's what the ancient neolithics did around the *Ring of Brodgar* so many prehistoric years ago.

'Commander, those were the words I heard.

'*Yes, Claire. I will have something for you then.*

At least one of the boxes must be specifically for her.

'*I'll be round this Friday evening, Livio, to cut your hair. Straight after you get the deliveries. About 9pm.*

'Livio is Italian does not want British citizenship. Livio Zanre and Claire Craigie are clearly in cahoots.'

I had to say something and did so. In the cold light of a darkening day it did all sound flimsy.

'Johnny, we must go through every box. At least one of them will give us what we are looking for.'

In the penultimate box, there are bags. Larger bags, heavier…Different in feel. Different contents. Hair Supplies. Mousse. Conditioner. Shampoo. Not for use in Zanres coffee shop but no hint of illegality.

'*Mama Mia,* I served you this afternoon. Was my crema coffee that bad and…the Cantucci biscuits?' It's the Colonel's turn to be in Livio's line of fire. *Stupido bastardo…Bastardo.*'

'Mister Zanre, any more monkey business from you and you'll be under arrest.'

Even though clearly the raid has been *disastro*, the Colonel is having none of this. The Colonel knows full well that authority once questioned permanently loses its lustre.

9.05pm. 'Remove their handcuffs now. Tell them to turn up at the Police Station tomorrow. They will be compensated, a bit of form filling required. Explain what the procedure is. Got it.' The Commander barks out the request to the Constables. They are left to do the cleaning up, the *scaffie* work.

The Commander then turns towards me. 'At least we've left a calling card. You can't choose your cock-ups in life, young lad.' His words didn't make me feel any better.

From the Colonel, no kind words. He just glares at me.

No back-up police vehicle is required tonight.

That run-a-way, aerodrome job *Faether* has been bending my ear about, I shouldn't dismiss it after tonight. Bridge Street-Albert Street-Victoria Street. Maybe I should have stayed put with the Aldwych-The Strand-The Adelphi run. Maybe what with me walking out on Kirstin, I fully deserved this. You sow and you reap.

Little more than one hour and a half out of my life but I now have nothing to live for. Even Saint Magnus Cathedral can't help put right what I had started. Why me? Why me?

SATURDAY 8TH JULY 1939

No *mither's* full fry up for me this Saturday morning. No *faether's* questions to duck and dive. I spent the night at my Albert Kinema hideaway, licking my wounds and looking in a completely different direction for solace.

The washbasin in my room? It'll do for a regular Monday to Friday spruce-up but a Saturday demands more than the scrub of my fingernails and a slapdash shave. My bib-and-tucker is there neatly folded in my duffel bag, to be called into action this Saturday.

King-and-Country stuff is for Mondays to Fridays. Saturdays are what life is all about. As for Sundays, its purpose in the scheme of things is to sleep off a rollocking good Saturday. I won't be sleeping alone tonight. I know that. This game gets easier and easier…and I'm not even 20.

07.30am. Early doors, I'm walking down Albert Street, then Bridge Street and there is Kirkwall Hotel on the corner. The Kirkwall Hotel, top spot for a soapy bath. I will be fresh and ready for action and we're not talking about someone acting as the Nation's Saving Grace, this'll be for pleasure, real personal pleasure.

Saturday morning, breakfast being served at the Kirkwall Hotel. A night porter will be finishing his shift, less than a handful of other staff on duty and they will be in the kitchen or dining room. Only Mister Night Porter at the desk will have to be tackled. Be confident. If challenged, just say 'Commander' and stare the bugger out. Easy-peasy.

Reception at the Kirkwall Hotel is manned but I'm waved through. That's unexpected. The first I hope of many pleasant surprises today. I want to be at my carbolic-soap cleanest and freshest for Isobel.

Whatever she orders, I'll have as well. Mind you it's going to be frightfully posh in there. The waitresses'll be wearing a special uniform, like them *nippies* in the Joe Lyons Tearooms. Joe Lyons, the Corner House, my favourite eatery in London. I even saw Joe Loss, the bandleader, play there. *Ballantynes. Joe Lyons. Joe Loss.* The names all just roll off the tongue. After today I will add *Isobel* to my list.

I've got my game plan. I'll be able to seduce her with stories from around the globe. Johnny Sinclair, *Man of the World.* That's me. I'll be the one to pay, of course. I don't mind shelling out half a crown. What's that housey-housey call for number 26? "26. 2 and 6. Is she worth it?" Yes… Isobel…will…be.

Scrubbed and dressed. Hair with central parting. Topped off with a bit of brilliantine. Brilliantine has got that Frenchie smell to it, whereas brylcreem wearers just a two a penny, greasy British pong. Off to the Ballantyne Tea Rooms. Ballantynes at the start of Bridge Street, barely an aitchoo away from the Kinema.

Number 4, Bridge Street, that's Ballantynes not the Kinema. I hope you're paying attention.

I'm nuts about her but I'll play it slow and clever. Draw her out. Find out more about the-there-it-is/there-it-isn't wedding ring. Not straight in there like a mad bull in a china shop but subtle as a moggy purr-playing its owner.

If my tales of derring-do and of course *the Malacca Straits* don't get her to open her eyes, mouth and… I'll bring out my important top security role. Just titbits, nothing detailed. Just enough for her to realise that I'm quite a catch.

The old dependables always there to be taken out of the pack. "Here…Take a card…any card." First one out of the pack, always the queen of hearts quickly followed by the king of clubs and then finally the ace of spades. I get right flushed by the time I've finished talking about myself. First off, my adventures onshore in Shanghai and then a tale or two about Tijuana with the Mexican jumping beans and then…*The Malacca Straits.* I'm licking my lips, anticipating her excitement. Wait 'til she hears about them *Mallacas*. *Beuys o beuys.* I know how to play the fiddle.

Girls? They want nothing more than to be seen walking down the street arm-in-arm with their man in uniform. *Faether* told me about those Great War days. I'll be old enough to be a reservist in a couple of months but I'm getting my uniform in advance. That's what I'll tell her. It'll be of course the Special Forces...how could it be any other?

My Oxford bags with belt and favourite black shirt will do in the meantime. I like wearing black. I got the idea in London, seeing groups of young men on street corners, all in black. Blackshirts. Black, the in-colour for 1939. It makes me look really tidy, really smart. Black sets off my strongest features. Their fashion. My fashion. My good looks.

Early, it's just after 9 o'clock. I walk round the block once and once more. No way am I going to be the first Ballantynes' customer of the day. Needs must; a third walk round the block. I've been around the block more than a few times.

Five past nine and there she is. I can see her through the window. Isobel, sitting in an alcove, on her own, able to see all comings and goings from her vantage point. Ballantynes is serious posh. No-run-of-the-mill tea shop, the tables in Ballantynes have these blue, gingham tablecloths on them, blue gingham. Gingham, that's posh.

In for the kill. In I go. Ting-a-ling. Let's whistle *Puttin' On The Ritz.*

'*Aye aye* Isobel. *Saluton.* Well just fancy seeing you here…'

'Johnny, fancy that and *Saluton* to you too!' Her red ruby lips slightly parted. Beautiful white teeth. Is that the tip of her tongue? Ah…it's not her ring finger day. Promising…She's letting me know.

'*Whit-like?*'

'*Noh bad. How's yerself?*'

There's a silence but she's expecting me to make the first move, I just know it. It's odd I don't normally feel like this in the presence of a woman but…but…I'm tongue tied.

Isobel comes to the rescue. 'Let's order.' She attracts the attention of the young waitress. 'My normal pot of Earl Grey and it's a bit early but can I have a look at the cake stand, please?'

Hang on. Hang on. Ordering should be the preserve of *the man.* The girls yet to walk down the aisle from my Kirkwall Grammar class are either now behind a shop counter or in domestic service…always answerable to…

'Sir, and for you?' This one serving me. She's using a completely different tone to me than when taking Isobel's order. What's all that about? I'm properly spruced up.

She's a smasher though. Starch black dress. Black stockings. Black just gets me going. I've already told you, black is my favourite colour. Shapely legs. White apron. Matching hat. Ballantynes has to be Kirkwall's Joe Lyons. Unmarried waitresses only allowed to serve in Joe Lyons. He wonders whether Ballantynes applies the same rule.

Oh dear, I know I'm gawping at the waitress. I hope I'm not being too obvious. This one, whatshername, was in my class at Kirkwall Grammar. She's smirking.

'Sir, and for you?' How dare she?

'Same as the lady, please.' I put on a gruff voice just to swat her out of the way. Go away. Go away. You've got my order.

Isobel. Just by the way she said *Saluton t*o me, sends a shiver through my spine. Her voice is so gentle, so feminine. We're waiting for the teas and cake stand to arrive. Right, let's turn on the charm. No time like the present for Isobel to realise that I am quite *the* catch.

'…There's a world of difference between the teashops of Shanghai and those here in Kirkwall. Shanghai's in China, you know.'

This is so easy. I'm off and running. More of a steady canter than a whipped dash to the finishing line. Smooth as me leading my partner for the waltz, not flapping about like those who prefer jitter-buggering.

'Fancy that. How interesting.' She smiles and I just know that she's hanging on my every word.

'All those rickshaws.' I quickly then add for her information. 'You know them passenger carts for two being pulled by runners.' If I say so myself, I am painting a pretty good Far East picture.

'Women.' Isobel's interrupting me.

'Women? What do you mean?'

'Well, what about the women?'

'Of course, women are allowed in the rickshaw.' What's she on about?

'No, Johnny. Of course, I know that. My question is – Do women *pull* the rickshaws in Shanghai?' Isobel is continuing to speak in the same sweet tone.

This is harder work than anticipated. She'll be asking me the Esperanto for 'rickshaw' next.

'What are you saying? That women should be allowed to pull rickshaws here in Kirkwall?'

'No, Johnny. I'm asking...are women allowed to pull rickshaws in China?'

I take a deep breath, then another. Is she asking whether women should be allowed to pull rickshaws here in Orkney? Rickshaws here in Kirkwall? Plying their trade Bridge Street-Albert Street-Broad Street, to and from Saint Magnus Cathedral? I know I've been away for a few years but…

'…Now *the Malacca Straits*, a completely different kettle of fish. I was there on the…'

'How very interesting.' She raises her left hand and jiggles her fingers one by one, smallest one first and then… The empty ring finger has the stage to itself, motionless under the spotlight. In this game, there are hints and there are certainties.

'Johnny.' Laying it on the line with a voice like honey. 'James is away at sea at the moment. At least, I think he is.'

'James?'

'Yes, James.'

'Away at…?'

'Excuse me for a moment, it's stifling in here.'

Maybe I'm the one not Isobel in need of a breather.

Isobel moves her chair back and gets up to hang her coat and ruby-red scarf on the coat stand by the door. All done with a flowing delicacy. I'm transfixed by the sway of her hips…I wish all this was taking place in slow motion. She seems to know a lot of people here.

That London hostess club I went to… *beuys o beuys.* We had a few drinks and I thought I was in there but goodness the prices. I left an hour later, completely skint. London's a fierce expensive place. Isobel's more beautiful than that looker who made a beeline for me at that club in London Town.

She's talking to a man by the cash till. I am not happy. She's with me. She's now back sitting with me in our alcove, without her coat. I can see that Isobel's wearing a black blouse to go with her mid length grey skirt.

'Now, where was I?'

She doesn't just look. She stares full on at me.

The pots of tea are brought. Selections from the cake stand made. I'm missing my fry up. Isobel's finger circles round the second tier. 'A fondant fancy for you madam?' But no, she plumps for that sugar-dusted slice of apple strudel.

Table manners have never been my strong point. Fork in hand, with peas I tend to spear and not scoop. So, I'm saying to myself. 'Johnny. Don't make a grab. Treat the cake stand like a woman, with respect. Look at the contents. Eye them up and down. Be polite and not hasty. Do not make a grab.'

I think I am being both playful and refined by letting my finger slowly waft round and round the cake stand like a spinning top about to run out of steam. I point to the lemon meringue pie.

'No whipped cream please.' Now that's showing I'm refined. 'Too early in the day.'

Isobel is smiling, so am I. The waitress smiles and leaves.

I feel a soft brushing of leg against leg under the table. Kirstin's favourite signal in London when she wanted me to know that…

Damn and blast…that looks like Kirstin's mother at one of the far tables, Mrs. Rendall. Of all the bad luck. She's talking to someone sitting opposite her but lucky for me she's facing the other way from me. Let's hope she doesn't turn round.

Isobel's eyes are shimmering.

'You must be missing him.' I lay the compassion on thick with a trowel. A brickie couldn't do better.

Isobel. It's not what she's saying. It's the lack of. She is staring full on at me. She is smiling. Phew. It's hot in here.

An hour later. I have got her back to the Kinema. my top floor Kinema – my office. As we climb the stairs to my top floor room, to underline that I'm more important than she may think I am in the scheme of things, I tell her everything about the Commander and Colonel. She doesn't even have to prompt. She's really interested in what I'm saying. I can tell. 'He even hasn't got his own boat. Him, the head of the Royal Navy here.' We both have a good chuckle over that.

Well as soon as I'd unlocked the door…she's all over me. Isobel's tongue with lizard playfulness darting in and out of my mouth, making contact with and not making contact with the tip of my tongue. Her hands at the same time knowingly encouraging my erection. Outside of my Oxford bags. Inside my Oxford bags. Through the gateway of…and then…

I need to get down to business, fast. That's what a real man does, take charge. I am the first to remove my clothing. Off comes the black shirt and it's tossed to the floor.

Now for the pleasure. What's her name? Christine or was she Kirstin? No. That was London's. Orkney, I'm back. It's Isobel. The name and location are not what's important. It's the doing of it.

My hand inside her dress. The bra being decoupled. Her black blouse unbuttoned and then removed. First one sleeve, then the other. Her black blouse wafts featherlight to the floor. Comes to rest, covering in its entirety my black shirt.

Black blouse over blackshirt.

Her glorious breasts and nipples free to jiggle-play. She gets only as far as the bed. I'm behind her. Skirt and white knickers removed. Isobel invitingly bends over. I can't hold back. I climax inside her. 'Kin-e-m-aaaah.' Then a much softer, 'Kin-e-maaah'. The syllables come out of me like a shooshed outpouring of relief.

Isobel is *not* going to appear in my weekly report, certainly not.

She doesn't want to dally. Saturday is Matinee Day after all at the Albert Kinema. Too many prying eyes. Word would quickly get around if they saw her leave.

There is a smile, bordering on a grin, on Isobel's face. Always the smile. But now for good reason.

Her job has been done.

I couldn't find my door keys afterwards. Where did I put them?

MONDAY 10TH JULY 1939

8.30am. Monday. Start of the week. Home. *Mither's* breakfast. Tasty, real tasty. It almost made me forget Isobel. She was on my mind all weekend. Isobel that is, not *Mither*. *Mither's* a star. You couldn't wish for a better one. You know what. I've been thinking. They can be a pain in the nagging arse at times but every lad needs a *Mither*.

I had turned up Saturday afternoon, kit bag over my shoulder. I mean Saturday afternoon is when any dutiful son sees his folks. Albert Kinema to Clay Loan was hardly a marathon run away, more of a stroll in the park – fifteen minutes tops. I walked up the pathway and saw my folks in the front room. I was ready to play my favourite game.

I knocked on the window pane, followed by extending first my legs, then my arms as if about to be frisked. I was now in start position, spreadeagled. Then my nose was squashed against the bay window. Rat-tat-tat once again went the index finger knuckle against the glass. I played the fool, the daddy longlegs.

After Isobel had left, I couldn't find my keys anywhere. I mean, I must have had the buggers with me. I must have. It wasn't as if I'd done the heavy lifting, persuaded her to come back to my place, only to find myself fumbling outside because I couldn't find the damn things. I mean without my keys we wouldn't have done *you know what* in my room. *Beuys o beuys,* it couldn't have gone better. Sometimes I feel sorry for *them,* no not my folks. Irresistible. *They* are all putty in my hands, women.

No keys I'm confined to barracks, as constricted as a Great War invalid or as a boa in a pepper pot. I couldn't very well leave my hideaway room unlocked and step foot outside the Kinema. I couldn't leave the Kinema unlocked. With the outside side door left ajar, the young *Toon* scamps would seize the opportunity and have a field day playing up and down the banisters…no doubt causing mayhem on the top floor of the Kinema, my top floor.

Ill-trickit, scamps that's what they are, *ill-trickit,* The *Toon's* equivalent of the Outlaws and William and Violet Elizabeth Bott and you could bet your bottom dollar they would be 'cauthing abtholute' mayhem, lisp not optional.

Tuesday, that's my agreed reporting day but I'll have to go and see the Commander on Monday to thoroughly apologise, *to fess up.* I need another set. *Fess up,* I heard James Cagney say those words. *Fess up.* That's what they say in America. Some say I look like James Cagney and even if I don't, I can always play the part with my *bu"er* knife.

The truth is as sacred as a *99,* a chocolate flake (the beacon) of an ice cream cone (the lighthouse). I'll just tell the Commander that my door keys must have dropped out of my pockets during Friday night's fracas. I'll start off eating humble pie as well for my role in what ended up as Friday's fiasco. 'I just reported what I heard.' 'Eyes and ears, that's all you are my lad.' What a flaming fandango. Bloody hell.

08.30 am. Monday. Start of the week. *Faether*'s chipping away. Par for the course. Breakfast. Pearls of wisdom evenly spread on toast. One slice after the other. Never listening for a reply. Like wisps of smoke dissolving into nothingness. '*Buddo*, how's the job going?' 'We've come to a pretty pass.' 'Them workmen over in Lyness, during the week constructing a Fort Knox, but every Saturday night bringing mayhem to the *Toon*.' 'Then there's Stromness folk not knowing how to behave when they see the bright lights…'

But he does talk sense sometimes, so I can't ignore the daft bugger all the time. 'Take away Kirkwall from Orkney and what are you left with?' That's what he said. Quite right too.

I do not make eye contact with *Faether*. I know what's coming next. I'm focusing on what's still to be wolfed down my plate, a rasher and one fried egg to go. He's puffing his pipe. Ready, steady, go. *Faether*'s off on today's sermon.

'These West Mainland fellers, you know what they say about them, *buddo*? They're at the Stromness quayside waiting for their darlings to arrive off the St Ola, the Aberdeen–Orkney ferry. The boat docks and you'd think they'd be a lot of hugging and kissing and weeping and stuff like that but no: not even a smackeroo or a hug. All they can manage for a greeting is just an apology of a move of the index finger, a now-you-see-it-now-you-don't afterthought, like the first stages of Saint Vitus Dance.' In one ear is *Faether* out the other but always if you let him *in* you can't stop him...once he gets going…

'*Cold*, that's what they are the West Mainlanders, *cold*. They need a good south easterly up their…We don't see much of 'em West Mainlanders in the *Toon*. Well, *buddo*, they can just keep on keeping themselves to themselves for all I care. And if we do see 'em in Kirkwall, they need to mind their p's and q's, their manners.'

'You're right, *Faether*. Must rush. Mustn't be late for the boat.' I let out a big yawn. 'I've never slept so well. It must be because I'm back home in my own comfy bed.'

'*Buddo,* a few bob a week in *Mither's* pocket would be a nice gesture from you.'

'Will do.' I will *don't*. I'm only 19. Of course, I'd like to help out but I haven't got any spare cash. I exit sharpish.

09.30am – Kirkwall Hotel. Monday. 'I need to see the Commander.' Straight in there, knowing that any sign of weakness and the gatekeeper will treat me like a cigarette ready to be stubbed out in an ashtray.

'Your agreed day to see him is Tuesday. You may have travelled round the world but you clearly don't know your days of the week. Today is Monday. He is not *in*.' Miss Val Garson, true to form.

'I can hear him. It can't wait. I must see him and now. Whose voice is that next door then? Shirley Temple's? No doubt about it. The Commander is definitely *in*, on the *dog and bone. Dog and bone* = cockney speak, phone.'

And I am right. The Commander is not using top security, enigmatic language. You be the best judge.

'Today…*Tumbler*…five guineas each way…he's an outsider…25/1…good odds…7.30 tonight at Ayr… also…*Shiner*?...yes, yes…*Shiner*… ah…good…7/1…five guineas only…*to win*…yes, you heard me correctly…*to win*...2.30, this afternoon at Epsom…how am I?… having a bit of trouble with the inside molar…must go to the dentists…bloody thing needs yanked out…'

'Let's have a look at Tuesday's diary. Tuesday's, your usual appointment day.' Miss Val Garson barely deigns to look up at me. 'There's a spare slot. I'll pencil you in for 11.45am. The Commander always takes lunch at 12.15pm sharp on a Tuesday. You mustn't make him late for lunch.'

'I will not wait 'til tomorrow, it's urgent.' I am shouting now. My dander is up.

The adjoining door is opened.

'What's this *rammy* all about? Ah…Johnny, what a

pleasant surprise. Good to see you. Come through, Johnny, come through. Miss Garson if you please, a pot of tea for two…no… cancel that…I realise I haven't the time… what a pity! What can we do for you? I'm all *King Lears*. Isn't that how you Londoners say *ears?'*

'Commander. I've been having sleepless nights. What happened on Friday was all down to the intelligence that I passed on…I've let you down badly.'

'My lad, what is done with the intelligence is my responsibility. It goes with the rank. I get the credit. I take the brickbats…We can forget about that Claire Craigie, the one you call *Mrs Sew and Sew.* Her views may be ignorant but she's as dangerous as a constipated cockapoo.'

'Commander, in the state I'm in I need to ask for your forgiveness on a further matter.' I describe my embarrassment.

'Easily solved, my lad.' The Commander made light of my keys' difficulty and handed over a duplicate set taken from his main desk drawer.

'After Friday's operation not quite going to plan, we better have a rethink. Let's put your Wednesday attendance at Zanres on hold. I'd advise staying away from there in the meantime.' It is difficult for me to conceal my disappointment, less Isobel time.

'Esperanto?'

'Yes, continue with the Esperanto class…on tonight, isn't it? Eyes and ears, what's that in Esperanto? There's one student there who I want you to run the rule over. Just put Friday behind you. It's for me to take the flak…*tempus fugit*…see you tomorrow, at 2pm.' He was all smiles. He had everything worked out and made me feel ten feet tall. What class!

The Commander then made this beckoning gesture towards me as if he wanted to let me in on a secret. I was an old man's whiff away. The Commander whispered something in my ear. The name of the person who I should pay special attention to at tonight's class? A horse racing tip? The Commander would certainly know how to make a bob or two on the gee-gees.

'Johnny. Always be careful where you dip your wick.'

The Commander has had the final word…

8pm. Monday. Esperanto class. She's there. She sees me. She is smiling full on. *Beuys o beuys.* Saturday had actually occurred. It wasn't just a fantasy. I'm in love.

A few more words added to my Esperanto vocabulary but I was there for one reason and one reason only and that was to see my Isobel. We will talk. Hopefully, I will manage to persuade her to stay on after. Will she, though? This has never happened to me before, this self- doubt when it comes to women.

I must concentrate. The Commander was very keen for me to attend. He has provided me with *the where, the when* and *the why* but not with *the who.*

There is something suspicious about that Mister Oertel. Albert Oertel. Something I cannot put my finger on. This elderly man with those pebble glasses and a thick foreign accent is a bit of a double for that Hollywood Claude Rains feller. This Mister Oetel looks shifty but judging whether someone is a spy or not just on their looks is too shallow a test.

Eighty-Six Victoria Street, that's where Mister Oertel's watchmaker business is run from, a hop-step-and-jump away from my Clay Loan home and the centre of *the Toon.*

I saw Albert Oertel last week. I'm sure it was him. It was not in *the Toon* but over in Lyness, Hoy at the Royal Naval Base. He was talking to a young attractive lady for quite some time and then she appeared to hand over a book. All this was happening a bit of a distance away but I'm positive it was this Mister Oertel. He just looked f*oreign.*

There were only six of us in class, no sign of Micky Angelo the artist nor of Mister S.M.D Firth, he of the cloth and dogs sniffing up each other's backsides in search of peace between our two great nations.

'*Whit-like?*'

'*Noh bad. How's yerself?*'

We *Saluton* each other and I lose myself in Isobel's limpid blue eyes. They are as deep and unfathomable as the Scapa Flow and they draw me in until I am hypnotised. I notice with gratitude that today is once again not a ring finger day for Isobel. I look at her and even when I look away, I cannot stop thinking of her and her only. I want to have her again and again and again. I can't help but lick my lips with anticipation.

The lesson passes slowly.

'Class. Tell me what type of word *on* is.

'Is *on* an Esperanto word?' I am in there like a shot, out to impress you-know-who.

There is an intake of breath from the teacher, Mrs Janet Shearer. 'Not quite, Johnny. Nearly there. *On* is English. It is a preposition, a location preposition. Does anyone know the Esperanto for *on*? Yes, Mister Oertel?'

'*Sur.*'

'Thank you, Mister Oertel. *Sur la* is Esperanto for *on the*. If I was to tell you that the noun is feminine, then the direct article must be…'

'The article and noun are always the same gender, Miss.'

'Excellent, Mister Oertel. *Sur la*. Mister Oertel, can you help us with this? *Ship* is a noun. *Ship* is of feminine gender. So, the Esperanto word for *Ship* must end in a…? Now, who remembers what we learnt in last week's class?'

'A letter *o*.' Mister Oertel is in there, straight out of the blocks. He has clearly done his homework.

'Very good Mr Oertel and the Esperanto word for "Ship" is?'

'*Šipo.*'

'Bravo, Albert. You are so very clever. Bravo.'

It wasn't the teacher who was now complimenting Mister Oertel, it was my Isobel. My Isobel. How dare she…and she is calling him by his first name! I am getting fucking sick and tired of this Mister Oertel, him and his pebble glasses.

'Teacher, the adjective has the same ending as the noun, so *Good Ship* in Esperanto is *Bona Šipo.*'

Mister Oertel volunteers this information to the class. *Sur La Bona Šipo…*

Teacher's fucking pet.

'Thank you, Albert. So class, we have the words *Sur La Bona Šipo – On the Good Ship…*'

Miss Janet Shearer – Teacher of the Orkney Island Beginners Esperanto Class – realises that this final word would be impossible for the class, but with Mister Oertel there, who knows?

'*…Sučsukerajo.* I repeat. *Sučsukerajo.*' Miss Shearer throws it open to the class.

'*Lollipop.*' Mister Albert Oertel doesn't disappoint.

Sur La Bona Šipo Sučsukerajo.

On the Good Ship Lollipop.

The class break into song.

We made sure that we were the last to leave the room.

It was just a short walk across the landing. We were hungry for each other. Esperanto was the last thing on our minds.

I manoeuvre her, the man taking charge as always. No rough pushing on the bed. *Tenderness*, that's the favourite word in my vocabulary. I make sure that Isobel is standing immediately in front of me, the nape of her neck being caressed with my kisses.

My hands around Isobel's waist, initially anyway, not wandering but there to steady her…but in no time at all stray in search of a rewarding under her revealing clothing.

Isobel instinctively knows the movements that she must take next, leaning if not tilting forward. I enter her from behind and briefly catch her limpid blue eyes looking up at me in the mirror's reflection.

Before I could say *Lollipop*, I had climaxed.

I didn't fall asleep immediately after our lovemaking. Isobel and me, tender in each other's arm and saying whatever first came into minds. She, first.

'Johnny, there are so many ships in Scapa Flow, it's always been a dream of mine to go on a big ship…'

I can't remember my reply. I must have fallen asleep.

ISOBEL TULLOCH: 1

'I have my own story to tell.' – There, I've finally said it. Yes, I have hopes and dreams and desires for my life that go beyond finding a man, falling in love and getting married and having children. Yes, I'm not going to keep my story to myself. Why should I? Yes, why should I?

Where does it start? Well, my own story doesn't start at birth, that would make it too easy for you. I'll start it on the last day of the week, the Sabbath. Sabbath Day, the Sunday. Not any specific Sabbath Day, you can pick and choose from the calendar.

You will always see me on a Sunday morning in a Saint Magnus Cathedral pew, taking part but not part of the congregation. I am neither prayers nor holiness nor connection with the Lord. I make no claims to be a pious churchgoer. I'm there for one reason and one reason only, to show my face without apology and if by doing so some might say, 'I am rattling the *Toon's* cage.' Let them see me. So be it.

If this *wifey* or that *wifey* wants to say bad things about me, well I'm quite happy to look *fishwifey* straight in the eye. It's always the *wifey* and not her man who will talk about me behind my back.

The men of course look at me for different reasons. They don't put it away even on the Sabbath day. I know what they want and I enjoy their look and always return their interest with a smile. It's only friendliness on my part not encouragement…just plain friendliness. You don't need me to tell you that they're not getting what they believe they're entitled to at home but oh dear I have just told you so!

Everyone's character is shaped by their journey through life. If you're going to pass judgement on me first please hear me out, that's all I ask, *hear my side of the story.*

I'm saying this for your own good. I really am. If you feel you have the right to judge me, I expect – *no, I demand* – that you judge yourself. Can I make a suggestion just to get the ball rolling? What about love-and-happiness? Has it been ever-present in your life or have you found it as slippery and elusive as handling a bar of Pears soap?

Of course, having heard me out you may still decide that I'm a Jezebel, a disgrace, a traitor…but it'll be like water off a duck's back…because I know you would not have been properly listening to what I've been saying.

I am Isobel Tulloch and this is my story and you will do

me the courtesy of hearing me out.

Ten-year-old girls wear pretty dresses, help their *mither* round the house and wear pigtails. Not me. I wanted to be outdoors in the *Toon* with the boys and be naughty, a *Toon* tomboy. Tomboys like to climb trees. There are not many trees to climb in Orkney. Trees and strong winds are incompatible. So, more often than not, I had to resort to kicking a ball about with the boys and scraping my knees and scuffing my shoes.

Every night before I went to sleep, I would say a prayer for *Faether.* He was away at sea. I loved *Mither* and *Faether*, *Faether* more so. It feels wrong to say that I loved one parent more than the other but may the Lord have mercy on me, I did. *Mither* was constantly here, whereas *Faether*...

He came to me one night in my dreams, at least this one who looked like *Faether*. At first, he was smiling down at me from up in the skies. I was sure it was *Faether* and I was happy but then the dream quickly turned sour.

The-man-who-I-thought-was-my-*faether* wagged his index finger at me and then said, "Your *faether* is dead. Your *faether* is dead. Your *faether* went to sea because you have been naughty."

I woke up crying. This dream or nightmare which it really was kept on coming back, again and again.

I had many uncles. These *uncles* would give me sixpence to buy some sweeties and in return I would promise to play outdoors for a few hours. One time *Mither* went into a terrible rage, shouting and screaming at both me and *Uncle*.

This uncle had asked me to sit on his lap and I did. Mither came into the kitchen and saw us. What had I done wrong? I thought it was me that Mither was yelling at for being naughty.

Inga was my best friend. Mither would sometimes say to me, "Wouldn't it be a lovely treat if you spent the whole weekend with Inga?" Inga was much older than me. I was 10 and she was nearly 11. I would then stay at Inga's. She lived in a normal house – a *mither* and a *faether* ever-present under the same roof. Inga lived in Stromness.

June 21st, 1919 – a day I'll always remember. It was many months after Armistice Day, which marked the end of the Great War. June 21st 1919 counting back to November 11th 1918, you do the 'rithmetic. I better not forget to mention that I was top of the class at Papdale, I got gold stars for each of the 3 Rs!

The sun had been playing Orkney hide and seek. The sun in Orkney can sometimes behave like a spoilt child. The previous two days, it had refused to appear, the wind and rain taking centre stage. Saturday, June 21st 1919 was a different sort of day. The sun shined on brightly, all day. Saturday, June 21st 1919 was to be a special day…for all the wrong reasons. That's why I'm talking about it now as part of my story, those life events that have made me be the person I now am.

A treat had been planned for my friend Inga's school, the Stromness Academy. All the pupils were to go on board *The Flying Kestrel.* It was a school trip. Inga smuggled me on board with her. For the roll call I pretended to be someone else in her class. All her friends were in on the deception and did not give the game away. I discovered from then on that I had a talent at pretending to be someone else but that talent in being able to play the part isn't why I'm talking about it now.

The Flying Kestrel was to sail in and out of the captured battleships of the German Fleet. Floating Prisoners-Of-War, that's what they were these German ships. First World War booty in our Orkney Scapa Flow waters until them world politicians could make up their mind what to do with them German ships.

The route we were to take was to be as precise as needlework. Our supply boat was to cross stitch itself through the waters of Scapa Flow, getting close up to each German battleship and cruiser.

And that's what we did, weave in and out, taking a zig zag path through over 70 ships – the might of the German Navy. We were on the deck of *The Flying Kestrel.* and told beforehand not to do this and not to do that, in particular to signal or wave at the German sailors who were also on deck, enjoying the sunshine. These German sailors were prisoners. That's what we were told.

We were happy. All two hundred of us. Innocent days. Climbing trees and kicking a ball about in the street. Tomboy. Right and wrong decided by *Mither.* And now I was on a big ship. How can I make you understand? That film that I saw just a few years ago at the *Kinema* with Shirley Temple in it. *Bright Eyes.* You're then far too young to appreciate that those childhood days when there is always someone looking after you don't last forever.

The school trip was meant to be fun but looking back on it there was something darker afoot that we children in our innocence had no awareness of. We were being used. The school trip was not organised as an innocent couple of hours pleasure cruise. We were there to partake in the caging and humiliation of the *German Eagle.* We were there to rub their noses in it. Their once proud fleet now behind bars. Life and spirit and respect taken from them, without second thought. The German Eagle. manacled, anchored and laid low in the Scapa Flow. Their sailors like animals kept behind bars in a zoo.

The sun shined on brightly, all day. Saturday, June 21st 1919. Waters, calm as a pond. The longest day of the year. Coincidence. The randomness of it all. These large floating objects, as still as statues. An Orkney equivalent of a day at the seaside.

Then suddenly, everything changed. One by one, the war boats of the *German Eagle* listed to one side as if they were starting a synchronised manoeuvre that would end in them all turning belly up and having their tummy tickled.

We thought this performance was being laid on specially for us schoolchildren, like a school play on water. What were those big fish I saw at the Albert Kinema? Dolphins lined up in a row and each following what the one before did.

But…no…the German ships suddenly started to exit life's stage in a rage of froth and spit. Shouts and cries and rowing boats and debris and Germans filling the now choppy, foamy brine. And what did I see then? Calm seas in vanilla-white order keen to wish you fair sail, changed in an instant to choppy waters, stained with flecks of dark red blood, a harbinger of evil.

I wanted all this to go away. I put my fingers in my ears. I covered my eyes with my hands. I was crying. I wanted back my calm seas and my sunshine and the friendly sounds of nature and my happiness and *Mither* and *Faether* to be standing either side of me, holding my hand, protecting me and telling me that it'll soon be over.

I didn't want to have to deal with *soon*. *Now* was worse than the worst of all my nightmares. It was worse than the man who looked like *Faether* wagging his index finger at me and then saying, 'Your *faether* is dead. Your *faether* is dead. Your *faether* went to sea because you have been naughty.' This was no dream turned bad, it was being played out before my very eyes.

'How could the British have looked the other way leaving the Germans to do what they did on Saturday, June 21st 1919?' You have every right to ask. 'Why didn't our troops stop the German Navy from committing suicide? The British had a choice and chose to look the other way. By their inaction, they wanted it to happen.'

We shot dead nine of these defenceless human beings in the Scapa Flow, our own waters. The German sailors' only crime was to try to swim to the safety of landfall.

Yes…us…British…shot…them…dead…in…cold… blood. Not…in…my…name. Not…in…my…name. If this is the 'King and Country' that I am supposed to sing the National Anthem to every day, I wanted then and want now to be no part of it.

Of course, it was all hush-hushed up afterwards by the authorities. The German sailors' graves are lovingly looked after on the Orkney Island of Hoy. But nowhere on these grave stones do the words – *Shot in Cold Blood* or *Drowned at Sea* appear.

Can you understand the horror of what I saw? Are you even really listening to me? And you dare to think I am a traitor to my country. What gives you the right to feel superior to me? You won't even look me in the eye. All you can do is to sling words like *betrayal* and *treason* at me. If you're going to accuse me of something, look me in the eye. You and your kind are pathetic. *Wifeys,* all of you… men and women…*wifeys*.

Let he who is without sin cast the first stone at me.

Let she who is without sin cast the first stone at me.

I am Isobel Tulloch.

11TH JULY 1939 TO 26TH AUGUST 1939

Where is she? There's a fight kicking off in the back stalls. Some scamps chucking food about in the cheap seats in the front. Even if the main film had got going, forget it. You wouldn't be able to see the silver screen, what with all the cigarette smoke forming a mist strong enough to roll off the sea. You're at the Albert Kinema and it's the intermission and the *Toon* clientele are becoming impatient.

The B movie is over, the main feature to come and they're waiting and waiting for the lady. Here she comes, the usherette. Nothing to look at but she's carrying this trayful of delights, sashaying down the aisle with the choc ices and the ice creams and the Kia-Oras. Kia-Ora, that orangey-looking drink that comes with a straw for your mouth that looks orangey, doesn't taste orangey, and is always lukewarm and just sticky.

The Orkney *Jahr* is working its way round the clock, between twenty-five to and twenty to the hour. One month follows the next and we've had the longest day of the year. Autumn beckons with the return of twilight time, *grimleens* time.

'Johnny, you know that the Great War started at the end of July. Well, we passed that 29th July landmark nearly a fortnight back. Tuesday, the 8th August and dear Miss Garson is taking her annual leave and there's no one here to do the typing nor indeed to make the tea. She's a star, our Val. Well you and I are here, at least that's one certainty. It's Tuesday and it's debrief day.'

The Commander is bloomin' well relaxed about this. Keeping his cards close to his chest. Something's in the air. At least he hasn't ordered me to pack my bags back to London town...even after that Zanres debacle.

'Let me tell you, Johnny. I'm used to runs of success on the gee-gees. I can pick winners. That's why I picked you, Johnny Sinclair, to join our team. *Nil desperandum…nil desperandum* because we will *carpe diem*...and we'll be *carpe diem-ing* before long.'

Haven't a fucking clue what the Commander's on about, so I'll just nod.

'Do you remember a few weeks back that nag at Epsom, Katy Kustard, causing absolute mayhem? Five of them ended up throwing off their jockeys…all because Katy threw a wobbly at the starting line. All it takes is just the one to panic and bingo…we can pick 'em all off in go.

'I've got my eye on this dead cert. This particular stallion is currently holed up in his stables, snug as a bug in a rug on the island of Hoy but we're closing in on him. It'll just be a matter of time before our friend makes a bolt for it and brings a few of his Nazi spies with him.'

Listen closely. 'Our friend...brings a few with him.' A 'him'. I'm not being given any clear picture here but the Commander certainly knows his horses.

The Orkney *Jahr* and there's always work to do on the land and farmers are reaping what they've sown. Slow moving oxen are still pulling the plough. Peat being cut. It's the Annual County Show Week. We've reached the second week in August and farmers deserve a few days well-earned rest.

Johnny puts in an appearance at Dounby's West Mainland Show on Thursday, the 10th. The Commander's secretary, Miss Val Garson, is there. She sees him but chooses not to see him.

Well, Miss High and Mighty. You've every right to be on your hols but two can play at this game.

He stays long enough at the Dounby show to see the satin red rosette pinned on the Stromness magnificent Prize-winning bull.

Stromness always comes out on top for bull...

Johnny gives a wide berth to the County Show finale in the *Toon* at Bignold Park. It's held like any good finale on a Saturday, Saturday the 12th, but Saturday for Johnny is and always will be his day off and the County Show finale is work. Saturday is Isobel's day. As for Sunday, for most it's the Lord's Day; for Johnny, it's the 3Rs – rest, recuperation and redemption.

August and why is that main film taking so long to start? The ice cream tubs and choc ice wrappers and Kia-Ora plastic tubs and straws littering the Kinema carpet, objects without purpose, spent like used fireworks on bonfire night.

Ps and Qs are now being minded at Zanres' weekly blether. At least Johnny's Esperanto's coming on, though numbers on Monday have taken a nosedive. It does bring into question whether the class will continue.

Johnny hasn't recently seen Mrs Sew and Sew at the Esperanto class. Too matronly, prim and prissy for his liking. Mind, Johnny wouldn't have said 'no'. Had considered her at the start to be a prime candidate, with her hairdressing salon in Lyness and the blousy, snip-snip of loose hair and loose talk.

Jolly's. Short for 'Jesus Our Lord Loves You So'. Funny name for a hairdressers' salon that! *Jolly's* with an apostrophe. *Jolly's* in Lyness. He really wants to pay a second visit to her salon, just to check things out. No, it's his duty to do so.

To Be Confirmed. Worse than a chatterbox, a real flibbertigibbet our Mrs Sew and Sew.

To Be Confirmed. Her top button always undone, allowing clients to keep abreast of matters.

To Be Confirmed. Just a bit more of a tidy up at the back please, missus. Would it help if I bend forward in my chair, missus?

To Be Confirmed. Nearly there…That final bit of tidying up with clippers and scissors at the nape of the neck…Mrs Sew and Sew is always willing to bend forward just a bit more…and then a bit further.

Johnny's right tempted to sit in that chair and everyone knows Lyness is leaking like buggery but Mrs Sew and Sew is not the spy because the Commander said the word 'him'. The Commandeer is looking for a him and not a her.

I need a haircut, well sort of need a trim...and it's Friday the 18th August and it's been a dull week and I'm in need of a bit of a lift. She can chatter away till the kye come home for all I care. It's now my turn for the hot seat. Twenty minutes tops. That leaves me just enough time for the ferry. It'll be a bit of a rush. Can I spare the time? Well...

Nearly finished. Where am I going to pin the Prize-winning rosette? Difficult to decide, equal candidates. She's Mrs Sew and Sew. What a star!

A spring in my step as I head for the pier and there he is three in front of me, Albert Oertel – the foreign watchmaker. Him with his pebble glasses who's a dab hand at all things Esperanto and doesn't he want the class and my Isobel to know it. He is the spy the Commander was referring to. He will appear in my next week's report. I'll stitch him up…one way or another. I bet his Aliens Registration Card does not pass muster.

Livio Zanre, he's almost one of us. Albert Oertel never will be.

———

'I wouldn't be at all surprised if things start picking up in a week or two, say from next Friday August 25th, I just know it. I can feel it in my water.

'In the meantime, all of our military preparations are well in hand. You listen to this, Johnny.'

The Commander with pretend swagger stick in hand runs down his list of why everything is tickety-boo.

'Anti-submarine nets acting as booms have been laid across the main entrances to Scapa Flow. Impenetrable.

'Blockships sunk in the smaller channels in between. Impenetrable. One hundred percent. Impenetrable.

'Don't forget the Fleet Air Arm as well providing protection from the skies. If those U-Boats and *Luftwaffe* have ideas, they…better…think…again. Impenetrable.

'Last week of August, the Hatston runway will be operational. Even more protection from the skies. Our air base just over the waters at Wick on the Scottish Mainland now has a kid brother here in Orkney. Impenetrable.

'Im-fucking-pene-trable, our Scapa Flow.' He concludes with his word of the moment. *Impenetrable.*

There's a bit of Mister Rennison sir about our Commander.

The Commander's going to look a right berk if he's being over complacent. Maybe he's had some good news about getting his own launch.

'And I save my last point 'til last.'

Is the Commander going to turn his voice up another notch on the dial?

'Miss Val Garson is now back from her hols. Refreshed, she has returned to post…and here she is.'

In walks my nemesis, as if on cue. She must have been allowed a late start this morning.

Val…would…you…be…so…kind? The Colonel will be honouring us with his presence…A pot of tea for three would do just the job…Val, those daddy longlegs on the window, can you just get rid of them for me…irritating spindly buggers…I mean what purpose do they serve?'

No. Our Commander exudes bonhomie. That's what separates the Commander from the Colonel. With one, you never know when he's being serious. With the other, you just know that he's always being serious.

'Commander and Johnny, this is a pleasure.' The Colonel has come straight from his legal practice and is dressed work-immaculate.

'Colonel, so good to see you…'

'And *aye-aye* in return. Good to see the both of you.'

'…and here comes our pot of tea. Miss Garson, you always do us proud. That usherette's job at the Albert

Kinema, it has your name on it. I can just see you bringing the ice creams and choc ices and Kia-Oras during the intermission. That would be the moment you've been waiting for all your life, walking down the aisle. Just say the word. Never mind the Orkney *Jahr*, 1939 will be *your Jahr*.'

Miss Val Garson has heard this one before. The Commander gives a nervous chuckle and quickly moves on.

'Gentlemen, with this new Special Powers Act you are now looking at *the man* who's got complete control over the lives of the people in Orkney. *The man at the top.* We're in an emergency. You need to have complete control over people during an emergency. It's for the general good that I have these powers...to keep us all safe… these powers...only temporary…of course.

'There is no better man than me to carry out this responsibility. I am a veritable Jason of the Argonauts with an ability to steer this ship away from those leeches attacking our state. My oral powers have never let me down. Command and control.'

The Colonel rolls his eyes, well aware of his friend's flights of fancy.

This is the Commander's Office, after all.

Why shouldn't it also be the Commander's Orkney?

SATURDAY 26TH AUGUST 1939

Johnny and Isobel. Intimate words are spoken, confidences being shared. It's pillow talk. Before or after? You guess. They're in Johnny's room, upstairs in the Albert Kinema and it's late Saturday morning, the last Saturday in August, the 26th.

'I'm sure I'm not the first, Johnny.'

'Well…'

'It's easier for you men. The more women you've bedded, the more your reputation goes up. With us, Johnny, it's the opposite. How can that be fair, my darling?'

Silence.

I'll tell her about the Malacca Straits.

'We have to hold back on what we really think in case a man feels he's being undermined. It makes us women appear secretive…as if we're planning something, as if we're laying a false trail, as if we're being two-faced.'

I feel uncomfortable. She may have a point though. Them Malacca...

Silence.

'Do you get on well with your parents, Johnny? I never knew mine…'

Silence.

Johnny's hopeless at innermost thoughts and personal hinterland, he tries to steer the conversation towards a more familiar landfall.

'Why can't we just spend more time together, Isobel?'

'I must work throughout the week. Saturday is really my only day off. Oh, there's Wednesday as well when I can. I must pay the bills. A roof over my head…food on the table…to live comfortably.' Flirtatious, now. 'Johnny, do you find me attractive?'

'Isobel!' Johnny kisses her.

This conversation malarkey. Faether putting the world bang to rights and now Isobel...when all I want to do is...

'I love clothes. I want to be the first woman in Orkney with the latest look. I'll show them. Everything though comes at a price.'

Christ. My Isobel? One-of-those-women-of-the-street? Ten a penny in the Malacca Straits...I'd never pay...

'I will help you, in any way I can.'

'You already are, Johnny. You already are. I've seen the way you look at me, naughty boy.'

She playfully wiggles her ringless finger above the sheets

and then makes a stubbing-out motion with this same finger under the sheets. He can feel her light touch on his knee. If only her finger and hand would stray a little bit further north.

'I'm a married woman. Why should I be taking help from you when James should be the one…?' The playfulness in Isobel's tone no longer there, fitful like the Orkney weather.

'James, when he took a drink, was a brute. He'd hit me. I'd need to use foundation and blush to conceal the bruising.' Her voice still gentle, but…the sadness.

'The swine.'

Let me just see him in Kirkwall, he'll be sorry. My Isobel.

'It was a blessing in disguise that he lost his job at the Naval Base in Lyness.'

'My brother also lost his job there. What happened to James?'

'He was fired over something or other. It's not important. We don't need to go into it now. He then signed on and went off to sea in a 'beautiful pea green boat', as a merchant seaman.' She nibbles his ear. 'James going away…it was a blessing in disguise.'

Johnny nods. An image of Kirstin has appeared. It is discomfiting.

If I'm kind and supportive to Isobel, it'll make up for how badly I treated Kirstin...and the others before her. I'll be putting things right. Me and Kirstin. Me and Isobel. Her and that James. What a lark. Funny how life works out. A right do-si-do.

'I once knew a girl called…'

No. He mustn't let on.

'I was on the *Dunster.* I know exactly what the game is with merchant seamen and how they're paid. Casual labour: no notice, no rights nor payment when the owners decide to lay you off. It shouldn't be like that… should it, Isobel?'

'The *Dunster*...was that your boat…Johnny? As for James...'

'It took time for any money from James to trickle through but what little there was, soon stopped. In truth, it wouldn't have made a ha'penth of difference to me if his boat had well and truly sunk with him on board.

'All seamen were never paid a farthing after any ship sank. James wasn't giving me money, anyway. This *wifey* was getting nowt; this widow would have been getting nowt anyway. I don't care whether he's still alive or not. No tears from me. There, I've said it.'

Johnny gives her a hug.

'If he were legally declared dead, would you marry me?'

'You know I would. Isobel, I love you.'

'If we were married Johnny, you do know the authorities couldn't make you give evidence against me in court and *vica versa*. What do you make of that?'

'You are the love of my life, Isobel. *When I was in the Malacca Straits…*'

'…I'm sure those sailing under the German flag are treated better than our boys, they must be. I heard somewhere that the Germans insist on giving *their* merchant seamen the same pay and conditions as those serving in the German Navy.'

Johnny is no longer listening. He holds Isobel tight but tenderly in his arms, her eyes are closed.

'The Germans are not bad people. You know, I've been reading the life story of Adolph Hitler in the *Orcadian.* What a strong leader he seems to be…The Germans call their leader, *Der Fuehrer*…did you know that Johnny?

'I had to provide for myself. Finding work was nigh impossible. Who in Orkney would offer a job to a married woman? It's so unfair. Why should a woman have to depend on a man? Why should a woman be punished for getting married?'

A woman's place is in the home. That's what Johnny's been brought up to believe.

Johnny is all-in-one-ear-and-out-the-other listening. His mind is elsewhere, hovering round and round like a pin circling to find its target on a map and then finally lands on his nom de plume job in Lyness.

I'm going to leave my mark on Lyness.

Isobel speaks to him softly. 'There are German sailors buried here on the island of Hoy, at the Lyness Cemetery. Part of the history of Orkney, whether the powers-that-be like it or not, is now indisputably woven into Germany's.

'You have no say over where you are born and the

nationality that appears on your birth certificate. This is the randomness of entering this world. With every randomness of birth comes the joker of death.

'These poor souls barely out of their teens are not just driftwood, flotsam and jetsam but have as much right as anyone else to rest where they are buried. There's a little bit of Germany that belongs in Orkney. *They* got a raw deal.

'It wasn't Orkney folk who gave the orders to shoot at the German sailors as they jumped overboard. The German scuttling of their own fleet, that's what they called it. It all happened in Scapa Flow. Six months *after* the War was over, in June 1919.

Some of those ships are even now, twenty years later, patiently waiting their turn on the seabed to be brought up. Out of respect? Out of tradition? No, someone always wants to use Orkney to make a fast buck; that metal, those sunken treasures worth a pretty penny to someone.

'See my black blouse on the floor. It's resting on top of your black shirt. The one is no longer separate from the other, an intermingling. You and me, my darling. That's Germany and Orkney. *We belong together.* Do you understand what I'm saying?'

Johnny nods.

'So, this supporting yourself?' Johnny's worried that she's got another lover, maybe even a sugar daddy or she's on the game. He'd picked up those expressions from the flicks, Hollywood, the Kinema. Johnny fears the worst but doesn't know what is the worst.

I'm not having my Isobel turn into a beauty for other men to look at, like one of those stunners – a Barbara Stanwyk or a Bette Davis or a Joan Crawford. Any sign of that and she'll be staying at home and looking for her bit of fun in doing a bit of crocheting or knitting. That'll keep her happy.

'You understand. Because I have no news one way or the other about James, my status is married. If you're a *married woman*, places won't employ you. Is that right? How can that be fair…?'

Johnny's come over all hot and bothered. He fears the worst.

'…I need to earn my keep.'

There followed what felt to Johnny like a very long silence.

'I sell books through the post.'

Runs her own business? What? First a woman ordering a cuppa for herself, unchaperoned in a tearoom, and now this...Johnny has a look of horror on his face. It is a picture that tells a story.

'There's an insatiable demand for books about the Orkney Islands. You wouldn't believe how much interest there is in Orkney from the rest of Scotland and England and Wales – France and at the moment I have a lot of customers in Germany. It's just a small mail order business run from home. I advertise in the papers. A gal has got to look after herself in these times. I enjoy it.'

'Male order…men?'

'No Johnny,' Isobel bursts into laughter, '*mail order* as in selling books by post.'

Silence. Johnny nods.

'Do you…like…advertise in a regional or in a national newspaper?'

'National. Just the one. Not a newspaper that you'd think would bring in the business, for me but it does. The *Racing Chronicle.*'

3.20. Syrup of Figs. 5/2. Epsom.

'The *Racing Chronicle*?'

'Yes, Johnny, *The Racing Chronicle.* Are you deaf? Clean your lugs out.' Another nibble on Johnny's earlobe and an attack of the giggles.

'Why the *Racing Chronicle*?'

'You'd be surprised how many men who like a bit of a flutter, also like to read books.'

Johnny nods.

'Isobel, why do you think folk *Doon Sooth* are so interested in Orkney?'

Isobel is my future. Mrs Johnny, no-ifs-no-buts. I can learn from her. Not only is she beautiful, she's right clever too. Isobel's got a lot up top. That's important.

'The romance, Johnny. The remoteness. Skara Brae and the Ring of Brodgar and Saint Magnus Cathedral. Islands off the North Coast of Scotland. A wee dram in front of a peat fire. The midnight sun and the merrie dancers, the green winter lights in the sky. Islands and their mystery.

'Those Germans, they may appear tough brutes but we

can soften their Nazi ways. Just think of what good they can do to our economy, with their neat and tidy farms and buildings and wide roads without potholes.'

Silence. A long silence.

'What was the last book you sent by post and to whom?' He blurts this out. It is a two-for-one sort of made-up-on-the-spot question.

Silence. This time from Isobel.

Maybe she hadn't heard? I just want to hear her voice. I'll ask a different question.

'So, James. What happened to James?'

'James?'

'Yes, your husband James?'

'Johnny, if he was next to me now, I would put one of these soft pillows over his face and suffocate him.' There is nothing half-joking, nothing playful in Isobel's tone now.

Silence.

'Haven't heard from him for nearly two years. Maybe he's dead. Maybe I should try and make things legal and divorce him?'

Divorce. He remembers as a child, *Mither* and *Faether* over the dinner table talking about some mister and missus in the next street. It sounded really serious, this divorce thing, like someone dropping down dead in front of you in the street for no apparent reason, just keeling over.

She gives him a long, lingering kiss. Her hand is no longer static, starting to move up and down his leg.

'You've asked me so many questions, Johnny. Please, I

know so little about you. You see quite a lot of this Commander and this Colonel. You must tell me more about them. They sound very important.'

His body is willing to tell her anything she wants to know and he'll get his reward and some. He tells her about them…everything…even the layout of the Commander's HQ at the Kirkwall Hotel.

It's Saturday.

Isobel is everything that he wanted Saturday to be. *Never mix business with pleasure.* That's what one of the old fellers told him when he worked in the mailroom in London. Aldwych-The Strand-Adelphi Hotel.

Monday to Friday, one thing. Saturday, a different kettle of fish. He doesn't need a topper-upper of a Saturday job. He's on £3.10s.0d. a week. Yes. £3.10s.0d. That's not bad for a 19-year-old, not…bad…at…all.

Beuys o beuys. Saturday never disappoints for Johnny but Johnny just knows that Sunday will be the day that he and Isobel will tie the knot and walk down the aisle. Why on a Sunday? Because Saturdays are sacrosanct for Johnny. It has to be a Sunday. Sunday's his Redemption Day. One day soon. Not far off. *One Day Over the Rainbow.* You can always count on a rainbow in Orkney. You always get a rainbow after a storm.

August 1939, coming to the end of the month. There's a beautiful rainbow in the sky, inviting you to reach out and touch it. Purple-blue-green-yellow-orange-red bright, those are the colours of this rainbow.

The rainbows are no different in 1939 than they are in any other year. But there's something not quite right about the appearance of this rainbow in the sky.

This rainbow has arrived not after but before the storm clouds.

TUESDAY 29TH AUGUST 1939

It's as if Johnny's only closed his eyes a moment ago but the Orkney *Jahr* continues to tick away and a few more days have passed.

He's back in the Commander's Office, in the Kirkwall Hotel. There's the weekly report to be delivered. So, it's Tuesday morning and it's 10 o'clock on the dot. But it's a different Tuesday, not just because it's a 29th August 1939, Tuesday. Usually just the two of them there but today a third person is present, Colonel Victor.

Now this is a change. What's up? Why is Colonel Vic here? The whole purpose of my morning briefing to the Commander is to give him a heads up before I have my afternoon meeting with Colonel Vic. What's going on?

These Tuesday meetings, official but so informal and it's this informality that Johnny is ill at ease with. The Commander behind his desk, that's to be expected. But it's the smiles, the charm in spades…the 'Good to see you, Johnny'…the 'Val, you're looking particularly lovely today'…et cetera, et cetera…that unnerves.

The Commander gets up from behind his desk and joins Colonel Victor, already ensconced in one of the comfy chairs. That leaves Johnny standing, feeling like a spare part at a Scottish country dance.

Looks towards Johnny, does our Commander. Palm open; one. Smiling face; two. Gestures without needing to speak. The Commander doesn't need to say a blinkin' word. Please do take a seat entreaty. That's class. That's the military for you. Something's up though.

Johnny sits down in one of the pastel-pink, comfy chairs. Pink is certainly not Johnny's colour. It's just… not…well…manly. Both senior officers are fully kitted out in their number ones. No legal-beagle civvies today for our Colonel Victor, it's army regalia day. Something's definitely up.

The Commander waves a newspaper in a once-and-for-all flourish as if he's a horse racing steward about to start the 3.20 at Epsom but the newspaper is not the *Racing Chronicle*, it's the *Orcadian*, last Thursday's to be exact, the 24th August's. The Commander then proceeds to read aloud something that's caught his eye in the newspaper.

'GERMAN DIPLOMAT'S PRIVATE FLIGHT OVER ORKNEY

'Purely A Private Flight.

'A German plane, with the Swastika on its wings, flew

over Orkney and practically the whole of Scotland, during last week. It was not until the weekend that the identity of the pilot and his companion was discovered in London.

'It was the German Assistant Air Attaché of the German Embassy and his wife.

'They flew up to Scotland for this pleasure trip. Captain Spiller pilots his own plane, a small Messerschmidt two-seater.

'"It was a purely private flight and nothing else.

'"We did not go near any prohibited areas and, in fact I know of no regulations which forbid a plane from flying to Scotland.

'"It was for pleasure only, to enjoy the beautiful scenery of your country. My wife and I were celebrating our anniversary."

'Johnny, will you just shut the door please. I will be using words that I don't want Miss Garson to hear.'

Johnny has only just this second retaken his seat when the now stern looking Commander well and truly blows his gasket. A stream of bile. 0 to 100mph in less than 10 seconds.

What...the...fuck!

Johnny is taken aback. Mouth open. Johnny is completely *scunnered*. This outpouring is completely unexpected from someone of the Commander's breeding.

'That is fucking *it*. The Germans are taking the fucking piss. Taking photographs of our military installations and calling it a *wedding anniversary treat* for the missus. Enough is fucking enough.

'We'll get Winston Churchill when he comes here…oh fuck…forget I said that…top secret…to shoot a feature film of our own military capability in Orkney; hand deliver it wrapped up and tied in a nice red ribbon bow; ring the fucking doorbell at the German Embassy in London; give a fucking *Zieg Heil* salute and sing "Happy Birthday, Dear Adolph…"'

'…I think we've got something to discuss, Commander, don't you?' The Colonel measures out his words and glares but not at Johnny.

'Let me finish…We'll even throw in Lancashire's finest – Gracie fucking Fields and George fucking Formby for a fucking song-and-dance routine on the pavement outside.'

That George Formby, he gets right up my nose. I can't stand him with his ukulele grin, the stupid fucker. George Formby's latest, 'I See Ice', is on at the Kinema, even a free ticket wouldn't tempt me. And pardon me for lettin' off, but Gracie Fields. 'Walter Walter, Lead Me to The Altar.' What tripe! What fucking tripe! Tripe, they eat the stuff in Lancashire! That says it all.

Why doesn't the Kinema bring back 'Angels with Dirty Faces?' James Cagney? Cagney'd sort out those Germans. 'Back by Popular Demand from next Sunday – September 3rd.' That's what'll be on the Kinema billboard. September 3rd, as good a date as any for the return of my gangster hero to the silver screen.

The Commander takes breath.

So, Churchill's coming. If only the two of 'em were to have a go at Neville Chamberlain, wouldn't that be a larf. The two of them, having a right old ding-dong. Go on. Go on.

All the lava has spewed out of the crater. The eruption is over. The budgie has had its trill. Our Commander is now counting up to 10. Our Commander is taking deep breaths. Normal service has been resumed.

'Johnny, if it isn't too much trouble, could you please now open the door to the outer office. That's very kind… thank you…thank you ever so frightfully.'

The Colonel is still glaring at the Commander.

'Johnny, I'm sorry, this may seem as if I've completely lost my marbles but could you possibly spare myself and the Colonel a minute. That's right, just wait in the outer office with door closed. Miss Garson will be only too pleased to talk Esperanto with you. We'll call you back in, once the Colonel and myself have had our little confab.

I've been home in Orkney for just two months and what have I got to show for it? Just that fiasco at Zanres. I don't think my new lead of Mister Oertel will save me. All things must pass. They're going to dispatch me back to Aldwych-The Strand-Adelphi House. As for my darling Isobel? Of course, she'll follow me to London. She's completely smitten. They always are.

'Full apology, Colonel. "Top secret visit." I was too free and easy with the tongue. Now, the boy. "Could we get a better Intelligence Officer than Johnny *in situ*?" That's the question. He came with such glowing endorsements.'

'Time isn't on our side. The getting-security-clearance-palaver would mean we'll be one down if we move him on now, Commander.'

'Let's call young Johnny Sinclair back in.'

Johnny, more of a resigned, head-down shuffle than an *atten-shun* recruit on the parade ground as he takes his seat.

'Now, where was I?... Colonel…Johnny…things are moving apace. Hatston airfield. I was at their opening shindig last Thursday, the 25th. A lot of young bloods but *ours*, not those Johnny-come-latelies, those brylcreem-RAF-upstarts. *Our* top brass from London, Admiralty through and through. The Fleet Air Arm always was and always will be Royal Navy…goes with the name…*The Fleet Air Arm.*

'Johnny, your father's work in delivering the stone from the quarry, helping to build the runway has borne fruit. We're now fully operational. There are now 44 Royal Navy warships in the Scapa Flow; that's right 44. Scapa Flow is impenetrable. Let the Hun just try…'

Don't remember ever telling the Commander or the Colonel what Faether does for a living.

'Johnny, the Colonel and myself have had a chat and we've come to a conclusion about you. You're a valuable resource but not being fully utilised. Your *modus operandi* is about to change.'

This is it. I'm being sent back to London Town with the tail between my legs.

'Esperanto classes – you carry on with them. Never know what flotsam and jetsam are going to wash up. Great news for you. Our Miss Garson is excited at the prospect of learning Esperanto. She'll be attending the class from now on.

'Zanres on Wednesdays – we can put you to better use.'

That seems to put the kibosh seeing Isobel on Wednesdays. That just leaves as a dead cert Saturdays. Doesn't look good for Monday evenings with Miss Garson now to be sniffing around.

Hello. Was that a wink the Commander just gave the Colonel? A nod's as good as a wink to a blind horse. They're just softening the blow of telling me to pack my bags. I'm the blind nag in all of this.

'Your report mentions this Mister Oertel.' The Commander says almost as an aside. 'We've had him on our list for some time.

'A consignment of goods was handed over at Lyness Pier, from an army van to an old jalopy which a Mister Oertel was driving. How did you know that the handler of stolen goods was Mister Oertel? Did you get a close look at him?'

'Not only a close look. I even jotted down in my report the number plates…this Albert Oertel…always had my doubts about him…each week at the Esperanto Class… shifty…he's hiding something…that watch repairing is just a front...yes…caught in the act…loading stuff in the back of a jalopy van.'

'We've got enough to lift him anyway. He's bound to have contravened something or other under the Alien Registration Act 1920. Buggered if I can follow all the *must do* things that these foreigners are supposed to comply with. He's bound not to have all the requisite police station stamps. It's about time I started to flex these Special Powers that I've been granted.'

I've managed to stitch up Mister Oertel but I'm still on a shoogly peg...Aldwych-The Strand-Adelphi House.

'Both myself and the Colonel are so delighted at how you've settled in that we've put your name forward and good news, young man, no…not just good news…but… excellent news…We've just heard this very morning that our recommendation has been accepted and Johnny, you are to be promoted. You are to be 2IC – Second in Command – of the procurement, assignment and distribution of gas masks throughout Orkney. It's a position of huge responsibility but you're up to it…no doubt about it.'

Me? Second in Command? Me? Wait 'til I tell…

'Johnny, call them gas masks or any fancy dan name you like…even respirators will do. Everything has to be ready to protect the Orkney population. We have full confidence. Probation period complete. Those delivery and courier days are consigned to the mists of time.

'Johnny. Visible. Respected. A pillar of the community, in charge of the ordering and distribution of. Making decisions, not just merely acting on the decisions of others. Life and Death. People will be coming up to you in the streets, wanting to thank you for your service and shake your hand.

'Poison gas will be dropped from the skies. Mark my words. We learnt from the Great War that poison gas is no precise sniper. Especially up here with the winds answerable to no one. All of Orkney is to be issued with gas masks, the children as well.'

Me, in charge. Must tell Isobel. I'd like to see the sneery faces of the nippies in Ballantynes now.

'Folk just don't see the danger here. They get muddled. Their geography goes to pot, as does their judgement. They believe that we're safe here because London's closer to Germany than is Orkney. Some even have got it into their head that because only a few Orkney households use gas, why should we bother with gas masks anyway?'

'Commander, you just tell me where to report to and when. I'll not let you down.'

'Both the Colonel and I have been very impressed, Johnny. Welcome on board and properly. You're officially our equal. I've said my piece. Well done. Well done. I'll pass you over to Colonel Victor.'

'Johnny, we have someone for you to cast your eye over.' Colonel Victor's monotone voice, not giving the game away and every word spoken is doled out as miserly as a daily tablet intake.

Colonel Victor slides a large white manilla envelope

across the coffee table towards Johnny. Its flap is tucked in, not sealed.

Johnny untucks the flap. A photo inside.

He's barely out of school...

'Just the one photo at the moment. The others are still in the dark room.' The Commander and the Colonel. Looks being exchanged. An eyebrow or two being raised.

Something's going on between them. There's more to this...

The Colonel brings Johnny up to speed.

'In Lyness, on Hoy, there's someone we want you to keep an eye on. His name is Thomas Dreyer. Tom. School assistant at North Walls Primary School. Has lived here for three years. German. On our watchlist. You are to find out what he gets up to and who he meets up with.

'Be discreet. The number of Germans I interrogated in the Great War. They would always talk in the end. In fact, they couldn't keep their *Von Trapps* shut. We don't want you to talk to him. We want you to keep an eye on him. Our MI5 boys want to pick up the whole cell in one foul swoop, not just the one man.

'Nothing incriminating on him so far bar his nationality. He likes photography, the Royal Navy Fleet in all its glory just up the road...convenient, that. Doesn't mean that he's in the *Abwehr*, German intelligence, but doesn't mean he isn't. Prime suspect. You're to dig a little deeper for us. You're a *weel kent face* and all. People will talk to you. You will report back to me—'

'—The chain in command here has not changed.' The Commander, dismissive.

There is a silence. You could cut the atmosphere with a knife.

'Johnny, respirators and our German friend…organising for the safety of every household and the gathering of intelligence…two completely different activities but both paramount…we have every confidence…well done, young man…well done…The defence of the land requires…'

The Commander stops midflow. He closes his eyes.

He's either lost the thread, normal with these old fellers, or he's having a vision.

The Commander opens his eyes and continues in a tone almost wistful. No levity now. It's as if he's talking in front of a congregation or of an audience.

'Two horses. The circus. One person riding two horses at the same time. Or is it just the one man walking on stilts, with the longest legs you'll ever see? There's only one place you'll ever see that happen…at the circus.'

'The circus. That's what my *faether* called the trenches. *He* served as well. The bible tells us that there were four Horsemen of the Apocalypse not just one. *Faether's* name for the Great War was the Apocalypse. I was there, as you well know. For me it was Dante's Inferno.

In Flanders Fields,
The Poppies Blow,
Among the Crosses,
Row on Row.

'Our country is in severe danger. There's no room now for conchies or free thinkers. People in Orkney must stand four-square behind Great Britain and against Hitler, a fight *against* Germany undoubtedly but at the same time a fight *for* the free world.'

Not straining the larynx, the Commander's voice. No gasket burst. No 0-100 mph. Every word carefully measured. A rallying cry but also a painful revisiting of something that should never be forgotten, the Great War.

The Commander's musings even catch Colonel Victor by surprise. The Colonel's head is tilted, mouth slightly open, expression thoughtful.

'That'll be all, Johnny. Would you be so kind as to close the door behind you on your way out?'

Miss Val Garson is typing away. She does not look up to acknowledge Johnny. Nothing changes there. He is about to say something in Esperanto to her but decides not to waste his breath. Johnny, *weel kent* by all in Kirkwall; not so *weel kent* nor appreciated by all in Stromness.

'Masterly performance, if I might say so. Commander Oswald, even I was blindsided.'

'Victor, it would have been cruel if the lad had seen all the other black-and-white pictures we have of our German friend, Thomas. Him and Isobel together in various degrees of undress. Starkers. Not bad lookers in the buff. I'd consider a rough and tumble with either of them or should the stars align with both at the same time. Astonishing what the fresh air of Hoy can do to some. If those are the delights that are on tap in Hoy, just try and stop me from pulling up sticks and leaving the *Toon*, regardless of what the Memsahib has to say about it.

'We'll hold on to those incriminating photos for now. Don't want to put an end to a burgeoning relationship between our two lovebirds.

'Thomas and Johnny?'

'Really, Colonel. Really? Behave! Johnny and Isobel of course. There isn't a better conduit for passing information, false of course, to the Nazis. While Isobel Tulloch is left free…anything we say to Johnny will get through to the *Abwehr*.

'Fancy that…and Commander don't forget that Johnny will also be our get-out-of-jail card if there's a cock up with the Island wide distribution of respirators, gas masks – call them what you will. He's our potential patsy. He'll be our fall guy, if necessary.

'Mister Johnny Sinclair of Clay Loan, Kirkwall, only 19 years old and there to take the shit. Serving King and Country but also serving *us*.

'Our Johnny riding two horses at the same time.'

Repeated, a second time in unison.

Both Commander and Colonel cannot stop. Red in the face. Tears from their eyes. Clutching their stomachs. Frothing at the mouth. In abject pain? I bet neither have had such a good laugh in ages. Unusual to see the Colonel letting himself go.

'Colonel. Please. Duty calls.'

‘Is it to do with one of the warships in the Flow?’

‘The HMS Nelson. Pip. Pip.’

‘Don’t forget to take the photos with you, Commander.’

‘No. Colonel Vic, you hang on to them. I don’t want the Memsahib to accidentally find them in my possession at home. They are rather nice to look at, though.’

ISOBEL TULLOCH: 2

I've been thinking about it a lot recently and even now, so many years on, it does seem so odd that… I'm struggling to find the right words, please bear with me…such a neither here nor there moment…could have had such a profound effect on me. I was in those years of no longer a child and not yet a woman.

I was always top of my English class at Kirkwall Grammar School and she was my favourite teacher, Janet Sinclair. I once overheard her say to a fellow teacher, 'that Isobel…she's so many voices in her head…always writing is that girl.' That made me feel ten feet tall. I enjoyed writing. I had the knack. I had discovered a world that I could retreat to, a world that offered me countless opportunities and freedoms and an identity. Writing enabled me to make my way out into the world. I was *Doon Sooth* without leaving the islands.

29th August 1939…yes, that's today's date. This week is my birthday week…but I cast my mind back to the 3rd September 1927…let's see, that would have made me 14 years old. *Mither* had bought me a wonderful birthday present. Where she found the money to do so, who knows? The question didn't even enter my head then but please don't judge me too harshly. How many 14-year-olds would consider thinking about how food gets put on the table. *I am hungry. It's mealtime. I eat.*

Mither would have had to really dip into whatever savings she had; or maybe it was bought on the never-never, a few shillings a week, hire purchase; or maybe one of my many uncles had given *Mither* a bit extra and *Mither* in return...

A typewriter. I loved to play at typewriters. I'd always dreamed of owning one. I would out of the blue sing *ping*. That's the sound the typewriter's carriage return makes. *Ping*, that's what I'd sing. *Mither* would join with the *falsetto. Ping.* Me and *Mither* for once were in harmony of sorts, a pair of contented mother-and-daughter cats. Writing to me is like typing, always at the far edge of the page and pausing, waiting for the sound of the release *ping* as the typewriter gives me permission to go on to the next line of *my* story. Writing to me is leading my own life. *Ping. Ping.*

A typewriter is not something that can be wrapped up in a bow, so I felt sort of cheated when the typewriter was just handed over to me on my birthday – no attempt made to mark my special day.

The typewriter was given to me as it was, not even inside a box. It looked brand new. It wasn't a hand me down. There was no surprise, no opening of...just handed over to me, no fuss, no kiss, no *happy birthday to you.*

And then *Mither* said, and it seemed at the time such a throwaway comment:

'Typing is a very useful skill to have, Isobel. You'll be up to speed in no time. A job in *Toon* as a typist awaits you. What with you then courting and getting married and starting a family…well *that's your future* laid out for you, my girl.'

Ping. Ping.

WEDNESDAY 30TH AUGUST 1939

The island of Hoy looks nothing like the Mainland nor the other islands in the Orkney archipelago. It's really two islands in a shotgun marriage. The wild, untamed North forced into holy matrimony at the end of a barrel with the house-trained, gentler South. The feral and the moggy.

Lyness and Longhope are in the south east of Hoy, the most populous part. Lyness is in North Walls; Longhope is in South Walls. Both towns, on the coast. Both towns, Walls' towns. There is a stringy land link between North and South Walls – the Ayre. Lyness to Longhope is only a half hour's sailing time.

With all this readying-for-war activity, Lyness has left Longhope far behind. Royal Navy base and all that. Lyness and Longhope, both introspective. Orkney definition of introspective – facing inwards towards Scapa Flow.

Between Hoy and the Mainland is Scapa Flow, the Flow. The Flow serves as the main set of water connecting Orkney with *Doon Sooth,* the outside world. The Flow looks in and the Flow looks out. Orkney's waters, replenished by what the tides bring in but these waters are ours. No one can lay claim to them.

Orkney's Scapa Flow.

North Walls Primary School is on Lyness' doorstep. Thomas Dreyer helps out a few days a week there as a student teacher.

A good egg is our Tom. Always willing to roll up his sleeves and muck in. Popular all round. Gentle soul. Bit of a nature buff. Knowledgeable. Good at leading walks. Likes his photography. Likes his flora and fauna. Camera and binoculars round his neck. Interested in birdwatching. Unassuming, our Tom.

Enjoys going to the North part of Hoy. Hilly and rocky, unkempt. Fascinated by the Bonxies, the Arctic Skuas. Tells everyone, they're dive bombing buggers. Tells everyone, they're *Arctic Stukas*.

This last comment always gets a laugh but Tom can't understand why. He doesn't get the joke but will always join in with the guffaws. Learnt that from an early age. Never stick out like a sore thumb. A universal survival tactic, no matter how old you are or where you live. Ever more important for our Tom, especially with where he's come from.

It's 1939. Tom's really happy here. Tom is in the right

place but at the wrong time. Him, wanting to fit in. Him, a German on Hoy, in Orkney and the dark clouds of war rolling in.

Takes a language class or two a week. Tom *takes,* that's important the taking of, the teacher of grammar, English grammar. Ironical when you think about it. Him being brought up in Bremen and his name Thomas, emphasis on the first syllable *Tooor* and then as an afterthought the *mass*. Tho-mas. His accent not of these parts but doesn't stand out as much as you would think. With Lyness' massive expansion, the majority of these voices wouldn't know their *Whit like* from their *morn's morning.*

RoRo. Rolled on to the SS Bremerhaven in Hamburg, rolled off of the SS Bremerhaven in Kirkwall. Cruise liner. A week after the end of the 1936 Berlin Olympics, it would be. Last week of August, 1936. Tom's three-year anniversary of living in Orkney just passed. Tom is happy to tell folk his story. People really like him, so people always make time to listen.

'I came here to finish off my Gaelic cultural studies. *Genau.* What a language this Gaelic is! They told me in Stornoway that Orkney was *the* place to perfect my Gaelic. A pack of lies. There is no tradition whatsoever of Gaelic in Orkney. Orkney is from the Vikings, from the Nordic Sea, not Gaelic…'

'So why did you stay?'

'Folk are so friendly here. *Genau.* Three years. Off a cruise liner from Hamburg in 1936. I'm not leaving here until my medal from the Berlin Olympic Games arrives in the post. I gave them my Hoy address.'

'Tom, a gold medal?'

'*Nein*. Bronze…for the breaststroke. I am getting in as much practice as I can for next year's Olympics. They tell me the Olympic Games are to be in *Vick*.' Words always accompanied by a swimming movement and a grin. Thomas has problems with his 'Ws'. Wick. *Genau.*

Tom is respected in Hoy for making the effort to fit in. His attempt at humour, disarming. He is respected as an excellent swimmer. Bookish looking. Wire spectacles. Bony. Angular. Shock of black hair. Wouldn't say boo to a goose. Everyone likes him in Hoy. South of the Island. North of the Island. South Walls and North Walls. What a unique island. Full of waifs and strays. Full of ferals and moggies. Tom fits in well.

Tom's at his favourite spot. Cantick Head. South Walls. The flat pancake part of Hoy. Longhope to Cantick Head, just four miles. An easy walk or bike ride. A clear day. The peninsula, jutting out as all peninsulas do. There's a lighthouse at Cantick Head. Every peninsula should have a lighthouse.

Tom looks through his binoculars, out to sea, away from the Flow. The Pentland Firth. That Pentland Firth, it can have a bit of a strop that strip of water. Outwards. Separating the Orkney Islands from the Mainland of Scotland.

Tom looks through the binoculars. Inwards, the Scapa

Flow, the sheltered body of water from the Mainland of Orkney to Hoy.

Hoy is the gatekeeper. Tom is the observer.

Through his binoculars he has a close-up view of a bonxie – the Arctic skua – in action. Must have strayed from the North part of the island. Nothing cute and fluffy about the bonxie. Its expertise is death by battering. These skuas don't mess about, a Nazi ruthlessness about them. Unloved. No surprise that the Arctic skua is also known as the parasitic jaeger. *Jaeger* is German for hunter. *Bonxies. Arctic Stukas. Dive bombing buggers.*

Funny that. The bonxie right in front of him. Tom looking at a bonxie eyeing up its prey. No chatting-up ritual, no need for dissimulation, unlike Tom in Hoy in 1939. In for the kill our Arctic Stuka.

With his binoculars Tom could be at the flicks, sitting in the posh seats, front centre-stalls, looking at the silver screen and a killing about to unfold. Tom is helpless as he watches and is unable to intervene, but because he is watching *and doing nothing*, Tom's own passivity makes him no less complicit in this murder.

The black-headed gull, the *baakie*, doesn't stand a slither of a chance. These bonxies really are the in-flight pirates of the bird world. There is a savage beauty in this rawness to marvel. The bonxie bulldozes into its prey. Nature in all its glory can be a ruthless beast. In its own way, the Arctic Skua truly deserves to call itself a *Luftwaffe* = air weapon. The black-headed gull falls into the sea.

Tom is checking up on something. It's the last week in August, 1939. Now there's a boat on the distant horizon. Could be the Aberdeen–Shetland Islands ferry stopping at Stromness on the way. No. It's the wrong time of day. Could be the new supplies boat, the *MV Hesperus*, due in at the lighthouse doing the rounds. Is today the day? That boat's important to Tom. Cargo off. Cargo on. But here's the rub, if it is the *MV Hesperus*, it's a day too early. Too far in the distance to make out this ship's markings anyway. His binoculars will sweep back to this speck in a few minutes time.

Tom is now looking inwards towards the Sound of Hoxa. Sound of Hoxa, lyrical in its pronunciation, and then the Flow itself. Cantick Head and the Sound of Hoxa, the south entry point to the natural harbour of Scapa Flow.

He's curious about the number of Royal Navy ships in the Flow. Could be an innocent hobby like trainspotting or collecting bus numbers. Binoculars now on full magnification. Better viewpoints elsewhere but still surprised he can only see a handful of ships. Not many there. Maybe they're out and about foraging and will be back at night time, like birds returning to their nest. Expected there to be more. Just curious. That's all. You'd be as well. Human nature.

Tom has found digs in Longhope, South Walls. Just up the road from Groats Stores and the Post Office and the Telephone Exchange and of course the Pier. Landside is the Old Customs House, the guest house and Tom's new home.

The landlady is a close friend of our friend, Mrs Sew and Sew, the hairdresser and Esperanto student. In her early forties, I would guess. No, not Mrs Sew and Sew but Tom's landlady. There's an air of sadness about Fran Kirkpatrick.

She's giving her friend, Claire Craigie – Mrs Sew and Sew, the 'I-said-and-then-they-said' lowdown, the blow-by-blow account, down the line – them sisters working the switchboard are bound to be listening in. All of Hoy will hear of this visit within the hour.

There were two visitors, one man and one woman. It's as if Fran already knows why they are on her doorstep.

'Our Tom told me everything about himself. He had nothing to hide. Nice boy. We of course have a guest lounge but he's happier spending the evening with me here in my front room. We'd listen to the wireless together.'

'May I say, Mrs Fitzpatrick, you have a fine collection of clocks on your mantelpiece.'

'Thank you there's just the nine, maybe room left for one more. Their tick-tock chatter does fill the silence. They are a comfort…ever since John…'

'Is there any reason for all of them telling different times?' She looks as if she's hanging on my every word.

'Of course, he's missing his family, especially his *Oma,* his grandmother. He asked me whether as a favour he could set one of the clocks to German time. It would make up for any homesickness, he said. Of course, I agreed. It's the one in the middle…'

'…Yes, Claire, they call granny *Oma* in Germany…'

'…Tom then asked me whether it would be alright to hang up a black and white framed photo of his *Oma* in his room.'

'Is that alright if we have a quick look round his room, Mrs. Kirkpatrick?' Her voice.

'Of course, let me show you. I was just about to give the room a clean. All our rooms are kept to the highest of standards. Gracie Fields' mother once stayed here.

His room is on the first floor. I have a spare key. Let me make you a cup of tea first.'

'That's very kind of you but later will be fine.' His voice.

Fran Kirkpatrick. The guide. After all, it is her Guest House. She leads. They follow. First floor landing. She has a spare pair of keys. They enter his room. She sees them studying the framed photo above Our Tom's bed, on the wall.

'That framed photo above his bed. He's a good boy, is Our Tom. *Bonnie lass,* the *Oma.* She's from Bavaria, you know. That's her, in her own front room. Her hair's done up in a bun.'

'Could you take the photo off the wall, Mrs Kirkpatrick? We'd like to have a closer look.' His voice.

Claire, they were jabbering away to each other, like you see them do in the films at the Albert Kinema. 'Front room.

Large wireless on the table. Looks new. Back wall, cuckoo clock. Photo hanging up. Well. Who do we have here? *His* face looking down on grandmother? *His* eyes, they're following you. Adolph Hitler. Well. Well.'

They had a quick look at the back of the frame and returned it. 'Our Tom is a good boy,' I said. 'That Hitler fellar in the photo. Probably his *Oma* has no choice in the matter.' That's what I said to them, Claire.

'He's a nasty piece of work that Hitler. The *Orcadian* telling the story of his life? Week after week. I don't believe any of that baloney, that's the word them Eyeties use. We don't want any of them Eyeties here. Oh, I don't mean Livio and Zanres. A nicer person you couldn't wish to find. But that Hitler. A good man? A life of struggle and service? No. No. Evil, he is. Pure evil. A nastier bit of work you couldn't wish to find.

'We were only married a year before my John was sent off to the trenches. He never came back. Just a boy really. What was so *Great* about the *Great War*? When he left, I was a wife. Before the year was out, I was a widow. But he did his duty my John as we all will again, if called upon.

Claire, that's what I told them. Them two asking questions about Our Tom. Them two with their frightfully, frightfully *doon Sooth* accents.

I'm pleased I married my John. Even though we never had time to really get to know each other. It's better to be a widow than a spinster. Whoever I meet, I can hold my head up high. Claire, if only life had been fairer but who knows what's around the corner?

'We'd most evenings listen to the wireless together in my front room, then I would go to bed early and leave him to the wireless and his favourite BBC programme. He likes the big band music. Victor Silvester is his favourite.

'Started recently to get more post. Official like. Typed envelope. Seemed to get him in a bit of tizzy. *Our* stamp on it. Yes, he would also get post from Germany. Just the one letter. Once a month it'd be and what's wrong in getting a letter from home? The last one looked as if it had been opened already. Oh yes. I know all there is to know about these letters.'

'Do you speak German, Mrs Kirkpatrick?' That's what the man asked.

Claire, I told him straight. 'My John did his bit but never came back from Flanders. He died for *our* country.'

'Please, Mrs. Fitzpatrick. I meant no offence. Your loss must have been such a hard one to bear.'

'That one letter a month sent by *Oma.* From Germany. Did you get a chance to read that letter?'

It was the man Claire again with his soft voice. A toff.

'What do you take me for? I told you I don't know any German. It had the same mark over the stamps, from somewhere in Germany. The *postie* here, he would back me up. Their stamps, about the same size as ours. They go on the top right of the envelope too. Their stamps have different colours to ours. The German franking mark, that Eagle, bigger than the stamp itself…'

I even banged the table with my fist to show them how the postie puts that mark over the stamp.

'…You see we always have our King on our stamps. Them German stamps never show their leader. We've got nothing to hide. What are they up to? Doesn't necessarily make them *all* bad, though. They're not *all* bogeymen. Our Tom's a fine lad. He's like a son to me. One final thing…'

The woman, no manners, butting in like that.

'…We want another look round the room. We'll make sure everything will be left neat and tidy afterwards, in exactly the same place that we found it.'

They didn't want me with them. They put on these very thin white gloves like doctors and nurses do at the Longhope Surgery. They came back downstairs after fifteen minutes.

'We'll leave you in peace now, Mrs. Fitzpatrick. You've been most helpful.'

I told them, so there would be no doubt. 'Left in peace? If only this time our country can be left in peace.' They wanted me to swear that I'd tell no one about *their* visit. Of course, I did. What sort of person did they think I was?

Mrs Sew and Sew had stayed silent for too long. She was just bursting to tell her news. Any mention of anyone doing a telephonist job and she's jealous. Plugs in; plugs out; sockets on a big board. Chest forward. I can do that.

'Fran, you know *that wifey* down the road. Yes, she's still carrying on with him. It's a disgrace. He's not the first…and I don't care if you, Lizzie at the Exchange, are listening in or not!'

Lizzie at the Longhope Exchange. Every call goes through her. Phone plug in. Light on. Glad news. Sad news. Courting news. Security news. Scandal news.

That innocent black-backed gull hunted down by the bonxie, *the jaeger…*

Yes. Our Tom is alright. Our Tom is enjoying himself. Helping out with the kids during their summer holidays. Not too onerous a task; not a must-be-ever- present obligation; more of an as-and-when-needed responsibility.

The summer holidays are not really a holiday for the kids. They're expected to help out on the family holding. It is as it is. Chores. They do get the occasional day off from stacking the peat or pulling up dandelions. That's when Our Tom is called upon.

Sunny day today but you're never too far away from a shower in Orkney. August must be the midges' favourite month. Wednesday 30th August. As good as any day for a treat for the kids, an excursion.

Our Tom takes a group of kids over to the North of the

island, the hilly part, for a bit of pebble and stone laying. Letters of the alphabet to be formed. Spelling can be fun like alphabet soup and it's a school trip.

He'd heard on the radio that someone in Donegal had laid down stones on the hillside with four letters of the alphabet – EIRE. Big bold capitals. *EIRE,* their Gaelic word for Ireland. County Donegal on the Irish side and not in Northern Ireland. Southern Ireland, certainly not in the UK but priest ridden. *EIRE.* White stones are laid out on their hills. Those giant letters can be clearly seen from the skies. *EIRE* has given Our Tom a pure *dead brilliant* fun idea.

'Kids, as you know, we in Hoy have got a crossing that takes us from North Walls to South Walls. The Irish also have a border. Northern Ireland and Southern Ireland. One side is independent and the other isn't. Different countries. Different laws. Different attitudes. The Southern Irish are our friends. They speak Gaelic. Who speaks Gaelic? Well it isn't us Germans. *Mein Gott.*

'Kids, wouldn't it be a good idea if we played this same game of putting down stones that made gigantic letters?'

'What for, sir?' Excited. All at once.

'Can any of you guess? Hand up anyone who can. Yes, you Maisie.'

'Sir, it'll be a message that'll be seen from up in the skies for Mister Rain to leave our island well alone.' Everyone laughs.

'Quite right too, Maisie. My suggestion is that it could

also be a message for those looking down on us from above. A flying saucer from another planet.

'Sir, what about making it easier for planes to know where they are flying over.' Our Tom remains quiet.

'What word shall we spell, sir? *Orkney*?'

'Who can spell Orkney?'

A loud chorus. Great fun. 'O'…'R'…

'No, Maisie, "Orkney" has too many letters in it. This'll be too much like hard work. What about something easier that still stands out?'

'Hoy?'

'That's it. "H" "O" "Y".' This is met with loud cheers.

'I've got a farmer to help us, one of the Moars. He'll be bringing in his tractor and trailer all the stones and pebbles we need right up to the top, orange juice and chocolate biscuits as well.' The kids whoop with joy.

'Now, line up in three groups. Each group takes charge of their own letter. If you do a good job with this and it's fun, we'll do this on another Orkney island next. Fara.'

And they all do a good job.

Popular is Our Tom. He has a way with adults and schoolchildren. There they are, those three large letters in white stones on the hillside. H…O…Y… 'Well done. I'm proud of you, children. Hands up those who've had fun today?'

Our Tom's work never ends. After he's brought his kids back to the North Walls Primary School, he has work to do, something important. Those photographs that he took yesterday and the day before at Cantick Bay Lighthouse need to be developed. He'll do that in his school hut where he's converted one of the rooms into a dark room. Shh, that's supposed to be a secret. A top secret.

So many new Royal Navy ships to add to his photo collection.

4pm. *The Toon.* The Police Car pulls up at the bus stop outside Saint Magnus Cathedral. Two Officers. One is eating a sandwich, the other – the one behind the wheel – is pouring tea from a flask. Both in uniform. After a minute or two, the non-driver gets out and talks to an elderly man. He is one of four waiting for the bus. I am just a few yards down the way. I see it all. Click-click. Click-click.

A document is handed over to the Police Officer by the elderly man. The document, it looks like an Identity Card (ID), is inspected. The other Officer gets out of the car and joins his colleague. It is his turn to inspect this ID. I can see by the greyish cover of this pocketbook-size document that it is an Alien Registration Card.

The Police Officer opens the rear door and leaves it slightly ajar. He returns to his Driver's seat. The elderly man walks from the side of the car to the back and gets in of his own accord. The seats are bench-style. No handcuffs are applied at any stage of the arrest. No restraint is needed.

There is a grille between the front and back part of the car. The other Officer returns to the car.

It has started to rain. The wiper blades on the windscreen move from side to side, as dogged as the Orkney *Jahr*. The wiper blades make a screeching noise. The Police Car moves away and takes a left turn, up Palace Road.

Goodbye Mister Oertel, Mister Albert Oertel. Never to be seen again.

THURSDAY 31ST AUGUST 1939

Today, the last day of August, is Johnny's swansong at the Golden Wharf. Just a few hours of clip board and overalls, issuing and receiving. An easy-peasy shift. He's the Stores gaffer, after all. Him behind the counter. Authority. A couple of Please-sign-here-and-here. Stamp, stamp, stamp on requisition and return forms. A bit like a *postie* in his own way, franking those stamps.

Catches the early afternoon boat back from Lyness to Scapa. Uppermost in his mind is his coronation as the 2IC, Second in Command, at the 6 o'clock official meeting tonight in *the Toon.*

All things respirators to be discussed; gas masks to me and you. 44 Junction Road, the Kirkwall Auction Mart's premises, that's where the Commander had said to turn up. It'll be held under the guise of a Freemason's meeting.

'We don't want to alarm folk here. I once had a tip on a horse called *Syrup of Figs*. It was running in the 3.20 at Epsom. Word got out and the odds quickly shortened to a miserly 5/2. Mum's the word, Johnny. Mum is the word.' The Commander has made his point crystal clear.

The transformation of this Clay Loan, *Toon* lad is well under way. Goodbye Johnny Mark I, hello Johnny Mark II. His remit is twofold, respirators and the bringing in of Thomas Dreyer.

Johnny's arrived at the Auction Mart, it's down Junction Road, just a minute or two from the Albert Kinema.

It's just gone 5.45pm. He's there outside the Mart. He would've expected some comings and goings but after a few minutes decides to bang on the front door, only to be told that the Freemason's meeting has been switched at the last minute to Temperance Hall, Mill Street.

Johnny runs like the clappers. It's a good five-minute sprint. Johnny's puffing, if not wheezing. He's disappointed with himself. Clearly, he is not as fit as he thinks he is. There is no sign of life outside the Hall, with the front door shut.

Banging on the door with his fists doesn't work. No answer. There are only a few people about in Mill Street. Johnny feels stymied. He can't ask passers-by what's going on or not as the case might be, because the meeting's supposed to be all hush-hush and there'll be hell to pay if he gives the game away.

I've been pissed about.

Johnny admits defeat. He walks from the Temperance Hall to the Bothie for a consolatory pint, then another and then another.

There's a good looker at a table near the bar. He is being given the eye, the come on. He knows so and goes over to join her. Buys her a rum and lime. Another pint for Johnny.

I'm in there. I know so. Let's start with the Malacca Straits chat-up line.

The boyfriend appears as if out of nowhere. Johnny does a quick beery take on him. Johnny is not having what's her name's boyfriend muscling in.

Doesn't this lowlife know who I am? I'm not any ordinary Johnny. I am King-and-Country Johnny. 2IC.

Christ. This one's a big feller, isn't he? No. It can't be. It's Bob Muir. Battling Bob Muir. Kirkwall's finest. Speciality: hard blows to the solar plexus. Heavyweight champion.

A friendly pint with Bob Muir…well…well…well. Yes… the Bob Muir was with me…on a one-to-one…he was pointing to his girl…and said to me…'you go ahead lad…I don't mind…you deserve her after all that you're doing keeping Orkney safe.'

Time for Johnny to leave the Bothie smartish, stage right.

He stops at the chippie to pick up the newspaper. It is a

Thursday after all. That's the day the local newspaper, the *Orcadian*, hits the streets.

You know what. I'm going home, to sleep in my own bed tonight. No one does a tastier breakfast fry-up than Mither. Let's follow my nose. I can smell it. That gravy poured over a bit of black pudding. Mm…Aaah…Bisto. Something great to look forward to the morn's morning.

You know what. I'll miss August. It's been a great month.

FRIDAY 1ST SEPTEMBER 1939

Johnny's in no rush. He is of course hungover and reckons that there's no harm in having a bit of a lie in. He's going to be giving the Commander a piece of his mind but why not enjoy that extra hour in bed and *Mither's* breakfast?

How the hell did I get back home from the Bothie last night? At least I won't get the third degree from Faether. *He'll be at work by now, in his new job at Hatston.*

Johnny starts his breakfast, rat-a-tat-tat's the top of the lightly boiled egg with the underside of his teaspoon.

Off with its head.

Toasted bread cut into precise, oblong shapes. He's his *mither*'s *buddo* and she's a star. Dunks the squaddies one-by-one. Yolk dribbling down his cheek. Johnny's playing eggy soldiers. Johnny is in eggy heaven.

Her Johnny is not going to go hungry. She watches and

tut-tuts. 'Some more rashers?' What are we going to do with you, *buddo?*' Nothing's too good for her Johnny. It's a *mither*'s lot. It's great to have him home.

Something must have registered with Johnny, a feeling that he needs to be returning her love.

'Don't worry, *Mither.* I'm helping out a pal on some building site today. Here's a couple of quid. Should've given you something beforehand for my keep.'

Johnny hands over a couple of banknotes. Green not blue but don't judge him too harshly, every lad has to take those first steps for handing over board and lodgings money.

'Treat yourself to something nice *Mither.*' Johnny's guilt is there but fleeting.

At the Kirkwall Hotel, 9.30am. Miss Val Garson is busy typing away. She looks up, sees Johnny and gives him her normal disdainful look. 'You're not expected today. Tuesday is your day. If you haven't noticed, today is Friday.'

'I…don't…need…you…to…tell…me…what…day… of…the…week…it…is.' Johnny spells it out for her. 'And you're a fine one to talk. You just breezed in at the Esperanto class last Monday there without a by your leave.'

'I need to see the Commander. It's urgent.' The adjoining door is open. Johnny can hear just the one voice, the Commander.

'The Commander won't be free until later on today.' Miss Val Garson, in her role of gatekeeper.

'No. That won't do. Right now. I…want…to…see…him…right…now.' Johnny talks to her as if she's a foreigner, accentuating each word so that there can be no doubt.

'I'll wait here 'til he's finished his call, thank you.' Johnny's taking no nonsense.

The Commander has finished his call, puts down the phone and walks into the outer office. 'Johnny, good to see you.' Charm, as always, with a capital 'C'. 'Please come through. Miss Garson; a pot of tea for two, please. Johnny, please take a seat.'

'Now this is unexpected, what can we do for you? Sorry to have kept you waiting, Now, where were you last night? The meeting still went ahead. Not the same though without you.'

Flustered, Johnny can't get his words out.

'I hope you haven't come down with something. Here, a sip of water…in your own time.'

Johnny tells the *story*. That's what he feels it comes over as, a story. It all sounds a bit lame.

'Look, please don't unduly concern yourself…last-minute change…bit of a blip in letting everyone know.'

Johnny is about to apologise for the umpteenth time, for what he doesn't know.

'Even though you weren't present, let me bring you up to speed. Colonel Victor shares my foreboding. It doesn't look good, does it? This morning's news…world events…what a dreadful start to the month…Poland's been invaded.

'Procurement matters were to the fore last night. You were *in absentia* appointed the Procurement Officer for Orkney.'

'But…but…' Johnny starts to protest.

'The last job lot of 4,000 respirators, useless, bloody useless. Can't breathe when wearing them. Needs sorting, there's no time to waste. Johnny Sinclair, Procurement Officer for Orkney. Not even 20 years of age. How good is that?' The Commander gives Johnny a congratulatory slap on the back.

Johnny basks in the moment, like a seal sunbathing on the rocks. Johnny feels a million dollars. If only *Mither* and *Faether* had an inkling of how highly their son is regarded.

The news, darker by the hour. All signs of optimism snuffed out. 'We are only doing this to protect our kith and kin in Danzig,' say the Nazis. Forget about the Judy Garland song, *Somewhere Over the Rainbow.* Not even the Orkney *Jahr* can fast forward to a time that would lighten such a sombre mood.

September 1939 is going to be different from any other September. Herr Hitler has been left in no doubt by Neville Chamberlain that the Anglo-Polish Alliance will be invoked. There is no turning back now. The Fleet, the Reservists and the Territorials have all been mobilised. Twenty-five years after the start of the Great War and now this.

'Air raid shelters are being built in Kirkwall. As for Stromness, they need a good kick up the arse. Why is

Stromness taking so long to get going? Kick up the arse. The Commander makes sure Miss Garson hears in the outer office. The Commander's voice is so loud that you can bet they can even hear him in Shapinsay.

'Johnny, I mustn't keep you…first assignment…ferry to catch and all that. Oh, it may pay dividends if you pop into the Post Office in Longhope. You never know…'

Post Office in Longhope? He knows something.

The Commander accompanies Johnny to the adjoining door. Leaves him to the tender mercies of Miss Val Garson. Picks up t*he dog and bone = phone.*

'Well it's about to happen again, Colonel Victor. Unprompted. Veterans of the Great War, singing in harmony. The *Parlez Vous?* song, that Great War trenches song – *Mademoiselle from Armentières, Parlez Vous?* – given a Tommy twist. The *Inky-Pinky Parlez Vous* song.

The Commander and the Colonel, a veritable Flanagan and Allen. The Commander taking the singing part, the Colonel, the speaking…*basso profundo. Parlez Vous?...* effortlessly followed by *Run Rabbit Run.*

One more call to make, important but it won't take long, then the Commander will go out for some fresh air.

He picks up the phone.

'Five guineas each way on Fortune Favours, the 3-o-clock at Thirsk.'

The Toc H hut, as it's known, stands just beyond the far end of the North Walls School playground. Bars are placed over the window. The glass is opaque, its frostiness letting in the afternoon light but that's all.

The hut's outside door is padlocked – no surprise there. Tom being responsible for out-of-school-activities is designated as one of the only two official key holders, the school caretaker being the other…but only Tom has a key. 'Haven't got around to getting a spare one cut.' That's what he tells them if they ask and they don't anymore. The school caretaker, well he's getting his out of hours allowance from the Council. Whether he is putting the time in or his feet up should be of concern but heigh-ho.

'I am having my cake and eating it,' says Tom, still navigating his way round this curious new language with rules but with more exceptions than examples. English does like its funny expressions and so does Tom. He'll squeeze the juice out of any new one he's taken a fondant fancy to. 'I am having my cake and eating it.'

'Your English is coming along grand. Just make sure the hut is locked. You know what kids are like,' the caretaker says to him.

'If I catch any messing around, I will give them six of the best.'

The hut consists of two small rooms; access to the second is through the front. The front room, a few trestle tables and chairs stacked up. The back room is much smaller but secured by a heavy mortice lock. No window round the back. It is full of photographic paraphernalia. From the natural light of a front room to the darkroom, that's the Toc H hut.

Tom hasn't been asked to explain what he gets up to in the hut. He has a perfectly good explanation at the ready, should he be asked. He is good at producing perfectly good explanations. Remember his default answer to 'What made you first come to Orkney?' – 'Gaelic.' It has stood him in good stead. They feel sorry for this *dummkopf*. He is German, after all. Gaelic has never been spoken in Orkney.

Tom has two explanations at the ready to bat away interest as to why he likes spending time in the hut. Clockwork is the common denominator. Either/or. Depends on what takes *his* or what he thinks will take *their* fancy. Like being a circus act riding two horses at the same time. Thomas Dreyer has no difficulty being Billy Smart amongst the hoy polloy of Orkney.

Watchmaker. Tom is only too happy to elaborate.

'I learnt my craft from *Vater*. He liked to bring back to life things that tick tock and cuckoo on the hour. It's the clockwork mechanism, how the second hand activates the minute hand and how the minute hand reacts with the hour hand. *Precision* and *accuracy*, those are the words for watches. You need a strong eye and a steady hand to be a watchmaker.'

The second. *Photographing lighthouses.*

'Why has such a great country as the *Vaterland* ended up with such a small coastline and so few lighthouses? Its

Fresnel lens and flashes of light and strong beam and heavy rotating clockwork mechanism are a thing of beauty and don't forget their white exteriors. Orkney and your beautiful lighthouses. I love to take photos of lighthouses. Without the darkroom, I would be…just…'

Tom's right. There is a fascinating lighthouse at Cantick Head. Cantick Head, Hoy, the southern part of the island, on the peninsula. Cantick Head, not too far from the North Walls Primary School, where he works.

The Toc H hut belongs for all intent and purposes to Thomas Dreyer.

When they broke down the door to the small inside room, they were not surprised by what they found.

Concealment? Thomas Dreyer might as well have left the whole job lot in glass display cases, exhibition items for all to see. No effort had been made at concealment.

On the large table was a morse-code transmitter, no wording to denote origin. In plain sight, a microdot reader. The Imperial German Eagle insignia on its underside is a giveaway and over there a polythene bag containing £5 notes, some with George V's head, some George VI's. Genuine, not counterfeit.

In the drawers? A diary with a Prussian blue cover. Inside are entries, some sort of code denoted by Greek letters of the alphabet, *Delta* appearing time and time again.

A photo… framed…just the one man…a *weel kent face…* back in his home…*Deutschland…Deutschland…Uber*…No prizes for guessing. At the back of the picture frame are row upon row of small shiny black dots, pinhead size.

Oh yes…and all that's just the sideshow. They didn't expect this. There is a dead body on the floor. Blood spilled like red paint carelessly splashed from a tin. Face contorted. Autopsy definitely required. Plenty of fingerprints to keep forensics happy.

All this to come. Foreknowledge. Prescience. 1939, at the time, a year just like any other. Foreknowledge. Prescience. Hindsight. Not unexpected.

It's the start of the month. Friday, 1st September. Isobel is on the late morning boat from Scapa, outside Kirkwall, over to Longhope, Hoy. She is dressed very smartly. She's wearing that Lana Turner *They Won't Forget* sweater. Tight fitting. Lana, in *that* film, just a year or two back. *Beuys o beuys*, did she cause a sensation.

Isobel's got the figure. Chest forward. Thin black belt above waist height. Accentuating those… features. Black three-quarter length, tight fitting skirt. Many would want to. Not many could pull it off.

Orkney's Lana Turner, that's Isobel with her red lipstick. Shame about the shopping bag. Inside is a pinny and some flat shoes and two Orkney books from the same author, Eric Linklater. *Juan In America* and *Juan In China.* She is on the boat to visit her Aunt Aggie, though the books aren't for her auntie.

Chances of bumping into Johnny, she'd put at less than five percent. Just in case, she has her cover story ready. As if she ever needs one. Isobel can just smile her way out of anything, those pearly white teeth.

Aunt Agatha isn't able to do as much as she once could but fierce house-proud. Will not employ a helper to keep her house spotless. There's a lot to do – windows to clean, a carpet or two to hoover and bedroom linen to wash – she manages. I come over on the boat twice a week to help out.

Funny that, both Isobel and Thomas are skilled at having stories at the ready, effortless in the trotting out. Alibis, all part of the training.

'Fran Fitzpatrick? Yes, I know her. She has taken in a lodger but he's no more than a boy.' Aunt Aggie is helping that very nice man and lady who are continuing their enquiries in Longhope.

'The perfect nephew. Tidy and polite. Company of sorts. It hasn't been easy, what with *her loss* in the Great War. I take people as I find them. Some good, some bad. Even here in Longhope, there are certain families that are rotten to the core. Kids out of control and their parents… Yes, Thomas is German…so what?'

Friday, 1st September. A few minutes after 3 o'clock.

Isobel rings the bell of the Old Customs House. 'The perfect nephew' answers. They wait until they're inside before they embrace. Tom whispers in her ear, 'we have a few hours to ourselves, let's make the most of it *meine Schätze*.'

Isobel is well versed in negotiating her way around a small room and a single bed and an inexperienced lover. She makes sure this time though that her clothes are carefully folded. Keeping up appearances is important. After all, Lana Turner always looks immaculate in public. But first Isobel needs to get a few things straight.

'I'll leave these books with you, Thomas. Once you've attached the microdots, hand them over the counter at the Longhope Post Office. Our friend in London, Doctor Dinglestoeford, is a good German like ourselves. He'll know what to do.'

She pauses. Thomas is looking at her. He is avoiding eye contact. 'What's the matter? I thought you'd be pleased to see me.'

'Isobel, of course I am.'

'You can get either Aunt Aggie or your landlady, Mrs Fitzpatrick to drop these books off after you've done your bit. The post from Longhope still has to go through the sorting office in Kirkwall but they're not going to be interested in a couple of books from a *weel kent* Orkney writer?'

'*Weel kent*? I...have...not...that...expression... heard...before.'

'Sorry, I keep forgetting. I should have said Eric Linklater is well-known here.'

'Isobel, I am having doubts about what I am being asked to do...serious doubts (the silent 'b' is pronounced). The German Embassy said that if I help the *Vaterland,* they would make no problems for my family. I haven't received any news from *Vater* and *Mutti* for some time now.'

'Thomas, they are true to their word...as you must always be with me. Sometimes I think you take your *Schätzchen* for granted. Maybe your Isobel needs to find a more loyal *Don Juan* in Orkney to help her.'

Thomas grabs her wrist and brusquely snatches the books from her. Yes, even affable Thomas can get riled. He studies the books' dust covers.

'Eric Linklater? We always use Eric Linklater's books? Do they sell well here? Are his books, how do you say, very *racy*?'

Johnny is on the boat to Hoy; the Lyness-bound ferry from Scapa, Kirkwall. The repurposed Johnny. Johnny Mark II, on Thomas Dreyer's case.

Tomorrow, he'll see Isobel. From one Saturday to the following Saturday. A week's a long time to wait. Ballantynes. Checked gingham tablecloths. Waitresses in their black uniform. Air of civility and good manners. Johnny expects a bit more respect from them given his importance now, perhaps…just perhaps…the best table.

Ballantynes – the Joe Lyons of Kirkwall. The Harrods Tea Room of the North. Isobel will be dressed to the nines; to start off with, anyway.

He gets off the Scapa to Hoy ferry at Longhope, the one before the final stop at Lyness. Longhope, that's where the search for this Thomas Dreyer starts.

Longhope and Lyness. There's a bay between the two towns. Two-and-a-bit miles as the crow flies. Eight miles by road, just follow the mouth of the bay, the Ayre. The journey can be cut down by taking a boat from South Ness to North Ness. You wouldn't really call it a ferry, it's a boat and the timetable, a bit at the harbourmaster's whim.

It's late lunchtime. He's hungry. Longhope Pierhead and if you fancy a sandwich just pop into JMF Groat and Sons, General Provisions Stores. Groats. Johnny sees Aunty Ida behind the counter…two birds with the one stone.

'Well. Well. Johnny Sinclair. Haven't seen you for some time. How's Kath, I mean how's your *mither*? Been away at sea, have we now? I bet you have got some exciting adventures up your sleeve just waiting to spill out…'

'…Well funny you saying that Aunty but…*the Malacca Straits, beuys o beuys…*'

'…Just look at you, haven't you grown. It's made a man of you, no doubt about it. Terrible news with what's going in Europe. We taught them a lesson then and, if called upon, we'll do it now. The *Huns.* Always giving us trouble.

'Thomas Dreyer, did you say? He's a lamb. What a nice boy. He'll do anything for you. See him in here regularly. "Please" and "thank you" and "are you keeping well, Mrs Downe?" Even took it upon himself to deliver some paraffin to my home after hours because I'd run out.'

'Aunty Ida, does Thomas use the Post Office much?'

'I'm not supposed to say. Them-in-charge-here don't like us gossiping about who we collect from and deliver to…but I can tell you this.

'Every month *his* letter arrives from *Germanland*, with that eagle or is it a swastika mark stamped on it?' Her fist makes contact with the table. The sound of impact, quiet as a dormouse though, a cushioned fist.

'Then there's the books he's just started sending to some foreigner with a London address; 88 Hillyfields, Brockley, South East London. Now, what's the name of the fellar? It's no Orkney sounding name. Dinglestoeford, or something like that. I call him *Dinglewhatsit.* Fran Fitzpatrick, you know Thomas landlady, sometimes brings in a book for posting to this *Dinglewhatsit.* What a name! It's a name that sticks.

'And then there's this *wifey* from Kirkwall. She's in on the game. No, I didn't say 'on the game', she's in on the game. Sometimes she's bringing in his books to send to this *Dinglewhatsit.* Not a job lot, only a single book at a time. This *wifey* in Kirkwall…Isobel…Isobel *whatshername.*

Sometimes she comes in with *him,* hand in hand, like a pair of turtle doves.

'This selling books by post, it'll never catch on.'

Time for the boat back to Scapa and the *Toon.* Just speaking to Aunty Ida feels like a day's work in itself. The weekend and Isobel beckons.

Commander and Colonel. Celebratory drinks? Why not? It's Friday afternoon and that's enough reason to celebrate. A Friday afternoon routine for them both, together. 'Chin chin' and 'bottoms up' for two o'clock. The clock says half past two and the Commander is late.

There is no hidden agenda behind his lateness. He's having to confront a sharp deadline, a-two-days-to-go deadline. After today, Friday, it'll be a one-day-to-go deadline. The deadline is not of his own making.

Sunday, the 3rd September. A glass exhibition case *with something pretty damn important inside* has to be collected from *HMS Nelson* in the Flow and taken to Scrabster, the nearest Scottish Mainland port and the northernmost. The hush-hush item will be travelling by bullion van just a few miles from Scrabster harbour to be deposited into the Thurso Bank of Scotland vaults.

'Commander, what are we talking about here, the Crown Jewels?'

'Top secret but I can trust you, Colonel Vic. It's a lock of hair.'

'Hair?'

'Vice-Admiral Horatio's, the very. A lock from Vice-Admiral Horatio Nelson's head. Our British hero, "Kiss Me Hardy" and all that. Only one place to keep it, safely under lock and key and on land. In normal times it would be safe and sound, pride of place on the *HMS Nelson*. These are not normal times, Colonel Vic.

'What if the battleship *Nelson* is bombed by the *Luftwaffe* or holed by a sub? I know we're talking fantasy here, our defences are far too strong for that but imagine the Germans somehow got hold of Nelson's lock of hair… what a propaganda victory for Goebbels and his Nazi cohorts…I'll repeat…What…a…propaganda…victory.

'I give up…Horatio Nelson…*HMS Victory.* You're very slow on the uptake today. Colonel Vic… you need a drink…no…we…*both*...need…a…drink. I've brought the bottle of Highland Park with me. Rare and aged, a bit like the both of us.' The bottle is opened. Two generous drams are poured and downed. *Slàinte.*

'This could be the last celebratory drink we have for a long time.' The Colonel is reflective; the Commander nods vigorously at what the Colonel has just said. Both of them feel overwhelmed by today's serious turn of events.

'The Germans have invaded Poland. We're to all effects and purposes at war. Neville Chamberlain had been made to look a fool once before…and now this. He has only one course of action he can take.

The Commander does his Neville Chamberlain take, in Pathé News style, on the Prime Minister's triumphant return from Munich, just 11 months ago.

'He walks down the couple of steps from a two prop propellor plane. At Heston Aerodrome, 30th September 1938. The ecstatic crowd are cheering wildly. The PM is waving the signed agreement in his hand. *The settlement of the Czechoslovakian problem.* "This morning I had a talk with the German Chancellor. We will have *Peace In Our Time.*"'

The Commander takes out a large manilla-brown envelope from his attaché case, gives it a quick wave above his head in Neville Chamberlain style and hands it over to the Colonel.

'No need to open it Colonel, I'd like you to leave it with Johnny as soon as you can. I think its contents would do Johnny the world of good. Contained within? Instructions of a sort.'

The Colonel's curiosity gets the better of him and he opens the large manilla-brown envelope. The broadest of smiles appear on the Colonel's face and he chuckles.

It's just the one photo, Thomas and Isobel in Thomas' Longhope lodgings. What legal beagles would describe as being caught in a compromising position and Colonel Vic is the head of the most prestigious legal practice in the *Toon* and therefore the most legal beagle of all legal beagles in Orkney. Nothing is left to the imagination.

'Are you thinking, Commander what I think you're thinking?'

'Spot on, Colonel Vic. I've just noticed a slight casualness creeping into our Johnny. Maybe this appointment as Procurement Officer has gone to his head, as if he doesn't need to prove his worth here.'

'I know what you're on about. Johnny's started to light up in my presence without seeking prior permission. Commander, what you call "casualness", I call damn insolence.

'The contents of this large brown manilla envelope will help concentrate minds, don't you think?'

The *MV Hesperus*, the new supplies ship from the Northern Lighthouses is doing the West Coast of Scotland and Northern Isles run. The *MV Hesperus* is visiting Stromness on Saturday for a courtesy call but its first stop is Hoy's Cantick Head lighthouse.

The Admiralty have given clearance to do the run, even though War is imminent. Provisions have to be delivered, War or no War. It's strange though that the Royal Navy hasn't beefed up surveillance and on-board security to prevent stowaways.

Hermann Schneider is at large having escaped from

Toon custody and as for Our Tom, the perfect nephew, he'll not get as good an opportunity to cut and run as this.

On the MI5 list of suspects, Hermann Schneider is Category A. Thomas Dreyer has now been reclassified from Category C. This could be their last chance to get off the Orkney Islands, with their return to *Deutschland* being the eventual goal.

'Colonel, I'm going to get the lad involved on this one. Stromness, I can feel it in my water, that's where we'll get the greater joy. I'll leave it to him. If nothing else and it all goes belly-up, he'll be covering both our backsides.'

Johnny's off the Scapa Boat. An early tea in Clay Loan. Isn't *Mither* just the gem feeding her hungry *buddo* when it suits him? And then it's Friday night 'On the *Toon'* and time for some beer and a bit of chatting up, *Malacca Straits* to be trotted out at precisely the right moment.

Johnny is confident that he can see off any competition but he feels he has no chance with this lot. It is personal. You'd think the whole lot of 'em would be the object of Johnny's hate, Orkney being flooded with newcomers, in and out of uniform. No, it's just one group of… and we're all supposed to be on the same side.

RAF Blue. Them are Glamour Boys. They're Hollywood. A woman on each arm. Ex merchant seaman Johnny sees himself suddenly pushed way down the pecking order. A merchant seaman current or previous stands no chance.

Brylcreem Boys.

If that wasn't enough, Johnny's age counts against him as well. He is still too young to enlist. A woman nowadays goes for a sharply dressed man. In uniform, even better. If he's in RAF uniform, bingo.

Bastards.

An earlier than anticipated return to his Albert Kinema hideaway for Johnny. The Bothie Bar was packed and anyone worth buying a rum and lime for had already been snapped up by a Brylcreem Boy. Even a continuation of his chat with the heavyweight Battling Bob would have turned the evening into a success. At least he'll be seeing Isobel first thing t*he morn's morning* at Ballantyne's Tearooms as per usual on a Saturday and the thought of that blows away like a fresh northerly any disappointment at how this Friday evening has panned out. He gets into the building from the side alleyway and then goes upstairs, key in lock and light switched on.

That's funny, I'm sure that wasn't there when I left this morning. A brown manilla envelope on my bed.

Johnny picks up the brown manilla envelope, flap end first, turns it upside down and looks front and back for any writing to denote who it may be from. He leaves it for a moment dangling as he holds it between finger and comes to the conclusion that what is inside is little more than one sheet of paper and could quite easily have been slid under the door without all this brown manilla envelope faff and nonsense.

You know what it can wait until the morning, the morn's morning.

Brylcreem Boys...

Bastards.

ISOBEL TULLOCH: 3

Blood poured from my face. I was grabbed by my shoulder and headbutted. The broken nose wasn't enough for him, him with his beery breath and his inner conviction that more had to be done to prove his manhood. Both punches landed. My eyes swelled up straight away.

He accused me of things I had never done with men I had never met.

His *mither* often came to stay with us. I'll never forget those words of hers. I can hear her cackle now. I can see that face, a face set like custard.

'James, you shouldn't hit a woman when she's pregnant…mind, it's alright to do so…when she's not.'

He was the one responsible for me losing my child.

My James was an alcoholic. You know that alcoholics the day after don't remember what they've done. James kept on looking at me in amazement the *morn's morn*ing, couldn't understand where my black eyes had come from and why I was wearing so much foundation and blush.

No one came to my help, no one. Neither friend, nor neighbour, neither aunty nor uncle, neither pretend aunty nor pretend uncle. It was swept under the carpet. It didn't happen. 'You keep it to yourself, girl.' An *omerta*, a *Toon* call to silence. I in turn kept my silence when the *Toon*'s *wifeys* here tried to goad me, 'Your James, he's gone off to sea as a merchant seaman, hasn't he? You must be missing him.'

These Islands…the Orkney Islands…they should have taken me under their wing …they should have protected me against life's billowing waves that foam at the mouth as they crash against the sea wall…but they didn't. Unlike a man…I had nowhere to escape to. 'A woman's place is at home.' No chance of earning *my* keep *Doon Sooth* as a seafarer like my brute of a husband James or dear, impressionable Johnny and his *Dunster Grange*.

I did seriously consider *flittin'* to Stromness, as I found Stromness much friendlier than the *Toon.* I was not going to let the *Toon* get the better of me. I am not a person to give up. I would not go back and live with *Mither* and what passed as home. Digs had to be paid for. Still legally married and married women are not supposed to work. How could I be independent?

Ballantynes, the tearooms, didn't need to come to my rescue but they did. I started off helping out as a nippy, waitressing in the front and then doing office work at the back, ordering and payroll…never typing. That's why I get treated like royalty when I go there every Saturday morning, front of house, as a customer.

I worked hard there and had a few shillings left to spend on myself once the rent was paid. I like wearing nice clothes, who doesn't? I want to wear the latest style, to look like the film stars that I see at the Albert Kinema but fashion doesn't come cheap.

If only we could turn the clock back a few years. That service in Saint Magnus Cathedral when the two German liners, *the General von Steuben* and *the Milwaukee* came to *Toon*. One thousand Germans at Saint Magnus Cathedral. The sermon was even delivered in German.

I couldn't understand a word of what they were saying but the Lutheran choir, Saint Magnus Cathedral and this heavenly music…I felt something…something that words alone will never do justice to. I knew then that I belonged to not only Great Britain… but something more… something greater…that Germany and Britain should be going forward together…hand in hand.

This man sitting next to me, was a cruise passenger off *the Milwaukee.* His English was heavily accented but impeccable. He was handsome as well. I'd say in his forties. We got on famously. He introduced himself as Hermann Schneider. Much to my delight he didn't leave *the Toon* after *the Milwaukee* set sail, on to its next port of call. Before long we became lovers. Hermann was so polite and cultured and caring towards me. It was the first time in my life that any man had treated me with such consideration. I was so much in love.

Love they say is eternal.

Love they say is eternal…until it's over.

I started doing small errands for him.

SATURDAY 2ND SEPTEMBER 1939

It's Saturday, 2nd September. Dawn and dusk times untroubled, answerable only to the workings of the Orkney *Jahr*. World events are not as important as they think they are.

Johnny wakes up really early, raring to go. Priorities, priorities. Everything though is not as it should be to *carpe diem,* to seize the day. *Beuys o beuys*. Two things on the to do list.

Usually Johnny's best bib-and-tucker already packed, creases in the right place. His duffel bag, ready to pick up and go for an early Saturday morning departure. Not so today.

The cleaner has been away on holiday and standards have dropped. The room doesn't need to be 100% spick and span but at the least presentable for when Isobel comes back with him after their cup of tea together in Ballantynes.

This Saturday is going to be a special Saturday for Johnny…and…Isobel. *Beuys o beuys.*

Everything's ready to go by 7.30am. Kit bag slung over his shoulder with best clobber inside. He's just taken a few steps from the Kinema's side door entrance, not even reached Albert Street and he's patting down his pockets. Damn. Something very important has been left back in the room, Johnny returns to the hideaway and something very important is on the bedside table.

It's the engagement ring he's bought for Isobel. He isn't going to pop the question at Ballantynes, all of Orkney would know within the hour. He'll be proposing to her when he gets her back to his Albert Kinema hideaway, in privacy. Romance, Hollywood-style comes to the Kinema. Where better?

But Johnny wants to savour the moment. He wants to take the ring with him to Ballantynes, his Saturday haven of checked gingham tablecloths and impeccable manners, basking in the knowledge that only he knows what's about to take place. The ring will be put in one of his front trouser pockets.

It's great to be alive. I've never felt like this before. Isobel, you are my sweetheart, the one for me. We've been courting for two months now. Darling.

Johnny takes the engagement ring and puts it in his pocket but out of the corner of his eye sees this envelope – brown manilla. His first thoughts are to ignore the envelope or even better to throw it in the waste paper bin.

This is, after all, going to be the most important day of his life.

But something tells him that he should address the envelope matter…and he does…he opens the damn thing.

Isobel and Thomas. The photo.

The ground has opened up…if only it would swallow him.

(Not yet 8am.) There he is, Johnny not striding not walking but old-man-shuffling down Albert Street, then Bridge Street and soon it'll be, take a left on the corner and there we have the Kirkwall Hotel. Something's different this Saturday morning, though. Not just in Johnny's frame of mind. It is the *Toon* itself.

The *Toon*'s shops are boarded up. It's September, so it's not yet Ba time, Xmas and New Year, when this traditional game takes place through the central thoroughfare of the *Toon* and windows are crying out for protection.

This particular Saturday is Saturday 2nd September. Most of the premises are slow to remove signs of last night's 'lights out' blackout trial run. Even the Albert Kinema was obliged to join in. No choice in the matter. Its eternal Hollywood light snuffed out. Is nothing sacrosanct? The films went ahead but a total embargo was imposed on light seeping out and light seeping in, seepage out being of greater concern to the authorities.

No outside Albert Kinema bright lights to tell folk what's on tonight.

Johnny notices that something's different this morning with the Bridge Street-Albert Street-Broad Street spine of *the Toon* but doesn't put two and two together. Misfitting black painted sheets of cardboard, like *troos* a size too short, cover many of the shop windows. Lights out? A blackout in name only. Johnny's mind is on other matters.

'Christ, you're making me look a laughing stock...with him, that Thomas...with that schoolboy. If it had been with a Brylcreem Boy I would have understood. I wouldn't have liked it but I would have understood.'

'It's got to stop.' That's what I'm going to tell her. I'm going to lay it on the line. 'You've got to give me your word.' And then if I'm not satisfied with her reply, I'll choose the right moment to say to her, 'Let me tell you that the number's up for people like Thomas. I'm on to him and he'll be sorry.'

Kirkwall Hotel, he's there. Washing facilities for the use therein. It'll definitely be a long soak for Johnny this morning, especially after the shock that he's received. He is waved through at Reception like a 365-days-of-the-year resident, like a *weel kent face* at the Hotel, like part of the fixtures and fittings.

Johnny will put on the Ritz and be the real man about town. White shirt. Snappy Oxford bags, dark green. Finished off with black winkle pickers. His only concession to the colour black. Don't 'alf pinch his toes, these shoes.

Country is on the cusp. In no way is he going to be taken for a blackshirt sympathiser. Black. That's Nazi uniform colour.

Johnny badly needs cheering up. He hopes his wash-and-scrub-up will do the job. Final touch, a dab of his froggy-frenchie brilliantine for the central parting. There's a lovely *eau de* not ordure to this brilliantine. Not much left in the jar that he bought in Saigon or wherever it was… somewhere off *the Malacca Straits.*

I know. I know. But at least brilliantine has got a nice smell to it. Whereas fucking, greasy brylcreem, common as muck. If a woman likes that hard-to-wash-off muck after she's run her fingers through your hair, well she's got no taste.

Parting shot, he looks in the hotel foyer's large mirror. That last minute reassurance that he's looking top dollar today, though he's feeling anything but. He needs an admiring glance to start off this Saturday, the 2nd September, the right way.

You know. Noh bad.

But the elements are conspiring against Johnny. The weather strictly out of a Christmas panto, Aladdin. Wishy-washy. Rain. Rain. Rain.

Not a gay day. Not a water-can-sprinkling-from-above day, more like a-volley-of-water-bombs-dropped-from-on-high day. It's chucking it down.

He certainly has a lot on his mind. These unwanted visitors, these dark thoughts. If they were gee-gees, you'd never rein them in…galloping all over the place. Thoughts trapped on that Hollywood carousel, round and round, faster and faster. No handbrake. Out of control. He'd like to but he can't get off.

Johnny is not going to stick to his strict Ballantynes routine. *Carpe diem.* Johnny's taking charge. Self-empowerment. None of this walking round the block once, twice etc. until she arrives. It's 9-o-clock. Saturday 2nd September 1939. He doesn't care if he's the first one through the door of Ballantynes today, not after what she's done to him.

He'll bloody well sit in *their* alcove table. He'll bloody well sit in *her* favourite seat so *he* can see what's going on and *he* can see out of the front window to boot. He'll bloody well get there first. He'll bloody well go ahead and order a pot of tea for two. He'll bloody well not order a fondant fancy from the cake stand just because it's good manners to do so. She'll see when she turns up who the boss is. He'll bloody well not lose his temper. He knows how to treat…

Nine o'clock. Johnny walks in. A ting-a-ling from the bell. He's Ballantynes' first customer of the day and sits down in *her* favourite seat, as he said he would. The waitress comes over.

'Pot of tea for two, please.'

'Anything with it, sir?' Christ, is that a smile or is that a smirk on her face?

'If I wanted anything with it, I would have said so. Give

me the menu and come back in a minute or two.' Johnny waves this nippy away. Miss Garson would have led the *encore…encore*. Johnny's brooking no nonsense.

After I've given Isobel a piece of my mind, I'll let her know how important I am. I'll tell her about my actual reason for being back in Orkney, that'll really impress her and top secret, military stuff and what I've been told about the Commander and the Colonel.

By wearing my best clobber and just by being here I'll show her what she'd be losing if she doesn't change her ways. I'm quite a catch you know. Christ, my hands shaking. I need a cigarette to steady my nerves.

The waitress he's just been rude to returns. She was in his class at school. Always seems to happen. His hand is shaking as he picks up the menu. Johnny gives it an exaggerated top-down scrutiny. Letters of the alphabet jumbled together, consonants and vowels. This scrutiny is pretendy. He is looking but not focusing on anything.

'No. That will be all.' Johnny plays the *I don't know you game* with the waitress. He must calm down. The state he's in. The tea will slop over the side of the saucer. Nothing for it. He lights up. Nerves to be steadied. Not his first Craven 'A' of the day.

Tables are starting to get occupied. The nippies no longer waiting *for* customers, waiting *on*. They are fully occupied. No time now to pass the time of day. Johnny's pot of tea is brought.

There it is, that smirk again. No tip for her. No. That's

too after-the-event. Take charge, Johnny. Take charge. No, it needs something to be said out loud and now. Some comment on the service.

Johnny's just stubbed out his cigarette in the ash tray. That's it. He'll complain that the ash tray hasn't been emptied. Johnny raises his hand and in a loud voice attracts the waitress's attention.

'Miss. Excuse me. Miss.' Johnny lifts the offending ash tray up in the air. His hand is shaking badly.

That showed her.

He takes his first sip of tea and just about avoids spilling it all into the saucer.

He looks at his watch. Five minutes past nine.

She'll be here soon. Her routine. She always comes to this tearoom on a Saturday morning. She'll be here.

It's now quarter past nine. Johnny, over a second cup and second gasper, has decided that the marriage proposal will be held over 'til next week. He just wants her to turn up. He is watching the door with greater and greater anxiety.

Phew. Relief. There she is. Just hanging up her coat at the entrance. Thank goodness. Her back to him now. Johnny knows what to say and he's bally pleased that she's here. Isobel turns round but it isn't Isobel. He's made a mistake.

Half past nine. His alcove table for four is being eyed by the waitresses. Johnny is made to feel that he's overstayed, just a tad, his welcome. The nippies' revenge.

They are doing the swoop. Taking it in turns. 'Sir, is there anything else?' 'Do you want a fondant fancy, sir?' 'Is sir happy with the ashtray?'

She won't come. I bet she's in Hoy. I bet she's in bed with Thomas Dreyer at his Guest House.

He is suddenly struck with self-pity. It is an overwhelming emotion. He is fighting back the tears.

If I was to see someone like me in a film, going through what I'm currently going through, I would weep for them.

Johnny looks at his watch. There's still time. Does a bit of totting up. If he hurries, he can rush back to the Albert Kinema, change out of his gladrags, get the bus and then catch the Saturday mid-morning boat over to Lyness or Longhope.

No. He's going to go straight to the bus stop outside Saint Magnus Cathedral. Why dress down? It's Saturday, after all. Saturday's always special. It would be somehow the proper thing to do to burst in on them in Longhope wearing his Saturday best. He likes to spend money on looking good. That's the reputation that Johnny feels he's cultivated, shame to spoil it.

Johnny's on overdrive. Johnny's going to be taking the Hoy boat from Scapa as per usual but this is his first time on a Saturday. He is nearly barged over at the bus stop by a bunch of kids who don't look old enough to be wearing the Royal Navy uniform. Those kids again from the *HMS Royal Oak*, moored in Scapa, larking about.

Drinking? At this time of day? At their age?

Johnny changes his mind, last minute. He's still going to sort things out once and for all in Hoy but…Saturday's a *special* day. Isobel has messed up his routine by not turning up at Ballantynes. Saturday's a day for not sticking to the routine.

Scapa can go hang. I'm going to catch the boat from Stromness. The SS Hoy Head. *I'm the one who decides how I'm going to spend my day.*

Stromness, West Mainland of Orkney. It'll mean a longer bus journey. That half hour extra will give him a chance to clear his head. Scapa Flow represents something more to Johnny than just a body of water. Fate. Johnny will be entering the Flow from the opposite direction.

While waiting for the ferry, I'll have time to check out this MV Hesperus, *the new ship that's serving the lighthouses. It's berthed in Stromness today, fresh from Cantick Head, Hoy. Who knows, perhaps Thomas is on board. The German is carrying on with my girl and he's an enemy to the country. I'll hunt him down. He won't get away. She…is…my…girl.*

A quick look round the *MV Hesperus* would suit Johnny down to a T. If he finds the German on board, there'll be no need for Johnny to catch the ferry over to Longhope but then again, Johnny's sixth sense tells him that Isobel must be in Longhope and he needs to have it out with her.

Should just have enough time. A and B. B will follow A. First, MV Hesperus. *Second,* SS Hoy Head. *The order is set, as sure as night follows…*

The Commander is on the blower to Colonel Vic first thing. Doesn't normally bother the Colonel the weekends but he is so excited and this is about 'Matters of State' not the '3.20 at Epsom'. He's just had word from MI5 that they are taking more of a back seat in Orkney. What has caused this change of heart? MI5 not prepared to go into detail. The Commander and Colonel are intrigued but not overly concerned. It means that with the Special Powers Act the Commander's writ *does* run large in Orkney.

Johnny's on the bus. Sheep on the road at the crest of the hill, just before prehistoric Maeshowe. That's the West Mainland for you, nothing ever's straightforward. Out of one field and the gate won't open to the other. Those sheep. Poor fencing. Poor planning. The road is blocked. Where's the farmer? Mind, it's more than a one-man job to round them up, even with a dog. The road is blocked. The bus is blocked. Six miles to go to Stromness and now this. He is going to be late.

That's all they deserve, those sheep, for holding me up. Mint sauce. Mint fucking sauce.

That's bad enough but something else is gnawing away and it's not the no-show of Isobel at the tearooms. Johnny looks out of the front and side windows of the bus. *He cannot see water* – neither sea to his left nor lochs to his right. He's firmly landlocked, in sight and soul.

Orkney folk, as a rule, like to be within sight of water. It is their oxygen. It's the air that they breathe. It frees up their way of thinking. Orkney is the gateway to the world. Orkney, with its Hudson Bay Company history is testimony to this *outwards - can do* way of thinking. Scapa Flow, one of the largest natural harbours in the northern hemisphere. Orkney rippling out to *Doon Sooth*, to the World.

The road is eventually cleared. The bus pulls into Stromness Ferry Terminal, well late.

Nearly midday. There are not two but four boats in Stromness Harbour. Two normal sized ones. Two extra-large. Like two pairs of twins.

One of the normal-sized babies is Johnny's *Good Ship Lollipop*, the *SS Hoy Head* to ferry him over to Hoy. Both normal-sized babies have engines running, for all to hear. The sound is of a low rumbling. He cannot see the boat's name on the side, so is having to go by instinct. Which of the two is the *SS Hoy Head*? Johnny looks at his watch. With the delay caused by sheep on the road, he's only got five minutes left before the *SS Hoy Head* is due to leave.

The *MV Hesperus* is one of the other pair of twins, the extra-large ones.

I can use the authority of the Commander to arrest Thomas…if he's on board.

MV Hesperus or *SS Hoy Head*? He has to choose, either/or. He has no time to board both.

Johnny vents all his pent-up frustration on the town of Stromness, easy enough target for anyone with any problems who lives in t*he Toon*, in Kirkwall. He's not picking on any one person. It's the town of Stromness *in toto* that stands in the dock.

What's Stromness for?

They've already got the main Aberdeen-Shetland Islands ferry stopping there and does that make them happy? No. You're just Orkney's second town, not its first.

Kirkwall this; Kirkwall that. Always moaning that Kirkwall wants to pull a fast one.

What they need is a marshal from Kirkwall to keep law and order in their Wild West. Mind, there's a lot of folk in Stromness who are quick on the draw.

Some towns always nippy; never happy. Stromness folk. You're well looked after. Stop whining. Stop seeing a conspiracy behind every bush or bollard. Do you honestly think that we in Kirkwall would ever have the bare-faced cheek to snatch the Aberdeen-Lerwick ferry away from you?

Come on, Stromness. Enough is enough. We always have your best interests at heart...

1939. September 2nd. Saturday lunchtime The Stromness to Lyness and Longhope ferry and let's throw in Moness and Flotta, as other stops on the service.

SS Hoy Head. Come rain, come shine. Embarkation and disembarkation. Wind or no wind. High water or low water. Peace in our time or no peace in our time. What starts out as that speck of landmass on the horizon, the *Hoy Head* brings ever and ever closer. The skipper can't afford to relax for one minute. By the act of boarding, your granting of trust to the skipper is implicit.

There are plenty of seats to choose from. Johnny will not succumb to closing his eyes, of throwing in the towel, of folding in his cards. He is brimming with an energy and positivity that's come from within. Thomas Dreyer will be found and in true Cagney style will be snuffed out. Johnny lights up and takes a deep puff and another. The Craven 'A' works wonders for body and mind. Four bells, two hours good thinking time ahead,

Johnny mulls over his life. Puts it into the context of what's in store for the nation. He's nearly 20 years old and it's just over 20 years since the end of the Great War. Folk can put two and two together. *Faether*, an early returnee from the Front; a few weeks before Christmas 1918. Johnny, the result.

Johnny, not born into sunny uplands but into a world of the Spanish Flu. Worldwide epidemic. There were less people killed in the Great War than in the Spanish Flu that ensued. The former regarded with horror and gritted teeth. The latter with just a shrug of the shoulders.

Should the next war start sometime soon, how long will it last and how and when will it end? Maybe another

plague. No, that was a one-off. These plagues are the stuff of the Bible. Mind, there's nothing wrong with the Holy Scriptures.

Life is Short

Death is Sure

Sin the Cause

Christ the Cure

What must it have been like to have been in the Great War?

First, the excitement of going off to war with your mates. Then the fear.

Then the worry about loved ones left behind.

The telegram, handed over by the delivery boy. 'It's my painful duty to inform you.'

Even then, the returnees, the survivors, are damaged, one way or another. No winners. Some even maimed for life.

Strange how such profound, adult thoughts could be included in the price of Johnny's Saturday ferry ticket on *SS Hoy Head.*

Johnny then sees a picture of himself. Not on the silver screen. Not in a mirror. It's almost a vision. This Johnny is walking along an asphalt track in the West Mainland of Orkney.

The skies are cloudless. Azure blue. The sea. Mediterranean blue. It's that time of day when there's a chill in the air. It is daylight but the sun has yet to fully establish itself. Definitely, morning. The light is sharp and eager.

Johnny looks sideways and then way ahead down the asphalt track. It is empty, not a nothingness empty but devoid of anyone else on the road bar one important companion. He sees his own shadow but his own shadow is five times his normal length. His head and upper body remain the same size but not so his pair of legs…elongated. Looks as if Johnny's shadow is walking on the most enormous pair of stilts.

Johnny stops to take in this reflection of himself.

The reflection has stopped as well.

The reflection is staring at Johnny.

This is no open-air circus. The blue skies are not Johnny's Big Top. He is not about to ride two horses at the same time. Johnny and his much larger shadow are not there for the purpose of providing entertainment. They are there for a reason.

Johnny is about to change horses. From one saddle to another. Johnny is about to change persona.

Just being there at that moment. This opportunity to change and become a far more impressive version of himself is not one he knows he should turn down. Johnny and the shadow of. A proper reinvention. It's his future facing him. No 'ifs', no 'buts'. No words needed. Out of the chrysalis of a Johnny…

The offer isn't one to take any sort of time to reflect on. Any indecision and Orkney weather will put paid to this once in a lifetime opportunity. Island weather has a wilfulness of its own. Any moment now it will cloud over, the sun no longer given free rein and the shadow chased away.

Johnny does recognise the moment, acts and is reborn.

Maybe it's time for me to grow up. To look further than the end of my nose. To realise that I have to consider others as well as myself. To understand my place in the world and to take full responsibility for my decisions. To behave like a man.

Never mind that Ballantyne-merry-go-round of thoughts, of getting even, of being spurned, of seeking revenge for himself. Maybe with women he should have listened to them more than trying to impress with one aim in mind.

Everything is now crystal clear to Johnny He is travelling over to Hoy for one reason and one reason only.

Not to salvage some personal pride. Not to impress his beloved, Isobel with the authority that he feels he has assumed and with his stories about *the Malacca Straits*.

His objective is to aid and abet in the arrest of two enemy spies. This is September 2nd 1939 being played out in earnest, not as a cinemagoer in the Albert Kinema reacting to what's taking place on the screen from a comfy 1/9d seat. Action is required. It is his duty.

It dawns on Johnny that he's had nothing to eat so far today. Nothing to scoff down with his pot of tea in Ballantynes. He's peckish. What's in his duffel bag? A quick rummage around. Bingo. A bar of chocolate. He'll just have the one square. Be disciplined. Oh alright, maybe two squares…but no more.

Fry's 5 Boys chocolate bar. The wrapper is dark blue. The same cherubic looking boy on the wrapper pulling five different faces each portraying a different mood. It's all played out for Johnny. The boy on the wrapper has gone through an identical journey. From left to right. From tearful through to joyous.

A long word for each of the stops along the way. A lot of 'tion(s)'. 'Despera-tion.' 'Pacifica-tion.' 'Xpecta-tion.' 'Acclama-tion' and finally 'Realiza-tion'.

Johnny's journey, this Saturday. 2nd September 1939. On the boat. Many stops along the way. Then you arrive.

You know what. Johnny's not going to deny himself. This will be his reward. It's the whole bar or nothing for Johnny and you should never choose nothing as an option. It's Johnny's Saturday treat. It's Johnny's Day of Personal Reckoning.

The bar is to be scoffed down this very moment. He removes the top of the wrapper. The first squares of milk chocolate delight peep out. Gone. That was tasty. Farewell 'Desper-ation.' The wrapper slides ever downwards, revealing even more squares of chocolate until the gift stops giving. None left. All gone. 'Realiza-tion.'

Johnny is left with this empty Fry's 5 Boys wrapper. He's in the act of scrunching it up but then something about that cherubic boy's face on the wrapper strikes a chord.

That boy could have been one of those boys larking around in Kirkwall pretending that they were older than they really are because they are serving King and Country. What was that battleship's name again? *HMS Royal Oak.*

Johnny may have travelled from 'Despera-tion' to 'Realiza-tion' but what does fate hold for the boy on the chocolate bar wrapper or for those young boys on the *Royal Oak*? Those far too young to be expected to serve, you can see 'em in the *Toon*.

It's Saturday, 2nd September 1939.

Johnny's going through the gears. Johnny Mark I. Johnny Mark II. And now, Johnny Mark III.

The skippers' lot is not an easy one. It makes no difference if the skipper is the skipper of the *SS Hoy Head* or of the *Marne II* motorboat. Every skipper has more and more to take on board while going through the Scapa Flow. The Flow never stays still. Last week's navigational charts are out of date. An ever-changing feast, this Scapa Flow. The skipper's head is bursting trying to keep pace with it all. Mental gymnastics. Marked out tracing paper overlaying marked out tracing paper. Having to keep so many of these gossamer thin sheets in his head, the skipper can barely make out what's on the original sea chart.

Continuous change. A boat brought up for scrappage. A boat sunk for blockage. A boom here. A block ship there.

Obstructions not waiting to be cleared but added to on a daily basis. Deliberate obstructions. Obstructions for the good. Keep them U-Boats out. National Defence and all that. Then, there's the tides and the sandbanks and the winds and don't forget all those boats of every shape and size. One lapse of concentration and it's *Goodnight Vienna.* Mustn't do a Titanic. No time for a chit chat, a ciggie or a mug of tea. No time to enjoy the glorious sunrise and the glorious sunset over the Flow, nor the glorious vista. At the wheel. Concentration, 110%. Must be an easier way to earn a living.

Kirk and Skerry Sound, and Water and Burra and Switha Sound. Not on the route but in the Flow. As the boat nears Lyness and Longhope, Gutter Sound and Weddel Sound. The Sound of Hoxha. These *Sounds* separate the Flow from the Sea. They're important Sounds.

All the Sounds have names. They are rhythmic sounds. Onomatopoeic. Bang bang. Like a gun. Clickety-clack. Like a train on the tracks. Diddle-dee. That plant on the Falkland Islands, wherever they may be. These Sounds are magical. Telling you how long the journey's going to be. Ding-dong. Bells ringing. Scapa to Lyness. Four bells. Six bells, that's two bells more, when the winds are blowing against you and the waves are topsy-turvy. Stromness to Longhope. Shorter crossing, four bells should easily do it.

If the skipper had the time to take in the full panoramic glory of the Flow, he'd see an umbrella of gun positions on the shoreline. The reception committee for *them.* A gun salute, Orkney style, should the *Luftwaffe* come a calling.

As at today, 2nd September, they're just over 40 ships of the Home Fleet based in the Flow. Watch out *Luftwaffe*. It's our turn to shoot the breeze. We'll be joining in with our guns. Flak added to flak. Flak squared. The dishing out of. You Germans, you'll be sorry.

The skipper has to quickly change course. Avoiding action. A small boat. 'Look, leave me be. No time for a chat. If I end up ramming one of those small boats, there'll be merry hell to pay.'

These small boats ferrying folk to and fro. State of the art with all mod cons and technology? No. More likely, a motor and a pair of oars. Over to Lyness and the big ships and then back again. From Lyness and to the bright lights of Kirkwall and back again. From Lyness to the big port of Stromness and back again. Even small boats to-ing and fro-ing between Lyness and Longhope.

'It's like a pleasure park on water. They'll be out in those pedalos next. Pedalos; them foreign, *peedie*, two-seater jobbies that pedal away on the water. Seen them on Pathé News at the Albert Kinema.' The skipper is rueful. Didn't spend all that time studying to be a master mariner just to be watching out for nautical tiddlers.

The Commander would give his eye teeth to have his own bespoke boat. It's getting near to the stage where any boat will do. He needs one to do his job properly. Word has quickly got round. He's known as 'the Commander without a boat'. But a pedalo? Don't even think about it. That would be taking the *mickey bliss*.

'Bloody Admiralty. If you would be so kind. Miss Garson, get me the Admiralty on the phone.'

One of the new arrivals in the Flow, a battleship. It's just been there a week or so. That's what he was told. Moored not far off Scapa Pier. No longer front-line, no longer the pride and joy. Showing its age. Don't underestimate the *Royal Oak*, though. It can still carry a punch. Has the firepower. Those guns. When called into action, it won't let anyone down.

The *Royal Oak.* Seen some of its crew on shore leave. Larking about in Kirkwall. Wearing their navy uniforms. My goodness. Kids amongst them. Some couldn't have been more than fourteen years old. Just children in uniform. Staggering down Albert Street. Three sheets to the wind. Somehow managing to get served. Old enough for a sherbet dip, not for a pint or two of bevvy.

Johnny saw them in the *Toon* last Monday. These kids, worse for wear. Others from the *Royal Oak* keeping a friendly eye out for them, like older brothers or dads or uncles would do. These kids…

It's Market Day, the auctioneer's gavel awaits and those *kye* mooing away on their desperate bid for freedom down those narrow streets in the centre of the *Toon*. More than one bull…outside the china shop.

'Ladies and Gentlemen. In the right corner. In the left corner.' Pound for pound, *kye* versus kids. The animal equivalent of the *Battling Bob Muirs* of this world. There's only going to be one winner. Cruel, isn't it?

Johnny Mark III and this new status makes it easier for him to put a proper and not cobbled together action plan together. Everything is dependent on both Isobel and Thomas being on Hoy. No shadow of doubt. Call it *prescience*. Call it *sixth sense*. Isobel and Thomas, German spies.

Step One. Johnny'll go over and see Aunt Ida in the Longhope Post Office. She'll know what's going on. Aunt Ida's covering for Agnes, who's on the sick. Groats Stores are quite happy with this arrangement. Aunt Ida is as well. She'll be almost the first with the news. That's important bragging rights for a small community.

Step Two. Johnny'll be as bold as brass and pay Isobel and Thomas a visit at Thomas' Custom House digs. Will they be in? There's only one way to find out.

Step Three. If no joy in Longhope, odds are that they'll be in Tom's Toc H hut in North Walls School, within catching-ball distance of Lyness. From Longhope, Johnny'll catch the ferry from South to North Ness and walk the rest of the way to North Walls School. It's not far.

No prizes what they are getting up to. Yes, Saturday is that special day of the week for everyone. Saturday is canoodling day. This Saturday has not been a canoodling day for Johnny.

———

'Well young man, if it isn't you again!'

Longhope Post Office. No one is front of house. Aunt Ida has heard the tinkling of the bell and walks through from the kitchen to take her place behind the counter. She's stroking and whispering sweet nonsense to the Post Office cat. The cat responds by purring loudly. Aunt Ida smiles as she sees who the new customer is.

'Well young man, may I say you're looking better than when you left yesterday. You'd come over so *peelie-wallie*. I thought you'd seen a ghost. I don't see you for years… now twice in two days. Before the month's out, you'll even be in uniform. You better get ready to be measured up.'

She pauses, realising that she could have expressed herself better.

'It'll be all those over 18 who'll be conscripted when War is declared. The baton is being handed down a generation to your lot, Johnny.'

Johnny hadn't thought that he would be called up so soon. Keen as mustard though. He'd resigned himself to having to wait until he was 20 years old. Johnny wants to do his bit for King and Country. Wants to be in uniform. Wants to be seen in uniform.

'Aunty. On the off chance. Unlikely, I admit. Anything

more on this Thomas? Have you seen him around and about, with his lady friend?' Said in an off-the-cuff, casual manner, not easy for him to put on.

'Johnny, the interest? Has she been two-timing you? You've got a lot to learn. Men aren't the only ones who have the right to pick and choose when to walk out on their beloved.'

Christ, I knew it was hoping for too much to expect what I did to Kirstin in London to escape notice up here.

'No…it's…not…that…Aunty…this…Isob…' Johnny catches himself and stops just in time. He likes his Aunty but him and Isobel, that's none of her business.

'Your high society lady has been here. She must've been the first of my customers. Dressed to the nines, she was. Right on opening time, with a letter in her hand. I wonder where she was staying last night. More's the point, who was she staying with? Has she no shame?'

Johnny is concentrating like he's never concentrated before. He is having to put his personal feelings to one side. Johnny's being professional. He knows that Aunt Ida will give him the information he's after so he must be patient and listen closely.

'She was very friendly at first. I was chatty back. I said that she was looking very smart. She said that she was wearing what debs wear when they come out. Then I just said to her. Straight to the point is your Aunty. No shilly-shallying.

"You're in early. Your German friend, Tom, has already

been in and he's sent a telegram in English." You should have seen her face. It was like thunder.'

'Well, I did also say that "it was for his grandmother". She's poorly, you know. But I didn't know his grandmother had moved to London. 1/3d, it cost him. Just the minimum, the nine words.

'The contents of the telegram…well I did let on…I shouldn't really…what's the harm…*Not feeling too good. Thinking of taking a holiday.*

'There and then, she slammed the letter that she was about to send right down on this very counter, left a tanner and stormed out. Didn't even wait for the change. Well… folk in Kirkwall can be a bit precious at times…but really…'

'Who was that letter addressed to, Aunty?'

'It was birthday-card size, to one of the Tullochs on the Mainland.'

'And Thomas' telegram?'

'I told you it was to London…to this *Dinglewhatsits*.'

'Did you make a note of the time of the telegram and all, Aunty?'

'I'm only covering here for Agnes until she gets better. No one told me about having to record telegram address details. I wouldn't even know what book or where. There's not much call for telegrams here. It's the first one I've had to deal with.'

Not feeling too good. Thinking of taking a holiday.

Assumptions have become certainties in Johnny's head. Thomas is about to make a run for it.

No difference between Johnny's needing to think on his feet to steer a steady course and the *Hoy Head's* skipper. Both fully alert at the wheel. Events are fast moving. Johnny has to be ready to change course at any moment. Johnny has no time to waste. He has to act…*Carpe Diem.*

Carpe Diem – words you won't hear at any Esperanto class.

Johnny is back of a fag packet, making plans. Like a snooker player. The pink is about to be potted and the white ball must be nice and dandy for the black.

Catch the boat from Longhope. South Walls to North Walls. Ferry from South Ness to North Ness. An hour's walk tops from North Ness to North Walls School. Maybe get a lift on the way. But say the harbourmaster decides to take Saturday afternoon off and his boat is tied up and there's no ferry service?

I'll walk the long loop round the bay. Cross the Ayre causeway, linking South Walls to North Walls. A lift? Will need one. A horse and cart will do. If the worst comes to worst, Shanks's pony. The Good Lord provides us with a pair of legs for the use of.

One way or another, Johnny has to allow himself a good hour and a half to get from Longhope to North Walls

School. He checks his watch. It's well after two o'clock now. He won't get to the School much before four in the afternoon.

Saturday afternoon and he has plotted out his course.

But first.

The Old Custom House. Little more than half a mile. Ten minutes' walk. Off he goes. A brisk walk, not a run. If they're there, it would save a pointless onward journey. Another of those; don't need to do B, if everything is done and dusted with A. Don't need to pot the black, if the pink will do.

But wait a minute. Johnny Mark III is able to think through all the implications. If he were to strike lucky and catch both of them at *The Old Customs House*, what's he going to do then? He hasn't a gun. A citizen's arrest? Two of them; one of him. What's to stop them making a run for it? Johnny, even Johnny Mark III, needs back up.

It makes sense to have P.C. Plod close to hand but there's only one copper in Longhope. Would've been different if he'd got off the ferry at Lyness.

Lyness with its military camp and all and with more police than in Kirkwall. Police aplenty in Lyness, like a rash all over you, these military police. Different matter in the *Toon* on a Saturday night though when they're really needed, military police as rare as hen's teeth.

I bet in time Lyness becomes a moaning Minnie like Stromness. Kirkwall this, Kirkwall that.

Johnny's outside the Custom's House in no time at all.

Primed for action. The Custom's House front door is open. Nothing unusual in that. A quick knock-knock on the inner door and a 'hello'. In the hallway, Fran Fitzpatrick, Thomas' landlady.

'Oh Hello, Mrs Fitzpatrick. You know me. I'm sure you do. My Aunty Ida. She helps out at the Post Office. Ida, that's right. Hubby's a Downe. No, I said *Downe* not *Doonie*, the Downes from Wick. Sorry…manners. I'm Johnny. Johnny Sinclair. My ma' is Kath Sinclair, she's from the Narrows. We live in Clay Loan in Kirkwall.'

Johnny is bright and breezy, but it's all front. He has that treading-water feeling.

I'm spending far too long doing the talkin', tellin' her about who I am, givin' her the family history.

'Oh yes. I know who you are. Kath's son.' Fran's reply came after a pause, with more than one good look up and down needing to identify this stranger to her.

'Is Thomas Dreyer in?'

'You're the second one who's asked today.'

Johnny nods.

'And the fir…?'

'…She was a very well-dressed woman. She didn't give me her name.' Fran, anticipating the question.

Johnny nods once again.

'About half past ten it was. She seemed agitated. I didn't take to her. Not one bit. Red lipstick, too bright a red. She didn't even want to pass the time of day with me. A bit snooty.'

‘So, Thomas isn’t in?’

‘Haven’t seen him since breakfast. Yes. Since breakfast today. He always enjoys his breakfast.’

Johnny nods. *Well, that was a waste of time.* Starts to leave but stops to ask the follow-up.

‘Did Thomas tell you how he might be spending the day?’

‘Told me that he was going to be walking up to Rackwick Bay, but that would be the *morn*. Did you say “Kath’s son?” Been away at sea, haven’t you? What did you make of Asia? It must be different to here. Now hang on, don’t rush me.’

‘Today…not the *morn*. It’s today I’m after. Did Thomas say where he was off to today?

‘Asia, I once knew someone who had been there. Now what was his name? Mal Acker. No hang on, that was the name of the country he came from. It’s so easy to get confused nowadays.’

Johnny turns tail, good and proper now. Has to get up to North Walls School immediately. Intuition not guesswork, Johnny knows he’s there.

‘He didn’t even manage a polite thank you, must be off now. Young people nowadays.’ That’s what she’ll be saying over the phone to Mrs Sew and Sew.

———

Johnny doesn't just walk. He doesn't run. Something in between, call it a fast stride. In the direction of Longhope Pier and then more and some. He's North Walls bound on what passes as the main Lyness road. Longhope now behind him. Hasn't got any time to take any chances with the ferry from South Ness/North Ness ferry. The causeway, it has to be. The Ayre, circumnavigating the Bay. He'll get to North Walls school and pronto, a passing car will offer a lift. It's the main road. Mind. This is Hoy and a main road is little more than a track.

The first vehicle happens to be a Black Wolseley travelling in his direction but does not stop. Police Car.

The second, well it's a horse and cart full of stacked peat. The farmer stops and apologises for not being able to give a lift. 'No room in the trailer. Sorry.'

The third, a van. It stops. Black Morris Minor. On the side, the firm's logo. JMF Groat and Sons, General Provisions Stores. Driver is in uniform. Not Groats' but uniform as in Police.

'Jump in. I'm the Special Constable here. I can only take you as far as North Walls School. Where are you heading for yerself?'

'That'll do me grand, thanks.' Johnny gets in. He'll let the Special Constable do the talking. Folk'll tell you what you're after, if you just give them the time.

'Not looking good, is it?' The Special Constable, *chewin' the fat*.

'Why, has something happened?'

'Well, sunshine. What do you think? This invasion of Poland by Germany. Neville Chamberlain's got no choice in the matter. Has to declare war on Germany. Can't let Hitler get away with it. We caved in on Czechoslovakia. Warsaw's being bombed. Have to stand up to this tyrant. We're ready. The next time our paths cross we'll both be in uniform…and it won't be in my getup.'

'North Walls School you're heading for, did you say? Who's going to be at school on a Saturday afternoon?'

'I don't know what the world is coming to. I'm from St Margaret's Hope and you'd never get an incident like that in *the Hup.* Must be some troublemaker from *Sooth* or more likely from Kirkwall itself.'

'What could've happened at the School?'

'Third time I've covered this route today. First time in uniform. The last one I gave a lift to… she was a real smasher. I wouldn't mind giving her…the time of day. Kirkwall lass. Dressed to kill. Only an hour or so back.'

'Where did you drop her off?'

'Don't get me wrong. *The Toon* has its good points but some of the lads there are feral, pure feral. Mind, even them feral ones can't be arsed to travel to *the Hup* to lark about. There and back. That's two long ferry journeys. It's not as if you can just get in a car or get Dobbin-the-horse to take you and your cart from Kirkwall to the Hope. Dobbin would have to do a lot of swimming and Dobbin doesn't take kindly to swimming.

'You don't need to be a genius to know that South

Ronaldsay is an island. No different to Hoy, a bloody island…you've got it, surrounded by water. I don't know why they need me over here in Longhope. They've got enough coppers in Hoy to call on. Lyness is bursting at the seams with them. It's just a spit away. North Walls and South Walls. Why can't Hoy just get its act together?'

'Was she wearing bright lipstick?'

'She was a smasher, the one I gave a lift to. Properly made up. Very precise in her instructions. I offered to take her all the way into Lyness but no she was insistent. North Walls School, it had to be. So North Walls School it was.'

'Did you say an "incident"? What sort of …?'

'You'll see soon enough.'

We've arrived at North Walls School. Those fellers from Lyness lending a hand. A couple of military police cars keeping the Black Wolseley company. There's an ambulance as well in the school car park. No yellow gaffer tape cordoning off the area. Lax as fuck. Any evidence could get contaminated. Already a few prying eyes. Any excuse for a gawk. Word gets around quickly.

A wind has got up. It's autumn. The winds claim their right to cock a snook. This is Orkney after all. No respecter of the seasons, these winds. The September wind has a winter nip to it.

The Special Constable who gave Johnny the lift in

Groat's Morris Minor has taken up guard duty at the School. Johnny has got out of the car also but is just staying put. The Constable looks at Johnny. Johnny is looking at the school building. The Constable can't work out why the person he gave a lift to shows no willingness to *move on now.*

Johnny's stumped as well. It's not that he feels an undying debt of gratitude towards the man who gave him a lift but he doesn't want to make him look a right Charley by barging past him into the school as if he never existed.

He shouldn't have been talking about my Isobel like that...as if...as if...for the likes of him...she's no more than a notch in the bedpost. That is no way to speak of a lady.

Johnny doesn't want to take the next step because he knows that he won't like what he's going to see. Johnny fears the worst but as to what the worst is?

Both are dead. One of them is dead. If it was only one dead, what one out of the two would he rather have dead, the German agent or the love of his life…who's also a German agent?

Neither are here?

Both have never been here?

No one's dead and all this police malarkey is just down to a ne'er-do-well from Lyness breaking and entering the school for drink money and the police with nothing better to do but go for overkill.

Get a grip, man. Have a smoke. Think it through. You are perfectly able to, if you apply yourself to this.

If only Johnny had a letter of authority from the Commander or from the Colonel – *On behalf of the Security Forces I hereby grant full powers to Johnny Sinclair etc.etc.etc...blah, blah and blah.* Johnny does have his *nom de plume* work pass with him for the Golden Wharf. This pass of course entitles him to diddly squat privileges elsewhere.

Hold your horses. Calm down. I can get away with airily waving this pass at the Kirkwall Hotel for my Saturday morning wash and spruce up. Someone once told me. The world is ¾ water ¼ land. Isn't authority ¾ front and ¼ whatever?

There's activity. Two people emerging from the school building. A distance apart. Single file. One, at one end. One, at the other. One in front of the other. All hands occupied. Fully focused. Serious stuff. Completely and utterly inappropriate to engage in any jocularity now. Both carrying the same thing. The stretcher bearers doing what they do. There is a body on the stretcher. From tip to toe covered by a blanket. Dignity all important.

A gust of wind lifts the hem of the blanket. Wind has no sense of propriety. The wind plays by its own rules. Dangling down the now uncovered side of the stretcher, a hand is revealed. Manicured. Nail varnished. Bright red. A further gust of wind and the blanket reveals more, *her face.*

Oh my god. It can't be. My Isobel. My darling Isobel. Dead. Dead. Oh darling...if only I had been able to find the words to tell you how much I loved you. I'll never get the chance. Cover her up. My Isobel.

The stretcher bearers put down their load. Consternation from the other two officials at the scene. The driver rushes out from his ambulance to offer help. The Special Police Constable runs over to find out what the hell is going on. Why are the stretcher bearers to all intent and purpose choosing this moment to take a ciggie break? What's happened to respect and dignity?

The front door of the school has been left open. Johnny doesn't know what to do. He is distraught. He is not thinking straight but who can blame him.

Johnny starts to rush over to the stretcher…*I must kiss her hand. My Isobel. My Isobel*…but then stops like a mad coo looking this way and that. The school's front door is open. With others distracted, the moment presents itself.

That is the Orkney way. Johnny recognises his moment has come. He wishes, oh how he wishes that it was somebody else having taken their last breath on the stretcher but he like a mad *coo* has to get Thomas, the murderer.

Johnny's hunch is that the Toc H hut is the scene of the crime. The hut is bound to be out the back. However, he needs to check out the classrooms first.

Johnny makes a dash for it.

In through the door. Still open, despite the gusts of wind. The lavvy is at the top end of the corridor. Calling it a corridor is like calling a packed lunch a three-course meal.

He sees a policeman come out of the lavvy, top end of corridor. Johnny just gets the rear view of the policeman. The policeman is oblivious to anyone else being there in the main part of the school, so still has his back to him. *Carpe Diem.*

Between Johnny and the policeman are the classrooms and then the all-important side entrance. Johnny tip-toes up the corridor. The classroom doors are open. Johnny only needs to take a quick peek in each. No sign of life nor death. Check. Classroom Number One and then Number Two and then Number Three. All tidy and orderly. No topsy turviness. The rows of desks undisturbed. Johnny can eliminate classrooms from his enquiries.

A hairbreadth's distance away from the policeman now, half a hairbreadth away from a side exit. Easy does it. Almost on tiptoe. If only his boots aren't so squeaky. If only his breath doesn't sound as loud as a cuckoo clock chiming on the hour. The policeman's back is still turned. *Carpe Diem.*

Easy does it. I have got this far now. If he turns around, he will be within knockout range. Battling Bob, eat your heart out. I'll have the element of surprise too.

The policeman turns around. 'Oy you. What the blazes!'

No time for Johnny to be fannying around with his Golden Wharf work pass or with any verbal tit for tat. Johnny knows what he has to do and he has to do it now.

Johnny lands the punch. The boxer, *Battling Bob,* the

man himself – Bob Muir of Kirkwall – would have been proud. On the button. On the nose. The policeman falls to the ground. A knockout punch.

Was that a belter, or was that a belter?

Straight outside into the fresh air. The wind still nipping. A quick dash on a pathway to the Toc H hut, less than a 100-yard dash away. The door has a padlock on it, a brass padlock with a shackle at the top and a key attached to the underside. The inverted 'u' mechanism is not clicked into place. A useless padlock, free and easy and inviting to be removed. Johnny does so and he's inside the hut.

Him, originally in full pursuit of Thomas and Isobel. Certainly now, one of the two has been eliminated from his enquiries. He wished that it had been the other way round. Thomas is in his sights.

Johnny is already in trouble, serious trouble. Assaulting an officer is bound to lead to a stint in His Majesty's Pleasure, probably Inverness Gaol.

'What are you doing here?' Confronted by one of the military policemen inside the hut. Johnny has got that bit wrong. Thought it'd be empty, more like hoped it would be. Not thinking straight, no. Let's cut Johnny some slack here. Unlucky, very.

Johnny has to see this through for himself and is not prepared to hear a third-hand account from whoever. Johnny's here in Hoy, now. Johnny's here and not front centre-stalls, Kinema Cinema. Johnny's making the story not watching it.

'Stop. Don't move.' This man-mountain of a policeman towers over Johnny, as awe inspiring as the spire at the top of Kirkwall's Saint Magnus Cathedral.

Yesterday's Johnny would have taken on this giant of the law. He would have believed he was more than capable of acquitting himself in any rough-and-tumble.

The mature Johnny knows the game is up. Assaulting one policeman has really dropped him in it. A repeat performance would be stupidity of the n'th degree.

Johnny's Saturday morning Kinema hero used to be Zorro. Zorro, him in his black mask and Spanish cape and hat. A man's man who could use his rapier sword and bullwhip at the same time. Zorro never lost.

The mature Johnny knows that he doesn't possess those powers and any attempt at resisting arrest would make a bad situation, even worse. Johnny's deflated.

Realiza-tion.

Both rooms in the Toc H hut show sign of a struggle. It's looks like the angry bull has been in the china shop.

Fold up chairs on the floor, no longer neatly stacked. Papers strewn everywhere. A broken window. An acrid smell. Ammonia from those smashed photo development bottles. Is that a whiff of carbolic soap? Maybe a start to a deep scrub had already been made. Carbolic soap and hot water. Would forensics be happy with that?

Pools of blood on the floor. Vivid red, neither darkened nor dried by the passage of time. No knife to be found here, either it's still with the assailant or safe in the possession of the law.

There is no second body. Thomas must have fled the scene. Two and two has been put together. Could this be making five? Maybe the police have been at the school for some time and it's the ambulance's second trip to the mortuary.

'Stand still. Hands behind your back. No monkey business.' Authority in its rawness. No bluff, just orders to obey. All aggression drains out of Johnny. The aftershock of Isobel's death numbing his ability to react.

'Do not even think about moving. Do not go there, Sunny Jim. You are under arrest. Turn around. Keep your hands behind your back. You are under arrest for the murder of Isobel Tulloch.'

'What! You've got the wrong man. I haven't killed anyone. All I've done is hit a policeman. You've got the wrong man. I'm part of the Commander's team tracking down…I never touched her.' Johnny in disbelief, crying out his innocence to deaf ears.

Handcuffed, the click of the lock, the coldness of metal against wrist. A reminder of his attache case and his Aldwych-The Strand-Adelphi days. Stunned by the accusation and exhausted into silence.

The special constable brings reinforcements. There are now three members of the law looking down on their captured prey.

I have turned over a new leaf and this is what I get.

'I am here under the authority of the Scapa Flow, Commander In-Chief.' No last throw of the dice. Said quietly, with as much confidence as he can muster. Johnny needs the law to know that he has a military right to be here and that the accusation is ludicrous.

'Shut up. Only speak when you're spoken to. We only as a last resort gag difficult prisoners, with murderers gagging is the first thing we do. We've experience of dealing with murderers on our inner city beat, they're the scum of the earth.

Johnny suddenly feels very hungry. Images come to mind. An eggy dipped soldier, that breakfast treat. Even a bar of chocolate would do. But it's the wrapper not the bar itself that he sees, that wee scamp pulling five different faces.

Despera-tion.

He turns the wrist of his free hand to check the time. 5.59. One minute before six. There's still a couple of hours daylight left on this Saturday, 2nd September 1939. The sun low in the sky casting an apologetic and watery light over the North Walls School playground.

Before he can turn his wrist back…a punch lands…a direct hit to Johnny's solar plexus…out of the blue from the man in blue. As he falls, this is quickly followed by a knee to his groin. Johnny is lifted up, two pairs of hands not coming to the assistance of. The crunch of truncheon against the bridge of his nose – a North Walls kiss – quickly followed by the crunch of teeth…Coiling up in a ball gives him no protection whatsoever against the kicks. Short and savage. Beating up a suspect? They knew exactly what they were doing. With a different unfriendly arm under each shoulder, a limp Johnny is dragged not frogmarched through the playground and bundled into the back of the Lyness Military Police car. Johnny spews up…the colour of raspberry custard…options for revenge, limited.

Johnny spends the rest of the Saturday banged up in the large holding cell, initially the only guest. No fluffy pillows, no clean sheets, no blanket – I tell a lie, there was a blanket on offer but it smelt of something you wouldn't want anywhere near your skin. It is a Saturday night and although most of the action will be taking place in *the Toon*, Lyness itself will have its fair quota of drunk and disorderlies. Johnny will soon have company of sort in a cell sharing just the one piss pot.

The fish supper was right tasty. Wrapped up, as it was, in last week's *Racing Chronicle*. The pain of the beating temporarily forgotten but not the accusation of murdering the only lady he'd ever really loved. Johnny found his voice again and yelled and yelled out. 'It's not me you want…it's that German, Thomas…Thomas Dreyer.'

The Military Policeman's final words were that I was entitled to one call to my lawyer and that every detainee is allowed to receive visitors at set times.

7.30pm. There were three. The same three. Visiting time, 7.30 pm, an hour *after* the fish supper (with brown sauce) had been brought in. It would be after, wouldn't it? On a full stomach. Johnny is set about again with relish, official relish.

Who'd have thought it?

Johnny couldn't help but reflect on the irony of his day, in particular the eating establishments. Morning, Ballantynes and its air of gentility and now Lyness Military Police, thuggery *et al.*

Police 2nd September entry. 'Prisoner slipped whilst being restrained.'

Mither taught me that the *morn* is another day. Well, today has been a bloody painful one.

SUNDAY 3RD SEPTEMBER 1939

September 3rd, the first Sunday of the month. It's chucking it down. What would Orkney be without rain? No bringing in the hay today. Orkney farmers are not happy, not at all happy. See those *kye* over there, in the field. The *kye* huddling together doesn't stop the rain dripping from their noses, stalactites of watery snot.

There are less churchgoers in the streets of Kirkwall than usual. Church bells peeling away with their morning, come-to-worship invitation. Church bells pricking *the Toon's* conscience peeling away with the message, *immerse yourself in the Lord not in the rain.* Rain is rain. Rain is amoral like buying a secondhand car – sometimes you're lucky, sometimes you're not. Orkney and rain. Orkney and wind. That's Scottish islands for you. Bastions of amorality.

Serious faces sitting round the wireless set, this Sabbath day. Even farming folk knocking off for an early lunch or delaying their morning tea break. The Home Service, the BBC transmitting a clarion call to the Nation. The Prime Minister opens with the words, 'I am speaking to you from the Cabinet Room at 10 Downing Street…' It is Sunday morning, the 3rd of September. Quarter past the hour of 11.

The announcement will come as no surprise. A dead cert, not even *evens*.

The Commander keeps his hands in his pocket on this one.

Neville Chamberlain, Prime Minister, speaks to the Nation, to one and all, to toff and hoy polloy. Clear in delivery, no crackle over the airwaves to dilute the power or clarity of the message.

'This country is at war with Germany.'

Neville Chamberlain, Prime Minister of Great Britain, makes sure it's all done and dusted on the Sabbath day. He strikes the right tone. *No peace for our time* hubris. Sombre but infused with determination, no hint of triumphalism. A five-minute broadcast. Short and sharp. Soon over.

We are as much at war with Germany as is London. Orkney is nearer to Norway than it is to London but the Orkney Islands are a redoubtable northern outpost of Great Britain.

The Commander listens to the Prime Minister's broadcast at his desk in the Kirkwall Hotel. It would have been a surprise *not* to see him at his desk on this day of all days. There's thoughts and papers to be gathered for the lunchtime, 12.30pm meeting of the National Service Committee at Orkney Council Chambers.

Events, events. *Weel beuy, whit's deuan the day?* Neville Chamberlain's made sure that there's a lot *deuan the day.*

Commander. Sober in mind. Sober in deed. No après-prayers, chin-chinnery. Bottoms-up? Not today. Difficult to resist but must. This Sunday is neither for cleansing the soul with prayer nor taking a snifter or two. The Commander's secretary, Miss Garson, is also there. A shared sense of duty.

'Val, what's that? You're worried about your Stromness friend, Lizzie Brookes. She's just set sail for Canada, on the *SS Athenia*. She'll be alright. I'm sure she will.'

Twenty to twelve. 11.40am. The Commander, *Racing Chronicle* on desk, on the phone; not to who you may think, it's an incoming call. Miss Garson did not make clear while putting the call through whether it was local or long distance.

What? Yes. That's right. Sorry could you repeat, there's gremlins on the line…

'Is he working for you?' Commander is parroting what he's hearing through the phone earpiece. He is slightly putting on a voice, making it at the higher end of the octave range. He's a card, our Commander.

'Yes. He works directly to me. Is there a problem? Under arrest? Good grief. For what? *Murder*?' The Commander shouts out that last word.

Commander can't believe what he's hearing, three parts angry, two parts amused. He's brought our Johnny all the way back home from London. He didn't bring the young lad back for him to end up in the clink and some – on a murder charge. Giving a shellacking to a member of the constabulary, that's a minor aberration that he could well imagine the lad succumbing to… but a frenzied knife attack?

'You've got the wrong man. Did you hear me? Arrant nonsense. You've got the wrong fucking man.' The Commander shouts down the line. 'Thomas Dreyer, the German, he's your man.

'Release him. Yes, you heard me right first time. Release Johnny Sinclair. He's on a secret assignment. Can't tell you more. If you want chapter and verse, you'll need to go one up. It won't be coming from my lips. Yes. Yes. Haven't you ever heard of the Official Secrets Act? Don't give me any of your insubordinate flimflammery.'

The Commander's voice no longer amateur dramatic. He is about to expose the hapless caller to the full onslaught of his temper.

'Release him now or I'll go one up myself. *Aliens Order 1920 – Certificate of Registration.* I trust Hoy's total compliance is beyond reproach? Documentation, fully shipshape? Lyness is due a surprise visit. Of course, if you don't pass muster, the shit will hit the proverbial…

'What's that? You know damn well what I'm banging on about. Every hotel and boarding house is by law required to keep a record of *Johnny Foreigner* residing there. Don't play the simpleton with me. You know the procedure. Lyness, as does the rest of Orkney, comes under my jurisdiction. Yes, you heard correctly. Do you need me to spell it out for you?' The Commander is in full flow.

'*Form AR-E.* Name/Nationality/Dates of arrival and departure. Legal requirement. *Form AR-E.* Don't play the simpleton with me. Ah! Your memory has returned. *Form AR-E.* That's the one. Jolly d!' Blood rushing to his cheeks. Fully wound up our Commander now.

'Release him now or I'll make that phone call. Have you heard of the Sperrin Mountains in Northern Ireland? I'd advise you to become quickly acquainted. Godforsaken hole. See if you'll take to the outward-bound life, getting those raw recruits theatre fit. I'll throw in as well the added joy of keeping Protestants and Catholics apart.

'It'll be winter soon. Release my colleague or you can wave fucking farewell to the home comforts you've got used to here. No pets allowed over there. Bye Bye Fido. Say goodbye to your free cigarettes allowance. Say goodbye to your additional leave allowance and a quid or two in your pocket and any other Overseas Posting sweeteners you get at the moment for being lucky enough to be here in tropical Orkney, Great Britain. The Commander rolls his r's with relish.

'The choice is entirely up to you. Release him or you'll go down in history as the first Officer to be discharged from the British Army in the Second World War.' The Commander ups the ante.

'Your choice. If you want to face the sound of music, that is your fucking choice. Release my…2…I…C…this very minute.'

The Commander's voice has gone up through the scale and the roof, all the way to heaven in fact, as he rolled out the consequences of not releasing Johnny. So close to heaven he was almost knocking on the door. Louder and louder. Higher and higher. Doh-fucking-Re-fucking-Mi-fucking-Fa-fucking-So-fucking-La-fucking-Ti…

The phone is slammed down before he can finish off with the second Doh. The gasket of bad temper is well and truly being blown.

'Miss Garson, Pot for one just for your Commander, in your inimitable way. Pronto. If you please.' A softer cadence to his voice. A smile now on his face. The charm well and truly turned back on. A masterclass. Being able to switch that easily from strong-arm intimidation to smooth ingratiation. Deserves a walk-on part in any Hollywood gangster movie.

The Commander strolls through to Miss Garson's part of the office.

'I do apologise for using such un-Sabbath-like

language. Completely inexcusable. I know I can get hot under the collar but we have declared war and nothing must come in the way of ensuring Orkney is as safe as safe can be. You understand, don't you? Please say you do.

'Your-and-my-friend Johnny is in more than a slight spot of bother. He'll soon be released though. A night in the cells in Lyness. Him, a manic-knife-slasher-cum-murderer, I don't think so. I know he's a bit on the young side but you know *Miss* Garson, *you could do far worse...*'

The Commander rings the Colonel.

'So. This is it, Victor…as we feared. "It'll be over by Xmas." That's what they told us in 1914. The deeply-regret-to-inform-you telegram. Stiff upper lip and all that but you can't help but shed a tear or two at the news.

'There's been…ah…a few local difficulties with our young man, young Johnny. Did you hear about the murder at North Walls School yesterday? Shocking business. They arrested our Johnny as prime suspect, arrant nonsense.

'Have to dash, see you at the Council Chambers.'

'...We are fighting for Poland, though no nation could have done more. We are in the strictest sense fighting for ourselves.

'Not only would a world dominated by the arrogance of one country be intolerable for free nations but nobody can imagine that a Germany, drunk with power, will fail to attack sooner or later the free nations of the West. The smallest will be picked off first. Denmark, followed in short order by Holland.

'What we are about to face will test us like nothing before. This War won't be a distant conflict fought out on foreign fields. With Orkney being readied as a safe harbour for the Royal Navy, we will be in the front line of enemy attack from the air. A civilian war. Gas masks to be carried at all times.

'We will never turn the other cheek to Nazi evil. The most important resemblance between now and 1914 is a spiritual one. The Great Britain which rallied to arms 25 years ago will react in the same way. Danger and sacrifice knocks on our door today. We will answer the call.

'All domestic differences must immediately be put to one side. I say to those advocating *Peace and Moral Rearmament,* that boat has left port. Quietness and confidence and a unified sense of purpose will be our strength. Everyone must play their part.

'*God...Save...The...King.*'

The Commander had delivered the rallying call.

There was much loud table thumping and hear-hearing.

His words were *of the moment*, no reading from prepared notes. The Commander had said his piece. There was now nothing left in the locker. He had delivered the most important rallying call of his life.

Johnny must have looked a picture. He felt a picture. In pain from head to toe, raw and bruised. A poor night's sleep on the floor. Two other companions now in this large cell, snoring their heads off. From his only good eye he could just make out a movement at the top of the door, the spy hole. No thoughts of escape come to mind, just this dread of *breakfast*. Johnny can barely move his arms and legs, never mind curl himself into a protective ball.

The door opens. Johnny fears the worst. He doesn't remember seeing this one before.

'Police Sergeant Mowat at your service. Come on, rise and shine, sunny Jim. Christ, do you stink! Time for a shower. Breakfast can wait. If you want, you're not too late for prayers. It's a Sunday after all. Let's see, that's been a one-nighter. If you want to stay for a second night, we do give a discount. Let's see that'll be…you can settle the bill later.'

'War has been declared' and there's no rulebook to follow. The starting pistol has been fired but then what? Everyone wants to do their bit but no one has a real clue as to what they're supposed to be doing and how their life is going to be changed.

ARP (Air Raid Precautions) wallahs and pinned official notices, everywhere. A foot pressed hard on the accelerator for the distribution of gas masks around Orkney. All told, 21,000 masks to shift in short order. Should there be a fuck up, 19-year-old Johnny Sinclair is the one to be held responsible.

This is a new ballgame. What a to do. Good job it's the Sabbath and the shops are shut. Any other day of the week and there'd be a biblical plague of locusts descending on all of them, especially the ones selling food, clearing the shelves before you can say Jack Robinson.

My goodness, does it never stop? The rain, that is. It's still absolutely chucking it down. You'd think the weather would be a respecter of us being *at war*.

Crops to be harvested. *Kye* to be milked. You-know-what to be spread on the already harvested fields. New pastures still to be opened. Fresh, succulent grass to be gorged on. Peat still to be gathered for the open fire. World events be damned. The Orkney *Jahr* is still steadily ticking its way through 1939 and knows what's really important.

What will happen the *morn*? A dry day we hope, not much to ask for. Farmers just want the sun to return. Makes life much easier. Bringing in the crops. If only Hitler would wait…but he won't.

Police. 3rd September entry. 'Prisoner released.'

12.05pm. The Commander's late morning intervention on the Sabbath day has brought immediate results. Johnny is in the reception area of Lyness Military Police Station. Signing here, there and everywhere – signing in triplicate. A plastic bag has been emptied out on the counter, Johnny's returned possessions, insignificant at first glance but tell the full story -; a couple of banknotes (colour blue), a set of keys, a small photo of a foreigner who goes by the name of Thomas Dreyer, a 5 Boys Chocolate Wrapper , Golden Wharf pass…and the engagement ring. Police Sergeant Mowat starts to say, '…and who's the lucky…' but one look at Johnny's bruised face tells him that he should put this quip in his pocket and save it for a rainy day.

The law is taking its time, reluctant to say farewell to a long-lost friend. Maybe it's because it's Sunday and contemplation and reflection set the tone. The few homilies from the Lyness Military Police go completely over Johnny's head.

In walks the Military Doctor, dabs iodine on the bumblebee, yellow and black swelling above Johnny's left eyebrow and then rubs in some soothing balm and applies a plaster. Is that it? No. The bridge of the nose needs some attention too. More iodine and another plaster. It's Sabbath, a splash of holy water would have been a nice finishing touch.

Smiles all round. Everyone is so friendly. 'What a day, today. It's chucking it down.' The doctor has finished what he needs to do and the passing out parade is nearly complete.

12.10pm. Johnny – Prisoner.

12.11pm. Johnny – No longer a prisoner.

Johnny can tell that everything is going super well by the look on the Sergeant's face. The Sergeant is not just smiling, he's grinning.

'Now lad, you've had your hotel stay. No bill. On the house. Now be a good boy and just fuck off.'

It'd be rude not to join in the *bonhomie.* Johnny in return gives a Cheshire cat grin.

An apology would've been nice. A fry up, even better. An explanation. That's three things, for starters. One day I'll make you pay for this, you fuckers.

He's about to walk out but stops. There is a commotion, a veritable *stooshie,* just inside the front door. Just about minimum height this copper in uniform, less than 5 foot 4 inches tall, but appearances deceive and he is barking out the orders. The way the other officers are reacting to his shouting and yelling, indicates this man wields considerable power.

A handcuffed man is being pushed this way and that by four others. They are shouting at the prisoner, roughly handling him but, and this is the strange thing, calling him by his first name. A familiarity there.

Johnny's free. He walks out of the Lyness Military Cop Shop, in the direction of the Pier.

The Commander must have got wind of my arrest. I'll get that German agent, Thomas Dreyer. He's at large and has murdered the love of my life. No. I'm in no fit state to pursue anyone at the moment. Let's get back to the Toon to get further instructions.

A boat's about to leave Lyness Pier. Chances are that it's going to the Mainland but for Johnny anywhere off the Island of Hoy will do. Kirkwall or Stromness, Kirkwall, *the Toon,* better. On a Sunday, beggars can't be choosers. The ferry boat is revving up its engines. Johnny makes a mad dash. He is hurting like buggery but is pleased that despite everything, his body just musters enough slack to get him there in time.

Johnny keeps himself to himself on the boat. The last 24 hours have given him plenty of food for thought. He replays the events as they happened with a Kinema-goer's detachment. The film action that he is reviewing is brought to him through the projection lens of a Johnny Mark III. This devil-may-care, beyond reproach attitude of Mark II and Mark I is confined to history.

Back on terra firma. Back on the Orkney Mainland. Back in Kirkwall, t*he Toon.* Mid-afternoon. On home ground and the reassurance that that familiarity brings. Needs just to get back to his home, the Albert Kinema hideaway not Clay Loan with all those *Mither* and *Faether* questions. Whistles, as he strolls past Clay Loan and

Victoria Street and Broad Street, with Saint Magnus Cathedral before him in all its glory and he's now well and truly in the main spur of the *Toon*.

He gets a few looks and comments. 'You been in a bit of scrap have you, Johnny?' 'You still trying to get off with Battling Bob Muir's girl, Johnny? (News travels fast in the *Toon*). 'What a picture you are, Johnny. Did you get that from when you are in *the Malacca Straits*?'

Soaked through, a drowned rat, chucking it down, rain and rain and rain. Doesn't want to add pneumonia to his list of woes. There aren't many folk about on the streets this Sunday afternoon, mind the weather even for Orkney has an unparalleled *dreichness* about it. Given his patched-up face, Johnny wants to avoid further attention, so ticks-and-tacks through the last stretch, Albert Street, out of public view and accesses the Kinema side lane entrance from Junction Road. Key in the lock. It's good to be *home*. 5pm.

Puzzled is our Johnny. It's quiet, he's hungry but most important of all he must get out of his wet clothes; the sooner, the better. This he does. That's better.

From the top floor of the Kinema, he crosses the landing to the large front film-paraphernalia, storage room that also doubles as the Esperanto room and looks out from the window overlooking Albert Street. There are a few more people about in the late afternoon but *the Toon* is still as dead as a dodo.

Silence from downstairs but it's Sabbath and you wouldn't expect anything different. Never any Albert Kinema patrons on a Sunday. The Sunday is the Lord's Day. The Sabbath wins hands down when pitted against Hollywood. It's a bigger box-office draw.

He finds it a devil to keep comfortable, too many aches and pains vying for attention. A bit of shut-eye is called for. That'll do the job.

9pm, night-time. Johnny wakes up. He must have had a good five hours' kip. Hungry but he'll survive. A quick visit to the lavvy. Call of nature. Leaves the room. Door ajar. You can hear a pin drop. Returns to his room. A note has been slipped under his door in the meantime. *Commander's meeting at Kirkwall Hotel, 9.30 sharp, the morn's morning.*

All will be revealed there and then and Johnny, after trying to settle on his left side, his right side, his back, his front, eventually cries himself to sleep.

Pacific-ation, of sorts.

11pm. 'Val. Sorry to be ringing you so late. I've just heard and I *havered* as to whether I should ring straight away or wait 'til the *morn* and tell you at the office. They say "never be the bearer of bad tidings" but it's only right you know straight away. Please forgive me if I have made the wrong call on this.

'It's not good news, I'm afraid. At 7.40pm tonight the *SS Athenia*, Canada bound, was torpedoed off the North West Coast of Ireland. No more details so far. Yes. We'll hear more through the wires, the *morn.* Fingers crossed.'

Today's news, the War and it's immediately brought home. The first day of the War. Orcadian, Elizabeth Brookes from Stromness, one of our own. The Great War and now this must be *the Second World War.* Whatever designation you wish to use, it's just got personal.

MONDAY 4TH SEPTEMBER 1939

6.30am. It's Monday. Johnny wakes up early. He's had a tossing-and-turning night. Mind and body are as bruised as each other. The uncleanliness of the cells, like past transgressions, needs to be washed away. This will be his second bath at the Kirkwall Hotel in three days. If only it was to look spick and span for his beloved and not the Commander and the Colonel.

What a fool I've been.

Those empty chat-up lines. They'd always served him well in the past but they had come out of the mouth of a boy, not a man. His mission now, in more ways than one, is personal.

Thomas Dreyer murdered my Isobel. He's on the run. I'll get the bastard.

Johnny Mark III is only a couple of days old. This chrysallis of Johnny is no more rooted than a young sapling, vulnerable to the wind and frost of a late Orkney Spring. Johnny Mark I, and II are still there in the wings, ready to barge in, at any opportunity, putting a 'me-me' focus on everything. Johnny's head is still liable to turn every whichaway.

Say, Isobel was expecting...and the child's mine? I'd be mourning then for the two, not just for the one. Then again...pregnant?...Isobel would have been careful. Wouldn't it be just grand to have a baby son or daughter smiling at me and going 'Da. Da. Da'?

7.30am. The sun though is shining down on the *Toon* today, the rain having been chased away by the wind. The sun makes everyone feel good about themselves. The *Toon* is waking up.

I'm famished. Maybe, just maybe, the Commander will get Miss Garson to make me a round of toast. It's not much to ask for, given what I've been through.

Johnny slings the kitbag over shoulder, and yes there's the strap decision to make and unsurprisingly he can't find a place on either shoulder that is neither raw nor tender. He heads out the side door to go to the Kirkwall Hotel, turns right up the side lane to Albert Street but just as he joins this main Broad Street-Albert Street-Bridge Street thoroughfare doesn't, yes doesn't, take a left turn. His eyes look to the right and he sees a notice covering the billboard almost blocking the pavement, outside the Albert Kinema. He turns right and walks over to the billboard.

'Please note that the Kinema will be closed until further notice.'

No one told me. That's all of a sudden. It must have happened over the weekend. I'll have to look for new lodgings. I'm sure the Commander will have something sorted out for me but I hope for Christ's sake that they'll be somewhere in the Toon.

Walks further up Albert Street towards Saint Magnus Cathedral and then doubles back and loses his footing once on the pavement. This news about the Kinema and its closing has distracted Johnny and some. He doesn't pay a second glance to the blackout shutters not yet removed in Albert Street and Bridge Street. For the life of him he can't fathom why there are queues forming this early outside John Foulis, the butchers, in Bridge Street. Number 11.

Mince at half price?

Nearly at the end of Bridge Street. He passes Ballantynes but forces himself to look straight ahead. Blinkers on, a necessity given Johnny's fragility. A glance to the right would be just too painful, just too raw. He would see *her* face.

8.00am. Johnny has his bath in the Kirkwall Hotel. Takes longer than normal. Not easy getting in and out of the tub as you can well imagine and so once in enjoys a long soak. He feels all the better for it. No brilliantine today for the finishing touch, none left and he will *not* use that RAF brylcreem muck. Then a bit of time to kill. He goes for a walk round the block and then back into the Hotel, the Commander's HQ.

Fresh as a daisy now, providing he doesn't try to smile. The plaster and slight yellow colouration over one eye are a bit of a giveaway but he is fully shipshape and presentable. Smells fresh and soapy. More like a bouncing baby boy than an ex-gaolbird with a bit of an old lag's whiff. Even Miss Garson acknowledges his presence. The bush telegraph has clearly been at work. Johnny's got his swagger back.

———

9.30am. 'Young man, so good to see you. What an adventure you've had. Miss Garson…' The Commander raises his voice, but not in anger… 'Pot of tea for two, if you please.'

'Johnny. No need whatsoever to stand on ceremony, especially after what you've been through. You are a totemic figure of self-sacrifice and bravery, like Edith Cavell in The Great War. Please take a pew. I'll join you in a jiffy.' He indicates what seat Johnny is to take with the grace of a butler about to decant a fine bottle of red.

'It's just me and thee today; for starters, anyway. The Colonel has been called away at the last minute, 'his memsahib you know.' Johnny doesn't know but nods, an arrow of pain shooting up the back of his neck. 'He'll be joining us soon. Well, let's take a good look at you. What you've been through must have been even more traumatic than…the...the…?'

'…*Malacca Straits.*' Johnny finishes off the sentence.

'You know, Johnny. I've always been popular with the ladies and I certainly cut a fine figure in uniform, even now. A ratings mess do with the Memsahib. I was Guest of Honour, looking down on the hoy polloy. Them in their 2Bs, in their ill-fitting black cummerbund; me resplendent in my gold laced *troos*. You wouldn't want to take tea on the lawn with them. Servants, as noticeable as a towel-rail and if insolent to be discarded, replaced and quickly forgotten. The hoy polloy may aspire to but will never accede to respectability…Yes. I was quite the looker in those days, if I say so myself.'

The Commander waits for a reaction to his wistful musings. Johnny just gives a brief nod.

'Commander, the noticeboard outside the Kinema…it says…' A rattling noise of cups and saucers on a tray and Johnny is distracted as Miss Garson brings in the tea.

'But, anyway, I digress. Jolly good to see you, Johnny. That plaster above your eye indicates that it wasn't all smooth sailing. You've had a frightful time. Really been through the ringer. Please tell. What really happened?' Paternal concern. That Commander knows every trick in the book.

'…The Military Police were from *Doon Sooth*. I was given a right going over…' Johnny is just a few minutes into his account. In walks the Colonel, not really late at all. Johnny is cut off in mid flow.

'Colonel, greetings. My word you look as suave as Ronald Coleman, my favourite Hollywood star. *The Prisoner of Zenda*, wasn't it? Exceptional good looks. Fine 'tache on him. Hitler could take a few lessons in that department. The photo session went well?

'Sorry about that one and all. I was under pressure from *the Chief* to have the family snap taken. My goodness Thomson's Studio at King Street are simply being overwhelmed. There was a last-minute cancellation for first thing and it was that or having to wait a few weeks or so. Corralled the family early doors and we marched down there.

'We were given a list of the do's and don'ts. What a palaver for a photo. I jotted down the rules in my pocket book.' He puts his hand inside his jacket pocket and retrieves the list. 'You just listen to this—'

'—I was set upon by three burly men in uniform…' Johnny interrupts, keen to be heard. After what he's been through, this deserves to be his moment.

Commander raises his hand, the stop sign. 'Now Johnny, all in good time. Let's just hear what the Colonel has to say for himself.'

'One. Don't come straight from the hairdresser's salon. Hair will look too stiff.

'Two. Plain dresses look better in a photo than those checked frocks. I know they're all the rage now but…

'Three. If the pictures look too posed, they won't appear natural. You'll look as out of date as a German wearing a spiked helmet…'

'…I'd only just finished my fish supper when they gave me another good going-over. "I'm innocent…I'm innocent". One punch after another. "Why were you in North Walls?" I told them nothing. They could hit me as hard as they liked but you had brought me back from London and I wasn't going to let you down.' Johnny determined to say his piece.

'…Well done, Johnny. Well done.' Commander purrs.

'Four. Don't stare at the camera, you'll end up with a photo with a beady-eyed fixed glare.' The Colonel allowed to continue his run down.

'And finally. Five. A good trick. Women, smear the eyelids lightly with vaseline. It gives you that gleam of mystery. Five and that's it. That's your lot.'

'What a palaver, Colonel, just to have your mugshot taken.' Commander licks his lips in amusement.

Colonel can't help but stare, mouth open, at Johnny and his boxer's bruise, upper cut, left eye.

'What a to do. My goodness, Johnny. One look at that eye of yours. I should have brought that tub of vaseline back with me from the photographers. First casualty of the war effort, I'd guess.

What did the Colonel mean by 'first casualty of the war effort'? He's having a laff.

'Good to have you back, Johnny I'm proud of you. Let's shake hands'…and they did so.

The Commander follows suit. Doesn't want to be seen to be slow in coming forward to greet our returned hero.

'Thank goodness the children behaved themselves. They were as good as gold, stayed still, no larking about, said "cheese". The photographer didn't need a third go. *The Chief* was insistent about getting the photo done. "Just in case," she said. "What with War being declared." Pays to do what *The Chief* tells you to do.' The Colonel's voice trails away.

'We're at war? Why didn't those bastards tell me in Lyness? Everyone is trying to make a fuck out of me.'

Johnny doesn't keep these thoughts to himself. He yells out these words. The outburst is so sudden and of such volume that even the Commander is taken aback. Like the interregnum between a flash of lightning and peal of thunder, a few seconds need to pass. Johnny's payback for telling all and sundry what he really bloody-well thinks comes with an arc-of-a-flight-of-an arrow-of-pain that now works its way down his broken body, from head to toe.

10am. '...And they kept on calling me "The Slasher" and saying "Your sort like using the blade on women, don't they?" "A real razor boy, we've got here." It went…on… and…on…and…on.'

'Simply dreadful experience for you, Johnny. Cannot be undervalued in any shape nor form. Time though is of the essence and there's the important business of the day to cover. After all, this is the first full day of *the War*.

'Our friends up in the Shetland Islands confirmed that the *MV Hesperus* was searched thoroughly on arrival, two days back. No stowaways on board. That rules out our German murderer using that route to escape.

'I can't see the supplies ship *MV Hesperus* starting on its return leg soon. U-Boats and *Luftwaffe* are ready to pick off, at their choosing, any stray. The *MV* needs to be protected by a convoy and we can't rustle one up out of thin air for every merchant ship. It's confined to the port of Lerwick.

'Different ballgame now. We are at war. What's today's date? Yes, Monday the 4th. So easy to forget. Hoy is as tight as…as tight as…a woman's…We've seen absolutely no suspicious enemy craft off the Flow. So, *he* hasn't been expatriated by one of *his* own. Our Thomas Dreyer is on the run. He can only stay out of sight for so long. We must keep vigilant.'

The Colonel takes over the sitrep.

'Keeping a low profile at the moment, our German. Fran Fitzpatrick, *his* landlady, at the Customs House, Longhope, says that she hasn't seen hide nor hair of *him* since Saturday morning…

'We were straight round at Isobel Tulloch's home. Searched it with a fine toothcomb. No sign of a guest's belongings there. Keeping a watch on her place…it's in the Narrows in the *Toon.* You never know, Commander. You never know.

'Best guess is that our friend is lying low somewhere in Orkney. Put my last bob on Thomas Dreyer being here in the *Toon*. Have you checked the boats, Commander? Back to you.'

'We've tried to be thorough in our track and tracing of all the ferries plying their trade across the Flow. Nothing or rather no-one's come to light. The trouble is with the skippers themselves. They're likely to be half-cut. In no fit state to give a positive sighting even if *King Kong* himself had been on board.' The Commander criticizing fellow journeymen of the sea, a rare occurrence.

'Maybe Thomas has topped himself.' The Colonel throws that suggestion in.

'Always a possibility, Colonel, but no bodies have turned up. We're doing a thorough search of all the outhouses in Hoy. Could have decided to take his own life. Washed out to sea. The Sea giveth as well as the Sea taketh away. So, not dismissing that possibility.

'Even got on to forensics to double check that they'd not made a mistake in the report. No doubt about it. It was Isobel Tulloch. Stabbed six times in the back. Terrible. Compression of the neck, first. She must have put up quite a fight. This Thomas Dryer, everyone's favourite German...but quite the psychopath. My commiserations, Johnny. I gather you and her were…aah.

'Colonel. Our MI5 boys and girls have been watching Isobel Tulloch for some time. How can I best describe her role? She was the right-hand lady for a Doctor Dinglestoeford, who in turn is one of Oswald Moseley's right-hand men.

'MI5 tell me that the Doctor is a top wallah in the blackshirt chain of command, part of the inner circle. Doctor Dinglestoeford, a top player for their big get-together recently at Earls Court in London. Security arrangements…'

'There were 30,000 of those fascists *Sieg heiling* until their heart's content. Johnny? Were you one of those 30,000...joining in with your right arm at 45 degrees saluting *Der Fuhrer*?' The Colonel gave Johnny the stare.

How dare you, you fucker.

'I'll answer that for you, Johnny. Colonel you're talking completely out of your arse. Johnny's been here in Kirkwall at my bequest since the 28th June. That disgraceful rally took place in London on the 16th July, three weeks after our Johnny's return.

'Mosley and his sort can take their Jew-hatred with them. Doesn't matter whether his supporters are privileged toffs or not. Sooner they're all banged up at His Majesty's Pleasure, the better…Scum of the highest order.'

God, if I'm banged up in Inverness Gaol for hitting that copper, I hope I don't have to share a cell with any of those Nazi traitors.

'Colonel. Apology in order to our Johnny. Right now.'

God, Commander's giving the Colonel a dressing down in front of me and about me. Top man, Commander. Top man. Everything I may have said about him, I take back.

'Sorry Johnny, no offence meant, just a bit of friendly banter. Just to look at you now shows what you've been through to help defend…Let's shake hands and move on.'

The Commander doesn't want an awkward silence to develop. 'Johnny, that bruise over your right eye. Quite a shiner. Why don't you wear a mask over your eyes like that matinée idol? You know the one, Zorro. He, with his black cape and mask. Spanish like the Flu.

'Zorro. Top half of his face was covered, his eyes but not his whole face. Imagine folk going about their daily business wearing a mask just from the tip of their nose to the bottom of their chin. I know. Ridiculous isn't it. People would just look too stupid for words…as if everyone in Stromness were out to rob a bank.

'Not even Adolf Hitler could get folk to go about their day wearing a mask. Mind I look forward to the day when the *Fuhrer*'s head is fully covered with a black mask and there's a rope round his neck and he's swinging from…'

'Right. Now that both of you are here, let's tie up a few loose ends.'

There is no one better than the Colonel in providing a concise summary.

'Room for improvement with compliance to blackout measures. I tell you there was enough light coming from vehicle headlights for them to be mistaken for searchlights.

'Looks as if all the lighthouses have been put into purdah for the duration of the War. Better check that's the case. We don't want to give the *Luftwaffe* a helping hand.

'What is so difficult about understanding what *blackout* means? Curtains to be fully drawn. Shutters down. Stop and reversing lights masked. A hood to be fitted over the headlamps. Obvious. Bloody obvious. They've been given enough warning.'

The Commander ratcheting up his rage but then silent. He's lost in thought. Then from him, an almighty peal of thunder.

'We're at War, goddammit.'

'We've got that top table meeting at the Freemasons Hall, midday tomorrow. Why don't we reconvene here just before, say, 11 o'clock? Who knows what might come to light over the next 24 hours?

'That murder on Hoy. I must say the circumstances surrounding that *wifey*'s death were simply appalling…as for Thomas Dreyer…'

Day Two but the first full day of the Second World War.

The Commander's desk is clear today.

There is no copy of the *Racing Chronicle* on his desk.

Gravity and gee-gees don't mix.

Appearances as always are important.

TUESDAY 5TH SEPTEMBER 1939

Sirens, none. Not the beautiful, luring you on to the rocks and sandbanks with their heavenly voices but we're talking about those of ear-splitting type, air raid sirens. It's Day Three of the War. Them *Luftwaffe* can choose to try and drop their load from the skies at any time of their choosing but are biding their time. The blackout and its imposition, that is what is the most noticeable change in people's lives.

Car collisions. Lorry collisions. Motorcycle collisions. Bicycle collisions. *Collisions* – the word of the moment. Alright, we'll allow a second – *accidents*. Many a pedestrian coming into contact with anything on two or four wheels. All due to the blackout. No fatalities but it's just been too damn black in the blackout.

It's September 5th 1939. Sunset comes at 8pm. No difference to any other September but in 1939, it's now a wartime September. Many hours to be got through where artificial light will aid the enemy and this habit has to be stamped out. Folk though are folk.

Headlights to be dimmed, rear lights as well. Cyclists? For god's sake man, use your head. Rear reflectors, useless. *They* are not going to be able to see you just using reflectors. For god's sake…

You can never discount sheer stupidity, though. Some will always be drunk and incapable, vehicle or no vehicle, blackout or no blackout. If a Naval rating decides to go for a walk down the pier after a bevvy or two and falls into the harbour basin, whose fault is that then?

But the Orkney *Jahr* moves on. There will have been a death or two and a church to be booked for the happy couple to be walking down the aisle and a birth. Officialdom may have other ideas, *the Registrar of Births, Deaths and Marriages*…so be it…it's not a Golden Wharf, *nom de plume* job.

Earlier, much earlier in the day, in the wee small hours of Tuesday the 5th… Jimmy Rendall is woken from his slumbers because of the blackout. He is to put no finer point on it *not happy.*

Jimmy is Kirstin's brother. Kirstin, Johnny's London squeeze. Bit of a temper, the brother. Runs in the family. Mother. Four kids. Three girls and Jimmy. Different fathers for each.

The girls are a delight. Fran, Mags and Kirstin. Well, Kirstin's home from London, visiting. She's made something of herself, a secretary with the BBC in Bush House, right in the heart of the Capital.

The lad, Jimmy, is in and out of trouble 'cos he's out-and-out feral. A right handful is our Jimmy. But here's the odd thing, though. Jimmy is the cuckoo in the nest. He is in the family but not of the family. Adopted but in temperament most like the mother, Beth Rendall. Jimmy has one bedroom all to himself, the girls share the other. The mother chops and changes male friends. Always a new uncle for the kids to get used to. Jimmy will do anything for his mum and his sisters.

It's a brave ambulance driver to rouse Jimmy from his slumbers at three o'clock in the morning, the Narrows of all places in Kirkwall as well. The mother stands in the bedroom doorway. She expects the ambulance driver to get on with what ambulance drivers do. Her lad, he's entitled to his beauty sleep. Mags' waters about to break but the choice lands on her lad's pillow. Is he going to help or not?

Jimmy called into action, three o'clock in the morning. The ambulance driver needs a second pair of hands. That's why Jimmy's being slapped about. Wakey-wakey Jimmy. Not to deliver the baby but to help guide the ambulance driver and the soon-to-be mother safely towards Balfour Hospital in the *Toon*. He's seen it all before, especially the early morning fog but never as bad as this.

The hospital, a mile away, not far from Saint Magnus Cathedral but when the ambulance has no lights and there's no streetlights and it's pitch black and there's a morning mist that would be the equivalent of a London pea-souper.

Jimmy is more than not happy, *troos* on, ready to assist but only *Jimmy-ready*.

'Here, Jimmy, grab this.' The ambulance driver shouts the instruction.

'What do you need me for? I've no training. You're the fucking ambulance driver.'

'Don't be a berk, Jimmy. I'm not asking you to deliver the baby. I need you to stand in front of the ambulance and swing this magic lantern so I can see where I'm going.'

'I'm not the fucking father. It's my sis.'

'So, where's the lucky father?'

'You fucking tell me. When I get my hands on him … He was working in Lyness. God only knows where he is now but I'll find him. No one messes with my sisters.'

Jimmy walks ahead in the middle of the road. Sometimes sees the white line in the middle of the road, sometimes doesn't. Swinging the lantern from side to side. As if calling on the general public to bring out their dead. The ambulance is crawling behind, with the driver's window wound down. The driver is shouting out encouragement like a cat owner trying to coax their moggy through the cat flap. The outlines of Saint Magnus Cathedral can barely be made out.

'You're walking too fast Jimmy, slow down.'

'Don't you fucking tell me how fast I should walk...' Jimmy Sinclair, right belligerent, even at this ungodly hour.

'Keep swinging it. Keep swinging it, Jimmy. Nice and slow. Can't be far from the Balfour Hospital now. Slow but sure. Look out for bumps in the road. We don't want the baby to pop out, do we?

'You're a dab hand at this swinging the lantern, Jimmy. Tell you what. As your reward, after we've dropped the *mither* off at the Balfour, we'll go looking for the *faether*.

'Language, Jimmy, language.

'Think on this, Jimmy. Doesn't matter whether it's a bonny bouncing boy or gal. Doesn't matter whether it's born on September the 5th, 6th or 7th, 1939. There's a war on. He or she will be a *War Baby*. Maybe it'll be twins. What's so nice is they'll have their Uncle Jimmy to help bring them up.

'Temper. Temper. Jimmy. Sorry, I missed that. What was that again? No, I always wash behind the ears. You are mistaken. I am not a dirty fucker.'

Being an ambulance driver does have its moments.

09.30am. The Commander needs to use his launch. Well as we know it's not exactly *his*. Availability? Grace and favour of those Brylcreem Boys, the RAF. *Fucking penguins, a lot of flapping about but few get up in the air.* Ridiculous situation to be in. He must make another call to the Admiralty. Needs to be sorted out once and for all.

Wartime. How can he possibly do his job with one hand tied behind his back?

All of Scapa Flow comes under the Commander's jurisdiction – HMS Proserpine. Wags deconstruct this tongue twister of a word Proserpine. Those military serving in the Scapa Flow call our Orkney theatre of service, Proper Swine.

The Commander has to go to Lyness in person. He needs to get to the bottom of this. We're not talking about the matter of his *boat*, though I cannot repeat enough times how important this is to the Commander. We have an open criminal case. We have a matter of Wartime national security. Two rolled into one.

The Murder. The Enquiry. The Suspect. The Spy.

The Murder took place last Saturday, the 2nd September – the day before *The Declaration of War.* The one preceded the other. That's where we are now, this Tuesday. Day Four since *The Murder* in Hoy. Day Three since *The Declaration of War* in Europe. Isobel's family from the Narrows in Kirkwall. It's personal. This German, whereabouts unknown.

Speaking on the phone, just won't do. The Commander feels as if he's being spun a line. The Military Police will tell you nothing or they'll tell you everything. Words, they'll make you die of thirst through the lack of them or they'll drown you by the bucketful. He needs to visit the scene of the crime. An eyeball-to-eyeball session, not-necessarily-a-confrontation-my-dear-chap, must be had with the Head of Military Police in Lyness, over in Hoy.

So, the Commander is on board, on the Flow, but this *grace and favour* boat has to be returned by 4pm. It required all of the Commander's honeyed words and control of temper to wheedle even this far-from-generous return time.

His Majesty's Military Police are continuing with their enquiries. That's the official line. The Commander wouldn't put it past them to already have this Thomas under lock and key. Given what happened to Johnny, there's no doubt a mark or two on him by now.

Let them ignore at their peril that he's the Commander. Any more stonewalling from the Military Police and he'll pull rank. They're only Army Officers, after all. None at Brigadier level. None his equivalent. The Navy, of all the Services, has an unrivalled military tradition. *Trafalgar* knocks the spots off *Agincourt*, any day of the week. The Orkney tradition is a maritime one. *Let them ignore that at their peril.*

If the Military Police wallah is not there, a surprise call to the Golden Wharf will have to suffice; the Golden Wharf, *his bête noir*. The Commander fears the worst. Work taking place? You must be joking. It'll be like the *Marie Celeste.* What with men slinking away to their farmsteads to help bring in the harvest, if he sees a handful of men on the job, he'd be happy. Everyone knows that this is the best grain crop for many a year.

The Commander has just one word for his kith and ken putting family obligations above the Nation's, *deserters*. The truth hurts. No way round it. *Deserters*.

He draws parallels with the Great War, just 20 years or so ago. Men in the trenches under continuous fire. Men who'd left their post, they'd had enough. Shot before dawn. Could be their best mates in the firing squad.

The Commander starts to shake uncontrollably and is reduced to tears. Alarmed, he looks around. Thank goodness no-one has seen what he perceives to be an act of weakness.

The Commander, despite appearances to the contrary, is as fragile as every other person who served in the Great War. Remove the chaff and this is what you'll find, not a husk but the true person. No wonder *those who were there* don't want to talk about it.

Winston Churchill is back as First Lord of the Admiralty and it is said that although he has made a mistake or two along the way, he would make a great leader in times of war.

11am, Tuesday the 5th. The Commander arrives at Lyness. A cold call but he is in luck. The Head of the Military Police is in his office. It's almost as if the Commander is expected.

'Good to see you, Commander. Thank you for popping

in. I was delighted that my deputy could help in the release of one of yours. I was just about to ring you anyway. Your visit is most timely. An important matter of mutual interest to discuss…'

No nonsense, straight to the point, gruff but approachable, *oor Weegie.* Glasgow or Edinburgh? Straightforward friendliness over refinement? One genuine…the other…

The Commander doesn't like what he sees. The Military Chief of Constabulary can call on a staff of three in his front office. He has not one but two telephones on his desk. Mind, there is a dart board on the far wall and that does even things up. A dart board, strictly hoy polloy.

Pinned to this dart board are pictures of Wallis Simpson, 'that American upstart' and George Formby, the toothy light entertainer from Lancashire. The dart board and the photos say it all.

Tea poured into mugs, chipped mugs. Tea, sloshed through a strainer. The same tea strainer passed from mug to mug until the tea is tea in name only. Regulation military piss water. McVitie Digestive biscuits offered. The Commander's counterpart dunks, yes dunks, his biscuit in the tea. That says it all.

Accent…*Parliamo Glasgow.* Smacks of the Gorbals. *He* does lack class, definitely one of the hoy polloy. The Commander wonders what school he went to, probably a breeding ground for scavengers and thieves, probably left school before the age of 15, if lucky then straight into a job in the Clyde shipyards. Less than five foot five inches tall, this Glaswegian. Short stature. My goodness they'll take in anybody, these days.

'…The murder itself. No doubt whatsoever as to how the deceased met her death. Forensics only had to confirm the obvious. Strangulation and then a straightforward frenzied knife attack. No sexual penetration before or after death. Mrs. Isobel Tulloch's saliva and pubic hairs found on the accused. Her blood on his clothing. Open and shut…'

The Commander impatient. His time limited by when he has to return the launch to the Brylcreem Boys.

'So…you've got the German under lock and key. Excellent. That's a weight off my mind. This Thomas Dreyer. I need to question him on matters of national security anyway. I know everyone in Hoy will tell you what a wonderful chap he is but the murder proves how Germans always revert to type. He is dangerous. His country is *the* enemy.'

The Commander in full swing now.

'The law of the land since 1919 states that every alien must register with the police, anyone failing to do so will be…Thomas Dreyer has never registered here in Orkney. He has been on our watchlist for some time, perfectly placed to act as intermediary between his London masters and here. The man has covered his tracks well. Despite his schoolboy looks, his murder of Isobel Tulloch comes as no surprise…'

Mister *Weegie* is quite happy to let the Commander finish his say.

'…Thank god you've got this Nazi murderer under lock and key. I'm sure you'll have no objection to me interviewing Thomas straight away.'

There's a pause and the Head of Military Police breaks into a broad smile. The Commander is on full alert. Let him just try and question his authority. *Let him just try.*

The Head of the Military Police lets him stew. He is enjoying the moment. Past master at swapping good-cop-and-bad-cop persona. Whatever suits. Whatever works. Particularly good at using silence for maximum effect. Staple of a good copper.

Mister *Weegie* bursts into laughter, raucous and lots of it – *Weegie* spewfuls of it.

'This Thomas Dreyer can suit both our purposes but Commander, correct me if I'm wrong but I don't remember saying, "Thomas Dreyer murdered Isobel Tulloch". Where did you get that from? Certainly not from me.'

The Commander nods. He keeps straight faced as he tries to process what he's just been told. Doesn't take to the Military Head of Police's manner one bit. Certainly, doesn't like the way he believes he is being made a fool of, the cat with the mouse at the end of its paw.

'Well, let's have a word with this Thomas Dreyer anyway. That's why I'm here, to have him transferred over to my jurisdiction and then to MI5.

'Thomas Dreyer…mm. Can't help you there either,

Commander. I never said that we have Thomas Dreyer here under arrest. We certainly have a man under arrest but that man isn't Thomas Dreyer. Turn the man that we *are* detaining over to the MI5…mm. That *would* be rich.' He's laughing *spewfuls* again.

This is one step too far for the Commander.

'What the fucking blazes is going on? If you think I'm going to let you make a complete and utter arse of me, you've got another thing coming.'

Not the sort of eyeball to eyeball the Commander had anticipated. More of a confrontation. This upstart is toying with him. The Commander isn't the man he once was but he certainly possesses height advantage.

'Calm down, Commander. Easy. Easy. Just calm down, man. I'll tell you exactly where we are.' He pauses. Mister *Weegie* lets the silence go about its work, like swilling mouthwash round and round.

'I've never come across anything so devilishly complicated. I started this investigation naively believing that I was dealing with a cut and dried murder case. I think you've guessed that this is turning out to be anything but…'

The Commander is taken aback. The Head of Police is using language straight out of the mouth of Sherlock Holmes not of a *Weegie*. He is rubbing it in. The Commander is being played for a fool and on his own patch – HMS Prosperine. This man is a Proper Swine.

'Hear me out, Commander. Hear me out. We have…the

murderer of Isobel Tulloch…well and truly behind bars…I have…the signed confession.

'Before you ask, it has *not* been obtained under duress. We've all the supporting swab evidence we need to link… this man…to her. Her blood on his clothing. Our prisoner's name is…Graham Forester.'

'Forester, not an Orkney name.' The Commander is wary in tone. He doesn't want the Military Head of Police to think he's just a pawn to be moved at whim, an old stager to be easily brushed aside.

'Graham Forester. That's the name on his ID card. Whether it's genuine or not, it doesn't really matter, does it? He's going to be handed over to his MI5 bosses even if his ID card were to say that he was *Harry Houdini*. We do have a problem, a big problem though. I think you can see where I'm going on this.

'Graham Forester, born in Buckie, Banffshire; based in Bethnal Green, London – is *under arrest* for the murder of Isobel Tulloch, of Kirkwall, Orkney *but will not be standing trial*.'

That's two punches to the Commander's solar plexus, not just the one.

'…Forester? Forester?...So where the blazes does Thomas Dreyer fit into all of this?'

'You tell me, Commander. You tell me.'

Silence.

'Please let me finish.

'Isobel Tulloch had come to our attention some time

back. Her name kept on cropping up on the contact lists of fascists who are now under lock and key at His Majesty's Pleasure. By all accounts, Mrs Tulloch was liked and well respected in Kirkwall. We had nothing we could pin on her. Yes, she did visit Thomas regularly. Yes, there was her business of selling books by post but the books we looked at…nothing untoward was found in their contents. The poor lass didn't deserve to end this way.

'Operative Forester was sent by MI5 to gather information but committed the cardinal sin of getting *too close*. He was there to watch and report, not to…became as they say, *intimately involved.*'

'How did you find out?' The Commander's interest is piqued.

'This Forester has confessed to the murder. Quite brazen about it. Almost as if he knew that there was sod all we could do. Boasted that he could always count on his lord and masters, the MI5, to cover his backside.

'Sadly, he's right. MI5 against the Military Police. There's only going to be one winner there. I don't want to hurt your feelings but not even you and the Royal Navy would have a gnat's arse in hell's chance of pinning blame on MI5.'

'But…but.'

'She was seen more than a few times in the company of our German, Thomas Dreyer. By whom?… By ostensibly *our man* whose stock-in-trade should just be *watching*. Forester noting down her every move.

'The MI5 operative followed the now-deceased from Kirkwall over to Longhope by boat and then from Longhope to North Walls School. "Just doing his job", that's what he initially told us. Lots of winking and laddish references, telling us how she liked *it*. Motive. He was not at all happy that Isobel was spending a lot of time in Thomas Dreyer's company. His detailed reports could tell you what she was up to, timed to the minute… Sexual jealousy. Power. The idiot.'

The Commander needed to regain the initiative here. Life hadn't prepared the Commander for just a walk-on part.

'So why didn't the MI5 operative kill Thomas Dreyer at the same time as butchering Isobel Tulloch? In fact, why didn't he kill my lad, Johnny, at the same time? Isobel Tulloch, as we know, was already very friendly with my protegé…'

The Commander stopped midflow. He was angry with himself. He was committing the cardinal sin of telling a person more than they needed to know.

'You might well ask, Commander. We can't even establish that Thomas Dreyer was there at North Walls School on the day of the murder, last Saturday 2nd September. So, tell me more about the deceased's involvement with your Clerk of Works on the Golden Wharf, Johnny Sinclair. Sounds like they were more than good friends?'

The Commander mutters under his breath. If he was

back in the sanctity of his Kirkwall Hotel office, the Commander would have poured himself a snifter by now. A wee dram being just the job to put him back on even keel.

'You referred earlier to *a big problem.*'

'A few hotheads in Camp have already ruffled the feathers of local folk. The normal stuff. Lads-of-all-ages behaviour. Whether it's chasing skirt or fists raised, all comers welcome.

'A good scrap. For many this is as natural as a bellyful of pints. Orcadians will accept a bit of argy-bargy as being an ingredient of a great Saturday night out. Farm workers with bulging biceps. They'd fancy their chances. If it were just this…

'…But a murder of one of their own, though. Cannot be tut-tutted away. Cannot be excused like an auntie tut-tutting the behaviour of an errant nephew. If it ever got out that the murder had been carried out by a MI5 man and then hushed up by his bosses, we'd *all* be taking the flak.

'Think, Commander. We're only a few days into the War and Scapa Flow is to be used as the home for the Royal Navy…If ever we needed to put up a united front against the Nazis, we don't want to turn all of Orkney against us…do we?'

'I see.'

The Head of Military Police's tone suddenly softens. Bushy eyebrows raised.

'So, we have a murder…and we have…by all accounts this German on the run. *I repeat…this…German…on…*

the...run.' The Head of Military Police, Mister *Weegie,* emphasises the last few words with raised eyebrows.

For the first time, the hint of a smile appears on the Commander's face.

He is having to do a fast re-evaluation on the man who, only up to a minute ago, he had regarded as his inferior. *Volte face*. I would never sign him up to be a member of my Lodge but he's certainly got it up here.

The Commander suddenly sees before him a montage of films that he's enjoyed over the years at the Albert Kinema, many a twist and turn in a good Hollywood, Hitchcock thriller. This could beat them all.

And the Commander suddenly switches thoughts to Johnny's favourite Hollywood star, James Cagney, just five foot five inches of him. This man standing in front of the Commander. This man who comes from the Gorbals. He has all the characteristics of James Cagney.

Mister Cagney, in the mobster films, has no qualms in setting someone up as *the fall guy*.

The Commander and the Military Head of Police have found their fall guy, to be thrown into immediate action and not on a conditional basis. They shake hands on it. Qualms? None. This country's at war and the murderer is to be German, and even if he weren't German, being foreign is tantamount to the same thing.

A more than satisfactory meeting. Time for a quick gander round the Golden Wharf and finally a visit to Jolly's for a trim. Why not? Worth coming over for. Damn it, I did promise to have the launch back with the Brylcreem Boys by 4pm. It'll be a close-run thing.

Thomas Dreyer is on the run. It's been the story of his life since Hitler seized power in 1933. His family, coming from a strong trade union background, arrested one by one and sent to the *Arbeit Macht Frei* camps, never to be heard of again. It will be his turn next. Thomas knows it. He's not going to wait for the *Gestapo*.

The Berlin Olympics in 1936, with the to-ing and fro-ing of competitors from all over the world, and Thomas seizes the opportunity to flee the Fatherland. A student place awaits in Glasgow University and with forged press pass he has no difficulty in securing his berth on the SS Bremerhaven liner, sailing from Hamburg.

MI5 is taking its time over Thomas Dreyer, the case file being passed from agent to agent. The organisation snuggles under its comfy blanket of top security and gives itself license to take as long as it damn well likes. Thomas' case always seems to end up at the bottom of some other operative's pile.

Minds are finally made up. The buff folder is stamped and dated. *Closed. 1st September 1939.* It's Friday and the Friday liquid lunch beckons. Employees are not expected to return to their desk afterwards. The weekend starts early for MI5 staff at HQ.

The first document inside the suspect's MI5 folder is the ruling, white paper, punch holed, A4 and no more than a couple of sentences. 'Thomas Dreyer poses no immediate threat to Great Britain. He is not a Nazi agent but requires the same level of monitoring accorded to citizens of enemy countries. Low Priority.'

The folder is left for all to see over the weekend, not by design. It should have been locked away in a filing cabinet, a security breach. This is to be a weekend like no other. Friday… Peace. Monday…the Nation is at War.

Yes, the decision's been taken but it's the communicating of the decision that's all important, especially in the field, inside and outside MI5. Boring work, this notification part and invariably not tackled with the gusto that it deserves. Always a temptation to leave it to someone else to do the unexciting stuff. Always a temptation.

Aunty Ida calls him *Dinglewhatsits*. Doctor Dinglestoeford, a leading light on the émigré committee in London. German Social Democrat cells, scattered all over Europe, dedicated to fighting the Hitler tyranny but easy-peasy to penetrate. The Nazis are of course enemy number one, but the Soviet NKDV are not far behind.

Something has happened to our Doctor Dinglestoeford, Thomas is sure. Thomas unwrapping a large parcel placed inside the Old Custom House doorway just last week and being very surprised at its contents, the stuff of spycraft – a microdot reader, a morse code transmitter – no note inside as if the recipient has foreknowledge…then comes the request for photographs…and now this letter from the German Embassy.

Thomas' full address in Longhope, Hoy on the envelope. Unsettling. Distinctly unsettling. Getting the message over, the German Embassy. 'We know where you are.' The message is on letter headed paper or should I say German eagle headed paper. Brief, to the point.

'Thomas, we wish to invite you to attend a cultural evening in our Embassy in London. Please R.S.V.P or ring this number. STA 2754. Reverse Charges. Heil Hitler.'

Thomas fears the worst.

Like Orkney weather, MI5 make no apologies for changing its tune. Irony upon irony. MI5 have officially closed down the case file on Thomas Dreyer just as Thomas Dreyer enjoys *a second coming* as a threat to cover the tracks of… A false trail being laid away from MI5 and their operative's murder of Isobel Tulloch.

MI5 are keen to avoid reputational damage at all costs.

There he is. Post Bills of. 'Thomas Dreyer – Wanted for murder', suddenly appear throughout Orkney, one or two at a time, public noticeboard and shop, here and there. You certainly can't miss them in the *Toon*. Such an angelic face staring down at you. 'Wanted for murder.'

What was the name of that James Cagney film, the hoarding outside the Albert Kinema? *Angels with Dirty Faces*. In this case, just the one angel is sought by the law. *Thomas Dreyer Wanted for Murder. An enemy spy.*

THOMAS DREYER – MY STORY

Their attitude towards me. No longer pleased to see me, the suspicion. I try to make them laugh, 'Bronze medal for breaststroke.' Sometimes I don't need to try, it just spills out. 'Arctic Stukas' for 'Arctic Skuas.' That change. I can feel it everywhere I go. Longhope…Lyness…North Walls.

Mein Vaterland will invade Poland and there will be war between Great Britain and Germany, as sure as 'eggs *is* the eggs'. I am as laid-back as a clucking hen on the eve of a stormy tomorrow.

Ich bin Deutscher, the British authorities will pull me in for questioning and more.

Ich bin Deutscher, the German Embassy know where I live and can at any time disappear me.

If one side doesn't get to me, the other side will. What's

to stop one country tipping off the other? I cannot sit tight and wait.

I miss my Isobel. *Meine Liebe. Meine Schätze.*

'Always suspicious, Thomas. Trust me and trust Doctor Dinglestoeford. He wouldn't be asking you for this information without good reason.'

That's what started our row yesterday. Friday the First. It would be, wouldn't it? We've had our tiffs before but this one…well…we didn't make up, there and then.

Friday 1st September, in the School Hut at North Walls. Friday the First…these Orkney people and the strange way they speak. The *Gaelic*, I believe it is spoken here after all. Friday the First, not a good day for *flittin'*...for moving house…for anything. I'll stay put in Longhope until the *morn.*

14.00. Saturday 2nd September. A late lie in. I'm still at 'sixes *und siebens*'. Go to *the* ground…the other end of the island…North Hoy…one of the stone *bothies*...near to where I took the kids? No. That would just be putting off the inevitable, too obvious. Hide in a cairn, in thick undergrowth? Supplies would soon run out.

I'll get a lift late afternoon on one of the creel boats over to Kirkwall, the Orkney Mainland. That's what I'll do. With all the boats heading in one direction only for the good Saturday night on the *Toon*, my chances of not being spotted are high. My face scarf will be pulled up to the bridge of my nose, like a mask. I will be 'the knee of the bees'. *Genau.*

Let's just check in my jacket pocket. She gave me her spare key for the house in the Narrows, in Kirkwall, the waterfront. She asked in return for the hut key in North Walls School. I felt obliged to do so. If she's not at home, I can let myself in. Yes. Her key…under my handkerchief… here it is.

Isobel got me into this mess, she'll get me out of it. I evaded the Gestapo to board the SS Bremerhaven in Hamburg, just three years ago. I can avoid *the authorities* again. That Hoy lighthouse at Cantick Head. Three seconds of bright-white light. Twenty-two of darkness. The odds may be stacked against me but *Ich bin ein Überlebender.* I am a survivor.

19.00hrs. Not yet dusk in the *Toon.* I am in the Narrows and knock on her front door, wait a second or two, knock again and then push with the palm of my hand and the door opens. The front door is not even on a latch. Front doors are rarely locked in the *Toon.* This is Orkney. Her spare key can stay in my pocket.

'Isobel, Isobel.' I call her from the foot of the stairs. Hand is over my mouth, like an apology. I am a fugitive again. My three years on Hoy and that inner and outer peace is forgotten in 'the click of the fingers'.

Maybe she's out *doing the messages*, that's some more Gaelic that I have learnt. Her home has got that feel about it. Empty. A chill in the air. That hint of mustiness. I'm alone and talk to myself out loud, just to hear the sound of a human voice. Standing on the corner of the kitchen table, a wireless. I turn it on and am so pleased to hear Joe Loss and his Orchestra, at full blast.

It's difficult to know whether I am more hungry than tired. A quick look through the larder and there's just a few days' food. Ah. Some bread and cheese. A cheese sandwich, washed down by a cup of tea, no milk, so black tea it'll have to be. Isobel any minute will walk through the front door. My ears are pricked-up alert, like the long droopy ears of a bloodhound waiting for his mistress' call.

One thumb short of a handful of hours have passed. Should've shut-to the front door from the start. I do so now. No slamming. Shh. Shh. I wait for the click of the lock, like a safebreaker, bloodhound ears. I close the curtains. Totally secure now…Wireless now turned down to low volume. Better late than…

I sit on the comfy chair and wait…and think about the last time we were together sitting round the Xmas table, back in Hamburg…*Heileger Abend*…only three years ago…they are there now in the same room as me…a happy family…and I cry myself to sleep.

11.15am. Sunday morning, 3rd September. I turn on the wireless hoping to hear some Joe Loss and his Big Band or even Ambrose just to cheer me up. Instead I hear the British Prime Minister and he is declaring war on my country, or should I say *mein Vaterland.* What-was-my-Germany no longer exists.

As soon as I step outside into the pouring rain, I will be arrested on sight or shot *escaping arrest*. No, I will open the curtains and stay indoors. My Isobel will walk through the door at any moment. I do not want to miss her. Where was she last night? Who was she with? How does that Tommy song go? *Pack Up Your Troubles In Your Old Kit Bag.*

21.00pm. It's getting dark outside and no one in the street seems to have their lights on. I draw the thin curtains. Where is Isobel? Where is Isobel? I'm hungry. Nine o'clock, another hour and it'll be dark enough to go out but the fish and chip shop will be closed by then. A can or two of herring left in the larder, I won't starve. Herring and black tea. I will self-quarantine. Two large beams of light and the ever louder roar from a car. There will be banging on my front door soon.

22.00pm. Tuesday 5th September. I know it's Day Three of the War. I am trapped. The darkness. The hunger. No Isobel. Above all, the hunger. No, above all – *No Isobel.* That black scarf on her sideboard will have to do. I wrap it round the lower part of my face. This can only be a part disguise, a mere half-face mask, but there is nothing else. I escape.

Scott's, Bridge Street. The Chippy. Not the only one in the Toon but the nearest. If they've run out of fish, a patty supper it will have to be. Just a few minutes' walk. Along Shore Street. The waterfront. The sound and smell of the sea. Nervous. No light, a blackness. Orkney Mainland should offer more anonymity than Hoy. Let's hope so. I have to be anonym. No name. No face. No number.

Few people about. Head down, just in case. Car headlights dimmed. Streetlights off. The few people about keep on tripping over the pavement. I hear them say, 'Those curbs are a bugger.'

Scotts is open. There are only two or three people waiting to be served. That's strange. Must be the War. I get the last fish supper. Head down, I say nothing but just point to the last remaining just-fried piece of cod in the glass cabinet and pay. The fish and chips with brown sauce are wrapped in the *Orcadian* newspaper, last week's copy.

As I head out of the chippie, I see that there's a small poster in the window, facing inwards not outwards to the street.

'Wanted…'

TUESDAY 5TH SEPTEMBER – JOHNNY SINCLAIR

The Commander's HQ, Kirkwall Hotel. 10.00am. Johnny's bored. Johnny's frustrated. Too many years of perceived hurt. It's a young man's lot. A salty, salutary taster as to what life has in store.

The excitement of having received Lyness hospitality, courtesy of the Military Police has been elbowed out of the way by the hurt of having this wonderful yarn of derring-do to tell. It even tops *the Malacca Straits*. The Commander is so avuncular, he understands that Johnny is bursting to tell. Puts a hand round his shoulder. 'Top secret, Johnny…has to remain top secret.'

To his folks, the story has to be, 'I tripped over a plank at the Golden Wharf.' At least the plaster over the eye has now been removed. The official line paints Johnny in a stupid light. Tripping over a plank. Honestly. He, with justification, feels his bravery deserves that much better.

Yes of course he is blessed to have had that personal revelation, that realiza-tion. An adult now with responsibilities, our Johnny, self-absorption a thing of the past. He has turned over a new leaf but that Damascene moment isn't enough to brighten Johnny's mood. There is nothing really to look forward to, to get his adrenalin pumping. It has just turned 10 o'clock with the whole day yet to face, a whole day of responsibility.

It's a test. Just because I'm new and better Johnny, it doesn't follow that I have to be miserable. 'Patience,' that's the watchword. The Commander wouldn't have brought me back from London if he didn't see something special in me. I will not let him down. I will give my best shot at anything he tells me to do.

The day goes quickly but Johnny's treading water. Assembling. Assisting. Smiling. Cajoling. Just one of the lads and lasses (pretendy) Shouting. Laughing (pretendy), Rolling up his sleeves, Loading, Organising, Bunny rabbit energy, Non-stop. Et cetera, et cetera. All pretendy.

Johnny is putting on a front. Glad-handing, as politicians and royalty do. Johnny is leading from the front. Setting an example. Early days yet. Johnny'll get the hang of it. It's practice and practice makes perfect. Top honcho at the ARP Depot Hall to be followed by an early evening meeting at the Vets, Junction Road.

I'm bored as fuck. I'm in charge of the assembly and distribution of respirators, that's gas masks to you and me. One gas mask for each man, woman and child in

Orkney. 'Well it's necessary,' and that's the best I can say about it.

Johnny feels as if he's foundered on one of the sandbanks off Moness, North Hoy.

At least the location of the ARP Depot and Vets in Junction Road is handy, just a spit away from his hidey-hole in the Kinema.

Johnny feels short changed. Tuesday, 5th September – Day Three of the War. War should be about excitement. The only real impact of the War so far has been him being caught short in the middle of the night, having to fumble his way to and from the lavvy in the dark.

No light's out relief for the *Toon* either. The Kinema is still shut. Hollywood denied to folk. Surely there should have been an air raid by now. The *Luftwaffe* by repute don't fuck about. Them Vikings didn't fuck about either but the Nazis are bad bastards whereas them Vikings, kith and kin.

Bombing is a terrible thing but isn't that what wars are supposed to be all about? Isn't that why we're distributing gas masks? I hope this gas mask thing doesn't last long. How the fuck can you tell if she's interested in you or not? How the fuck can you make conversation if your words are muffled and you can't understand what she's saying? You come over like an old dear with a shawl, listening through an ear trumpet.

Even the Commander would have trouble with his gee-gees. Imagine them trying to get round the course at Aintree for the Grand National. Those Jockeys and nags wearing gas masks. It's tough enough for them nags being forced to wear blinkers in the first place. Handicapped? Too fucking right. 25 to 1. Long odds.

You know what? I'd rather just take my chances, not wearing 'em. What blinkers? No, gas masks...

Mind on. Johnny was just waiting his turn for his fish supper yesterday evening in Scott's, down Bridge Street, when he overheard someone spreading gloom and doom about 'them Hun bastards' having carried out a reconnaissance flight over the Flow.

You'll always get someone so keen to be first with the news that they'll come up with any gobbledygook. The gobby types. Those who'll prattle away about who's run off with whom. The Mrs. Sew and Sews of this world. They'll be telling us next that Nazi frogmen have under blackout cover emerged from the Bay of Kirkwall in top to toe black camouflage, right down to their flippin 'eck, black flippers and started the invasion.

There's a strange feel to the *Toon*. It's as if a *haar* has descended, enveloping the *Toon* in this damp squib of a cloak. A *haar* of a blackout. Outside of the *Toon*, there's the harvest to be brought in. The harvest is still top priority for Orkney, the War or not the War. In the *Toon*, everything is not tickety-boo. Folk are fidgety…through waiting.

I loved her. She's in my head all the time, Isobel. It was good of the Commander to tell me that that the German, Thomas Dreyer is the number one suspect. The German's face is on every poster in town. He is on the run and I will be the one to bring him in. That Hun bastard.

Unhinged. Sadistic. This Thomas. Bu"er wouldn't melt...This Thomas. I've seen a storyline like that at the Albert Kinema. The murderer can't keep away from where the girl he's murdered once lived. The Narrows, off Shore Street isn't it? That's where Isobel used to live. Somewhere round there. As gumshoe jobs go, it'll be easy-peasy to find her place.

I need some fresh air. Christ, it's night time. Who knows where the time goes? It's pitch-black outside.

Johnny's just a stone's throw from his hidey-hole in the Albert Kinema and he's *cream-crackered.* Johnny is knackered and fancies some chips. The ARP Depot Hall had put on a spread of sorts but Johnny fancies some chips. That's where he'll head to, *Scotts*. *Scotts* is his favourite chippie. Chips. He fancies them.

First though a stroll along the waterfront and some bracing Orkney air to clear his head. Out of town, that's the route he'll take. Just has to follow his nose, along Ayre Road and the delights of the Peedie Sea. You'll always get a strong whiff there, wind or no wind.

The Peedie Sea, the *Toon* refuse dump. Not picture-postcard stuff. Fresh air makes Orkney a go-to destination but you don't want to head anywhere near this hidden treat. Anything and everything is dumped in the Peedie Sea and *beuys o beuys* does it stink. An island shithouse. There is no escape from harsh reality, even in Orkney.

It fills twice a day, this Peedie Sea, with the salty sea water. You can float on this biblical Dead Sea on your back, if you want. The Peedie Sea, different class. Not for the better, I'm afraid. You'll have floaters for company. My god, this is where a gas mask would come in right useful, the stench.

Ten o'clock at night. It's pitch-black. Johnny is walking away from the *Toon* on the land side of Ayre Road. This 19-year-old *Toon* lad is clearing his head of the day's trials and tribulations but certainly not taking in a deep breath. Deep in thought but not sure of foot. Who can be sure of foot in the blackout?

'Pal, you watch where you're going.' A loud stranger's voice out of the murk and not friendly.

'Sorr…sorry.' Automatic response from Johnny, would've been even from Johnny Mark I what with his manners and Clay Loan upbringing.

'Easy enough to say, pal.'

This someone is with someone. Difficult to make both out in the dark.

'I said, I'm sorry.'

'Who do you think you are pal? You think it's alright to barge into anyone you want. *Who do you fucking think you are?*'

He's with his girl and trying to impress.

'I…said…I…am…sorry.'

'I know you, don't I?' The accuser takes a step forward. Not quite in Johnny's face but not far off.

He'll get bored with this soon.

'Maybe you do. Maybe you don't.' Johnny's reply, nonchalant and not backing down.

'Fellar. Deaf, are we? What's your name?'

I'm not going to get into fisticuffs. There's no point. But if I need to...I could easily see him off. The one he's with, she's looking at me. I haven't lost the touch, have I?

Johnny says nothing, a smile on his face.

'I say you…fucker…what's your name?'

He's had more than a few pints. Breath, beery. No. It can't be. I'll tell him, if that keeps him happy.

'Johnny Sinclair, my friend and yours?'

'Rendall. Jim Rendall and this is my sis' Kirstin Rendall. Does the name ring a bell? She's got something to say to you.'

'Kkk…kirstin.'

'Thank you for the gift, you bastard.' A lady's voice.

What gift? I know I left London sharpish and that... would never treat a woman like that now...but I don't remember giving her a going-away present.

'I'm in the family way, Johnny. It's yours.' Kirstin spits at him. She has every right to.

'Hear me out, Kirstin. What I did was wrong but I've turned over a new leaf.'

'You bastard…'

'You fucker,' adds Kirstin's brother, lunging at Johnny.

All Johnny can think about is removing himself from the scene pronto He trips up Kirstin's brother and makes a run for it, back towards the *Toon.* Doesn't look behind him. None of this 'Lot's-wife-bible-bollocks.'

I will not be caught.

Legs it back down Ayre Road. Takes a right into Great Western Road. Left turn, into West Castle Street. At Junction Road turns right. A hundred yards or so, stops at the Farmer's Mart to catch breath.

Silence. A pitch-black silence.

Johnny is confident that he's given Jim Rendall, *the bampot* of the brother, the slip. Catches his breath. Smiling to himself, he stifles this near overwhelming urge to let out a roar of triumph. He slowly walks back down Junction Road towards and then just past Castle Street. Castle Street, in the centre of the *Toon* but not quite.

There's someone walking towards him on the far pavement, the other side of the road. He can just make out the outline in the darkness but it's black on black in the black out, a silhouette against a black backdrop. The shroud of a blackout makes everything and everyone seem threatening.

What makes him do what he is about to do defies logic. He yells out in the direction of this amorphous shape almost now exactly opposite. Is it Kirstin? He can't tell. Now he can tell. It's no longer a silhouette, and no, it isn't Kirstin. All this is unfolding in the swirly mists of the blackout.

These decibels shoot out of Johnny's mouth, out of mature Johnny. Ear splitting in intensity and these decibels are without any prompt arranging themselves into recognisable words.

'*Sieg Heil.*' Repeated not once but twice, '*Sieg Heil. Sieg Heil.*'

The target of Johnny's invective immediately turns tail and runs back from where he came. It's Thomas and his worst fears are being realized. Thomas rushes towards the anonymity of blackness.

Johnny steps off the kerb.

For Johnny, the roles have changed. The 'hunted' becomes the 'hunter'. Johnny has seen off Kirstin's *bampot* brother but despite his newly appointed role *this hunter* does not give chase.

Blackout.

Johnny hears a car approaching. And the sound of this souped-up engine gets louder and louder in his ears. It is heading towards him at quite a speed, from the Tankerness Lane end of Junction Road, the top end.

Johnny goes by sound alone. The ever-increasing crescendo. This guttural, mechanical roar coming from behind.

Johnny stays firmly put. Johnny is in the middle of the road. No jumping back on to the pavement for him. No looking behind. Johnny is facing in the direction of the sea, as if it's every Orcadian's default position.

Johnny raises his hands up as if in surrender, waiting. A daddy longlegs fully extended. A soldier at the Front.

He entrusts his future to the Orkney *Jahr* clock.

A loud screech of the tyres.

The sound engulfs him. Johnny shuts his eyes.

He decides that this will be the moment to turn round and face the enemy. Him, in the middle of the road. Not in boxer's pose but statuesque. Arms and legs spreadeagled like a daddy longlegs firmly rooted to the tarmacadam. His eyes now opened. In defiance.

'Isobel. Isobel.'

Johnny's yells of pain are drowned out by the deafening noise of shell after shell of enemy bombardment.

'Isobel…' Johnny is sobbing. 'My love…'

This warfare crescendo of malevolent sound dissipates into the rat-a-tat-tat of a firing squad and then…stillness… the whiff of cordite quickly dissipates, wafted out to sea by the winds.

The car must have just managed in time to turn left, up West Castle Street.

The *Toon* returns to blackout silence.

Postscript

The callers. Uninvited. Don't make a sound. Not special. A puzzle there. Sadness for some. Two legs, spindly. Daddy longlegs.

Had their moment on the big screen.

These daddy longlegs. For only a short time. In their prime. Clamped onto the outside of the front room window. Suction pads, not visible to the naked eye.

Interconnecting parts. Walk on parts. Cog in the wheel. A marvel.

Set of antennae at the top. The head itself pin size. Stretched out spindly legs. Arms in crucifixion position. That's Mother Nature for you. A geometric beauty. Like a symbol to rally round.

Some felt the same about the swastika.

Their parts played. The actors link arms. Take a bow. No spotlight.

Even the one who didn't make it to the starting line quite rightly takes her place.

No rhyme nor reason why she should have been the one not to have made it.

Daddy longlegs. Husks. Spent like a Catherine Wheel. Rolled into a tiny ball. Powder puff.

Daddy longlegs. Waiting to be wafted away by the winds.

The Kinema's plush curtains now firmly drawn.

No film has been shown. No lights have gone up.

No National Anthem has been played. No *God Save The King.*

'Kinema closed until further notice.' A regulation.

What is good for the few, is good for the hoy polloy. That's what we're told.

It is to be observed by everyone, unfailingly, uncritically…even by those who make the rules and regulations.

Some become giddy through possessing this power and are always the first to deny how much they enjoy exerting it.

They lose sight of their own insignificance.

The Orkney *Jahr* works its way round the calendar clock face, at its own steady pace and is never to be rushed.

The Orkney *Jahr.* It has many stories to tell. All I ask you to do is to listen.

Those islands to the North of Scotland, the Orkney Islands. Orkney.

Addendum – Official Notice

Conscripts to Register at Labour Exchanges on Saturday June 3 1940.

For British male subjects who are between the ages of 20 and 21.

In order to spread out the work of registration and to avoid congestion and delay as far as possible men will be asked to come at different hours according to the first letter of their surnames as follows:

A between 1.30pm and 2.00pm

B—C between 2.00pm and 3.00pm

D—G between 3.00pm and 4.00pm

H—K between 4.00pm and 5.00pm

L—M between 5.00pm and 6.00pm

N—R between 6.00pm and 7.00pm

S—V between 7.00pm and 8.00pm

W—Z between 8.00pm and 8.30pm

Mass Vaccination clinics to be held for the Covid-19 vaccine on Saturday 13th and Sunday 14th February 2021 at the Outpatients Department in THE NEW Balfour for patients aged 65—69 registered with a GP Practice on the Orkney Mainland (including South Ronaldsay & Burray).

Saturday 13th February 2021

Time if your surname begins with:

09.00 A

09.30 B

10.15 C

11.30 D and E

12.00 F

13.30 G

14.15 H

14.45 I, J and K

15.15 L

Sunday 14th February 2021

Time if your surname begins with:

09.00 M

11.00 N and O

11.30 P and Q

12.15 R

14.00 S

5.30 T, U and V

16.00 W, X, Y and Z

About the Author

This is David Barnard's second novel. 'Chiff Chaff' was the first.

He stood in the 2019 General Election for the northernmost constituency of the UK in Orkney and Shetland as an independent, receiving many plaudits but few votes.

With Stushi his cat he kept the Argentinians at bay in the Falkland Islands under the name of Major Carlos Hopalong.

He has a regular DJ Dub Reggae slot in Istanbul as DJ Da-Da-Da but his home very much is in Stromness, Orkney.

If you've enjoyed 'Hoy Polloy', please spread the word and consider leaving a review on Amazon, Goodreads or any other online forum. These are a huge help to authors.

Printed in Great Britain
by Amazon

23999966R00212